MAGICAL MAKEOVER

MYSTICAL MIDLIFE IN MAINE

BRENDA TRIM

Copyright © May 2021 by Brenda Trim
Editor: Chris Cain
Cover Art by Fiona Jayde

* * *

This book is a work of fiction. The names, characters, places, and incidents are products of the writers' imagination or have been used fictitiously and are not to be construed as real. Any resemblance to persons, living or dead, actual events, locales or organizations is entirely coincidental.

WARNING: The unauthorized reproduction of this work is illegal. Criminal copyright infringement is investigated by the FBI and is punishable by up to 5 years in federal prison and a fine of $250,000.

All rights reserved. With the exception of quotes used in reviews, this book may not be reproduced or used in whole or in part by any means existing without written permission from the authors.

※ Created with Vellum

I would like to take the opportunity to thank my PR Agent, Veronica for being a rock star. You have the patience of Job and always have an electronic smile for me along with a slew of helpful suggestions. You make my books shine and for that I am forever grateful <3

CHAPTER 1

"What do you mean that was an irritated ghost?" I gaped at my patient as she lay on her hospital bed and shrugged her shoulders. Surreptitiously, I checked to make sure I hadn't peed myself a little. Ever since I had my daughter, my bladder control went out the window with sleep.

How was this my life now? I'd gone from being charge nurse at a respected hospital in the triangle in North Carolina, married to one of the country's best cardiothoracic surgeons to divorced and living back home with my mother and grandmother.

Hattie Silva, my patient and current employer stared at me with a furrowed brow. She was a ninety-year-old woman suffering from cancer of the intestines and required full-time care. After being fired from the hospital, my ex-husband ran me out of North Carolina and had managed to ruin my reputation, leaving me no options for work outside of in-home nursing with a hospice organization.

"I mean precisely what I said. Evanora isn't happy about you ignoring her. She's trying to get your attention. I struggle to hear her most days. I'm at the end of my life and running out of time." Hattie looked frail when she spoke like that.

She was older and suffering far more than was pleasant. It was difficult to watch her in so much pain, but when she talked like this it was easy to forget all of that and simply see her as crazy. I thought her doctors needed to add dementia to her diagnoses.

I reached up and grabbed the necklace Fiona had sent to me a few weeks ago. My best friend had moved to England after her grandmother had died and started a new life without me. At first, I kept busy with the kids and Miles, but when my ex informed me that he was leaving me for another woman and proceeded to tear my life apart like a wrecking ball, I missed Fiona more than ever.

We met in college and hit it off right away. We'd been in each others' weddings, got jobs at the same hospitals and did everything together. I was there when her twins were born because her husband Tim had gotten stuck in traffic. And she was there for me through both of mine. Miles had elected to continue surgeries both times saying it was too complicated for him to hand off.

My heart skipped a beat when the bluish image of a woman wearing a bonnet with a tall brim and a floor length dress that was cinched around the waist with big, poofy sleeves appeared in the spot where the remote control had fallen. Startled, I dropped the necklace and reached my hand toward the ghost. The image disappeared and I shivered with the chill in the air.

Great, now she was infecting me with her crazy. Ignoring what I thought I saw, I set the glass of water on the tray beside the bed and raised the head of her bed more. "There's no such thing as ghosts. Let's get you some lunch. I made some chicken soup today."

MAGICAL MAKEOVER

Hattie was so thin I could see her bones under her flesh. She felt very breakable when I shifted her body's position. She started coughing when she slumped forward to make it easier for me to arrange her support. As gently as possible, I laid her on the pillows and held the cup in front of her mouth then adjusted the oxygen flowing through her nasal cannulas.

After several seconds, she took a sip then sighed. "How is it you have an item of power, but you are ignorant as the day is long?"

This was a familiar argument. She would say something about me having some powerful object and being ignorant of everything important around me. "I like you too, Hattie. You ready for lunch?" At her nod, I left to get the food. The house was massive and most of the time I didn't notice the echo throughout the place, but I was jumpy after that conversation about spirits.

Rumors from my childhood popped into my head. Maybe they had been right after all. It would make sense for her to believe in ghosts if she really was a powerful witch. Although, I could see only brief glimpses of the power she must have once held. Whether or not that was true didn't matter.

She was ill and susceptible to being taken advantage of. I hadn't been hired to consider anything other than her health, but I would never sit by and allow someone to take her for a ride. Hattie was richer than God and had numerous companies to her name. All of which poachers were dying to get their hands on. *Not on my watch.*

Hurrying to the kitchen, I turned off the pot that had been simmering on low for the past half hour since I finished putting it together. I grabbed two bowls and paused when my gaze caught sight of the water beyond the window. The panoramic views of the Penobscot Bay were to die for and cost a fortune.

Hattie's house was called Nimaha. It reminded me of how Fiona had always called her grandmother's home Pymm's Pondside. Their generation must have named their houses or something. I'd heard several friends talking about names of their grandparents' homes. My generation had nothing as refined to lay claim to. We had crow's feet, liver spots and unwanted chin hair among other unpleasant signs of reaching middle age.

Wanting to shove aside thoughts that would only lead me to perseverate on how my life had gone to hell in a handbasket at the most inopportune time in my life, I refocused on the coastline. There was nothing on the more than three hundred feet of shoreline. Hattie had a serene sanctuary here. The waves lapped lazily against the pebbled beach. It was so peaceful and remote. Nothing like the hustle and bustle of the big city hospital where I spent twenty years caring for patients. I watched for several seconds until my mind quieted and I was relaxed.

Turning away from the big window, I grabbed the rolls my grandmother had sent with me that morning and headed back through the five thousand square foot house. Thankfully I didn't have to clean all of the bedrooms and bathrooms, or care for the three acres and its outbuildings. The gardening alone had to be a beast to maintain, although I had yet to see a gardener come and tend to the multi-terraced back yard.

A hiss nearly made me drop the tray of soups I had been carrying. Shifting my hold on the tray, I scanned the area for the little heathen that I swore was trying to kill me. There she was.

"Don't scare me like that Tarja." The tabby cat stuck her nose in the air as if she could understand me and continued

MAGICAL MAKEOVER

past me and up the stairs. She had the most beautiful coat I'd ever seen on a cat. Multi-colored with the oranges and yellows being vibrant and shiny.

The second bowl on the tray was to feed Tarja. I wasn't used to treating a cat like a person, but she ate the same food I fed Hattie. I swear Hattie invented the term crazy cat lady. Tarja was her princess and the only thing Hattie was forceful about during the job interview. I should have known Hattie wasn't entirely together when she told me Tarja was to be fed meals with her and her litter box needed to be cleaned several times a day.

I could deal with Hattie's eccentricities and bed pan and dressing changes without any problems. It was cleaning animal feces from a box that made me gag. Yes, I was aware how little sense that made. But c'mon it was a container filled with excrement that had been sitting for hours.

Shrugging off that unpleasant thought, I continued climbing the stairs and stopped short when I saw a large creature through the port hole window on one of the landings. It was dark green and almost as tall as the closest tree. And it looked like the dragons Hollywood depicted in countless movies. Only I didn't see any wings on this one.

What the heck was that? I swear something new popped up every day in this place. My heart raced and I was nearly hyperventilating as I tried to figure out what the large beast was. My breaths fogged the glass, making me use the sleeve of my top to clear the glass. When I looked back out there was nothing there.

When another scan didn't come up with the dragon, I continued up the stairs and hurried into Hattie's room where I deposited the tray and rushed to the window. Her room faced the side of the house where I'd seen the dragon. I hoped I would catch sight of it. Something that big wouldn't be able to disappear into the forest surrounding her without leaving a trail.

"What are you in a tither about now?" Hattie snapped at me like this more often than not. It was how someone talked to their child when they'd had enough of their odd behaviors.

I turned to my patient and pushed the table with the tray of food over to the bed. "I thought I saw a dragon in your backyard. I'm losing my mind just as much as you are it seems. Must be the stress of the divorce."

Hattie laughed, the sound like dry leaves rattling over a sidewalk. "You aren't seeing things, my dear. That was Tsekani. Oh, that soup smells delicious."

I was too tired to let my surprise show over her having named this imaginary dragon. *Are you sure it's not real? You saw it for yourself.* I was positive it was a bad sign that my mind was trying to rationalize my hallucinations.

I set the bowl I had brought for me on the plate where the rolls were. "Here's your lunch, Tarja."

The cat approached and sniffed the soup then started lapping it up. "She says the bay leaves were a good addition to the soup. That's not something I've ever added to mine."

My head snapped up to meet Hattie's smile. "What?"

"Seriously. Where did you get that necklace from? I'm beginning to sense you aren't magical at all." Everything in me froze with her words, including my heart for several seconds.

"My best friend, Fiona had made it for me as a symbol of my new beginning. Why are you saying it's magical? There's no such thing." Right? I wanted to believe I was open minded, but the past month of working for Hattie Silva and hearing her bizarre comments had me questioning that. There was no way I could jump on board with her and believe in magic.

Although, I had to admit I was beginning to have my

doubts. I'd seen enough in the past four weeks to really wonder. Problem was that I'm a scientist and relied on what I could prove and see. And while I had seen more than a fair share of oddities there was nothing I could hold onto or examine all that closely.

"You wouldn't believe me if I told you. Can you push the tray closer? I'd like to taste the soup Tarja can't shut up about." I shook my head and moved the tray over her bed and adjusted it, so she was able to reach the food easily.

I picked up a roll and tore off chunks while staring out the window. She had windows facing the forest and another on the wall above her head that overlooked the water. I was focused on the gentle waves and the pebbled beach when a dog raced across the area, kicking up rocks as he went.

My feet carried me closer and I watched as he bared his teeth. He wasn't like any dog I'd ever seen. He was big and dark grey in coloring. "Do you have wolves in this area?"

The clatter of a spoon filled the room. "Of course, Layla moved here first, but several others have taken refuge here over the years." I wasn't surprised to discover she named the wolves prowling in her woods. She had named her house after all. Wild wolves wouldn't have been my first choice of companions, but she had enough property to safely offer a place to as many wild animals as she wanted.

Dark coughing made me turn away from the window. I expected it to be Hattie, but it was Tarja. If she hocked up a hairball, I wasn't cleaning it. "When does your maid come to clean the house anyway? I've never met her."

Hattie cocked her head to the side and looked at me. "Mythia comes after you leave. She doesn't care to be around mundies. Why?"

"Mundies?" "I have no idea what that means, but I assure you I have done nothing to upset anyone. I haven't been here long enough to make any enemies. I was hoping to talk to

her about how she gets rid of hard water around the shower faucet. I have never been able to get mine so clean."

I thought moving home would offer me a few perks. Like not having to clean bathrooms anymore, but I'd been wrong. There was no way I could take advantage of my mother like Miles had me for so many decades. Despite working long hours seven days a week I always pulled my weight around the house.

After the hurt of his announcement settled in, I immediately began dreaming about what my life would be like without him. In my naivete I had dreamed of continuing my position at the hospital and staying in the house and hiring someone to do the cleaning.

Reality was an entirely different beast. After being fired I had spent weeks of job hunting before realizing I had no choice but to move home. Miles's little tart worked in human resources at the hospital and made sure I wasn't appealing to anyone interested in hiring me. I could have filed a suit for violating my rights, but after Miles had managed to fast track our divorce and screw me out of what I deserved I didn't bother. He had friends in high places.

"Oh, I know you haven't. I did my research before hiring you. Speaking of, how did you piss off Tara so thoroughly? She had nothing good to say about you when I called. And Mythia won't share her secrets with me, so she won't share anything with you."

My head started pounding and I clenched my jaw then balled my hands into fists. Miles got his little girlfriend to sabotage my only shot at a job in this area, too? "Tara is the jailbait that slept with my husband and blacklisted me at all the hospitals in North Carolina. My ex-husband didn't want to be reminded of what a jerk he is or that his girlfriend isn't much older than our son."

Hattie laughed so hard she started coughing. Tarja

jumped onto her lap and placed a paw on her chest. Their connection was more than obvious. The cat was always close and offering comfort when Hattie had bad moments. I shifted Hattie forward and rubbed circles on her back until she stopped coughing.

"I was right about that one it seems. When I saw the written record of your employment, it made no sense to me that you suddenly started making fatal mistakes after twenty years of pristine performance reviews. She did her best to convince me that you were stressed out and upset over your husband leaving you and could no longer be trusted with patients."

I gently set her against the pillows again and returned to the window. "I was upset that Miles left me like he did, but it never affected my ability to do my job. I can assure you I will not cause you harm in any way."

Hattie waved a hand dismissively. "Oh, I know that dear. What do you say we curse her with premature winkles? Or maybe make him impotent!"

That made me choke out a laugh as I turned away from the beach outside. "I would love nothing more, but that would make me like them, and I will never be so malicious. I believe that you reap what you sow. They will both get what's coming to them one day."

"You've got that right, dear. Fate gets her way, even if it takes years and several unexpected turns." I nodded my head in agreement as I gathered the lunch dishes from her tray.

I TURNED my Land Rover off and couldn't help but smile. Keeping the nice SUV along with half of the house when it sold were the only concessions the judge awarded me which was why I was forced to move back with my mom and grandmother.

I couldn't afford the house payments on the lake front house and no one would hire me. I couldn't buy a house on the money I would be given whether Miles sold or bought me out. We owed too much on the property.

Looking up at the house I had grown up in, I couldn't help but think about the differences between Hattie's house and the house I left back in North Carolina compared to this one.

My grandparents moved into this modest one-story Cape Cod style home almost seventy years ago. The yellow siding had been repainted half a dozen times and the windows were replaced with double-pained ones last summer. The kitchen had been updated fifteen years ago when my mom moved in with my grandmother but not much else had been done.

The wood floors were scuffed and scarred and the marks measuring my height were still in the doorway to the garage alongside my mother's. Unlocking the front door, I entered to the familiar smell of lemon polish and baking bread.

"I'm home," I called out as I set my keys in the dish on the table in the entrance. "Where is everyone?"

My mother poked her head out of the kitchen. "We're in here, just finishing up dinner. Did you eat with Ms. Silva?"

I headed down the hall and caught the door before it closed after my mother returned to the sink. "Hi, nana. How was your day?" I bent and kissed her cheek while she sat in a chair at the table. She was the same age as Hattie but in much better shape.

She patted my cheek and smiled up at me. "I made some rye bread for you to take to Hattie tomorrow and finished the book I was reading."

"And you got in a good nap," my mother interjected. "Anything new happen out at Nimaha today?"

Both enjoyed hearing about the events, saying the house had been haunted as long as they could remember. I shrugged my shoulders. "Hattie has given refuge to wild wolves living in the woods around her house and she has a dragon named Tsekani."

Grandma nodded her head. "She owns something like five acres, so she probably does think she is giving them a place to live. But a dragon? Is it dementia? Many of my friends have succumbed already."

My mother shut off the water and leaned against the counter drying her hands. "Good thing we have excellent genes, and you don't have to worry about that mom. You might want to start looking for another job soon, sweetie. Sounds like she's going downhill fast."

"Who's going downhill fast?" Nina asked as she entered the kitchen and approached me with her arms open.

"Ms. Silva," I replied and embraced my daughter. She looked a lot like me except her brown hair was longer than my short cut and she didn't have crow's feet around her brown eyes. I had always loved the fact that she looked so much like me. Until I was fairly certain that was the reason Tara didn't want Nina around anymore.

Nina released me and went to the fridge. "She's been cra-cra since the day you started there. You don't have to worry about finding another job." I could hear the panic in Nina's voice. She was by my side when I struggled to find a position and celebrated with me when Hattie hired me to take care of her.

"I am giving her gold star treatment to make sure she sticks around. Do you want me to make you a snack?"

Nina gave me a side smile and shook her head. "No, you sit down and rest your feet. You work too hard. I'll grab you some rocky road."

I sat next to nana and held back the emotion choking me.

I might not have the fancy house or the cushy job, but I had more love than Miles would ever know and that's all that mattered.

When my daughter asked my mom and grandmother what they wanted and proceeded to get them some vanilla ice cream along with a cookie, I realized Hattie didn't have this. She was all alone in the world and had no one to shower her with love and affection.

I made a silent vow to ignore the crazy and show her how much she was appreciated. She was cranky, and adored cats, but she was funny and made me laugh all the time. And there were times when she had these little nuggets of wisdom that were priceless. Like when she told me to stop complaining that my daughter was asking for a car of her own.

Hattie had just finished the cookies Nina had dropped off at the end of my first week on the job when I started complaining about her latest request. I would never forget the way Hattie had scowled at me as she said, *"Be grateful she doesn't want it to go joy riding. She wants to give you and your mother a break from taking her to and from practice, and a way to get to and from a job. Yeah, she told me how much she wanted to earn money to ease your burden. Most children her age are selfish critters with no care for anyone else, let alone how much their parents sacrifice to give them what they have."*

I blinked and shoved the memory aside when Nina kissed my cheek and placed the bowl in front of me. "Thank you, peanut. You're the best daughter ever born."

"Agreed." My mom and grandmother both spoke at the same time while enjoying their dessert. My midlife makeover wasn't what I had hoped it would be when I was twenty something, but I couldn't ask for more.

CHAPTER 2

"Another long day?" My mother kept her focus on the stew she was making for dinner, so she missed the grimace I cast her way.

I scrubbed a hand down my face as I debated how much to tell her. HIPAA protected any and all information about her health care. Not that I would ever share patient information. My grandmother shuffled into the kitchen far faster than her tiny body should move. Sure, I judged her based on Hattie's inability to move independently, but that didn't make it any less impressive. She was pushing ninety years old, after all.

Nina was right behind her. The smell of dinner having coaxed my daughter from her room. "Hi, mom." My insides warmed finally when she kissed my cheek.

I had been cold ever since a candle tipped over onto one of Hattie's old books in the library. I hadn't lit the thing, and neither had Hattie. She couldn't make it to the bathroom without my help, let alone downstairs.

"Hi, sweetheart. Yes, it was a very long day. I swear something very strange is happening at that house."

My grandmother braced herself on the table as she lowered her slim frame to her chair. Her grey hair was cut above her ears and fell into her bright blue eyes. "Why do you say that? You don't think Miles is causing problems for you here, do you? It might be a good idea to talk to Stella to see if she's heard anything. That woman has her finger on the pulse of this town."

"I've spoken to Stella several times but not about my work. I don't think Miles is behind this. It's far too much effort for him. He wanted me out of town, not dead. No, this feels like it's directed at Hattie." My stomach knotted at the thought Miles might be trying to destroy more of my life. Was I naïve to dismiss him as a possible culprit? No. If something happened to me, he would have to take Nina, and his girlfriend didn't want her boyfriend's daughter hanging around.

"She's rich and all alone. I have no idea precisely what's going on, but bizarre things are happening at that house. First, there was the dragon, that I now wonder if it was a projection of some kind. It matched dragons I've seen in the movies too perfectly for it not to be. They might think it was possible to frighten her to death. I think someone's after her. Especially when a candle toppled over on some books in Hattie's massive library today."

My mother gasped and swiveled around. "Did the house catch on fire? Is everything alright? You should bring her here and call the police."

I shook my head. "Nothing happened, other than some expensive leather-bound books getting wax on them. It was lucky that I was walking by and saw it fall over. I considered calling the police. What would I tell them? That I thought someone broke in to try and kill Hattie. I have no proof and what has happened gives them nothing to go on. Besides, it's possible, I suppose, that she managed to get downstairs

MAGICAL MAKEOVER

before I arrived and light that candle." I didn't believe that for one second. Hattie was a proud woman. No way would she use a bedside commode or bedpan if she could move around so well. Someone had definitely been in the house and lit the candle. But I had no proof, and calling the police would only make me look insane.

"What did Hattie say about the incident?" My grandmother asked as she leaned toward me, fully engaged in the conversation.

I grabbed a pitcher of iced tea from the fridge and put it on the table. "She said she had no idea what happened that she hadn't lost control of her magic and hadn't felt anyone enter the home." I barely kept myself from laughing out loud. The words sounded even crazier tonight than when I heard them a few hours ago. I left out the part where she promised she would reinforce the protections to ensure that didn't happen again. The woman needed to get a security system. I was shocked she didn't already have one.

Nina didn't bother to keep from laughing. "She's definitely losing her mind. I hope you gathered all the candles in the house so this can't happen while you aren't there."

My mother joined her before catching herself and schooling her features. "You shouldn't say that. It's rough getting old. Your body and mind betray you." I couldn't agree more with my mom. My back ached, and a hot flash flared at that moment, proving how true her statement was.

"Just you wait, young lady. It starts with minor aches and pains, then your body dries up one part at a time," Nana chided as she tried to point at Nina but ended up rubbing her hands together.

She wasn't wrong. Getting old wasn't pleasant. I had my share of complaints, but they were nothing compared to my grandmother. Her fingers no longer straightened. Most were permanently bent and crooked. Same with her back. And she didn't move very fast or sleep all that well. Despite the outward signs of aging, both she and Hattie had an inner light that spoke of life and vitality.

"If I look as good as you do at your age, I will count myself lucky, Nana." Nina bent and kissed my grandmother's cheek then did the same with my mom making both of them get teary-eyed.

"Back to the point. Nana, have you ever heard of anyone that hated Hattie enough to try and hurt her? I mean, it seems like someone is definitely out to get her." I was certain the incident was intentional and designed to kill Hattie.

My mom set the tureen of stew down, scooped some into a bowl for my grandmother and herself, and then passed it along. My grandmother poured a glass of tea, meeting my gaze when she passed the pitcher to me. "There have always been a handful that didn't like her. She wasn't popular in high school, and that has continued over the years. Particularly after she built a successful company."

My mom waved her spoon through the air, dripping stew off the sides. "That had to do with both the rumors about her being a witch. As well as her being rich. She refuses to help certain local politicians with aspirations for the Senate. She hasn't made many friends, that's for sure. Why else do you think she's all alone up there in that big house with only you to care for her?"

My heart cracked for the eccentric woman. It was one reason I agreed to work for her. I hated seeing people with no one there for them at the end of their lives. Besides, she wasn't an awful person. Grouchy at times, sure, but who wasn't? And she did have some friends.

There had been several women stopping by at different times. Although their visits seemed more like business meetings. For all I know, that's precisely what they were. She never allowed me to remain in the room, so I had no idea.

"What happens to her estate if she dies? Does anyone know?" I looked up at Nina when she spoke. I hadn't thought about that. Money certainly motivated people to do awful things.

"Surely, she has a will to make sure no one can take advantage. I can ask her tomorrow." I wanted to make sure her inheritance went where she wanted. I could just imagine the government getting a boatload if there was nothing in place.

"Be careful," my grandmother warned. "You don't want her to think you're fishing for information or looking to take her for a ride yourself. She's a smart woman, or she wouldn't have been able to make so much money throughout her lifetime. I'm sure she has her wishes documented."

I nodded my head, praying she was right about that. I couldn't shake the feeling that someone was trying to kill her to gain what she had. The idea seemed impossible, but the certainty wouldn't allow me to dismiss the idea. Besides the fact that there had been too many eerie incidents to say with confidence, nothing was amiss.

MY HIGH SCHOOL BEST FRIEND, Stella, smiled widely at me and wrapped her arms around me. Her impeccable suit jacket stretched over her shoulders with the movement. "It's so good to see you finally. Don't get me wrong. I've loved talking to you so often lately, but you've been busy since you moved home."

I released Stella and returned her smile. Seeing her took me back thirty years to when we met in middle school. We both joined a summer swim team and became fast friends. I missed those easy days of going to the pool for practice then riding around town looking for something to do until it was time to go in for dinner.

"Moving home has been a whirlwind of chaos. Especially since I started working for Hattie Silva the day after my daughter and I arrived in Camden. Let's grab a table so we can catch up." I motioned to the hostess stand inside the doors to The Waterfront restaurant where we had decided to meet. I loved their fresh seafood, and you couldn't beat their outside dining in the summer.

Stella greeted the hostess and asked her to sit us on the patio at a table closest to the water. Following the twenty-something woman through the restaurant, I took in the familiar décor. Little had changed over the last five years since I had eaten there last.

Our table overlooked the water and boats below, with nothing but a couple bars separating us. We took our seats then ordered drinks. I raised an eyebrow when Stella ordered wine. I stuck with lemonade. I had to go to work after I was done eating.

"So, tell me how you've been," I prompted when the hostess left. I felt entirely too underdressed in my scrubs and nursing crocs. Not that the Waterfront was super fancy, but next to Stella, I looked like a dump.

Stella's long brown hair was pulled into a ponytail, leaving her grey eyes clear. She looked great for our age, with few fine lines and wrinkles. And her makeup was spot on. I needed to ask about what her face care routine was. I swear my wrinkles had wrinkles.

And don't get me started on the dark spots just showing up. Or maybe I just needed a good lesson on how to properly apply makeup. I rarely bothered with too much because it always melted off by the end of a twelve-hour shift.

"I've been busy raising my kids and growing my business. Nothing terribly exciting."

MAGICAL MAKEOVER

I frowned, trying to remember what she'd said about her husband. For the life of me, I couldn't recall his name or what he did. "You own the local realty office, right? How has that been for you?"

She nodded her head up and down. "That's right. I just expanded and brought in two more agents. I've received more and more listings, but I don't want to work full-time, and even if I did, I would have needed help. Anyway, Todd and I agreed that I would be home after school when the kids get home. Neither of us wants them to get into drugs or worse. There are so many more dangers for our kids than when we were younger."

"You're right about that. Smartphones and constantly being connected have created a generation that doesn't understand downtime or delayed gratification. Remind me what Todd does again." Knowing his name didn't help me recall anything about him, which left me asking directly.

"Todd is a local sheriff. He sees and hears about the worst of humanity. Having a dad in law enforcement makes it next to impossible for the kids to get away with anything."

The waiter arrived then with our drinks and took our orders. I got fish and chips plus an order to go so I could take it to Hattie. Stella got their haddock sandwich. Taking a sip of the lemonade, I let my gaze wander to the boats. "I'll have to remember Todd is in law enforcement if anything weird ever happens again at Hattie's house or I need to threaten Nina or Jean-Marc." Jean-Marc was twenty-one and in college in the triangle. He lived close to his dad. Not that Miles ever talked to our son. Nina, however, lived with me. At sixteen, I was more worried I'd have to have Todd scare some sense into her.

My gaze flew back to her face when Stella gasped. Her full lips had rounded, and her grey eyes were flared wide.

"You work for the witch? How is that? What kind of weird stuff are we talking about? Ghosts and bats and stuff?"

I chuckled at her million questions. She had always been a talker, and when she got excited, you had to work to keep up with the words flying from her mouth at you. "Nothing that exciting." *Liar, liar.* I wanted to choke my inner snark. No way was I going to tell her I thought I had seen a ghost. And a dragon. I would be the insane one then. "But I do wonder if someone is trying to hurt her. There was an incident where a candle was lit in the library, but no one else was in the house, and she can't go up and down stairs without me."

The light in Stella's eyes dimmed some, and her mouth closed. "Well, I never did believe those old stories anyway. I'm not surprised someone is causing trouble, though. There have been rumors that she hasn't identified an heir yet for her billions of dollars."

My stomach knotted. If there was no one chosen, I was likely on the right track. "How does anyone know if she has declared an heir or not yet? Isn't that private?"

"Well, yeah, but you know how it is. Someone finds out somehow. In this case, Liz saw Ms. Silva's attorney and asked what he was there to do. He said something about filing paperwork for the company's latest merger. That made her ask how she was doing. That was when her attorney mentioned she was looking for an heir."

"How does the fact that she is looking for someone translate into having nothing set up already? I can't imagine that wily woman not having a backup plan."

Stella nodded and waited until the waiter delivered our food before replying. "Perhaps. But she's put a lot of work into her business. She has her hands in more pots than I can imagine. I can see why she wants it to continue. It's her legacy, and without her, it would just disappear."

I shook my head. I knew very little about businesses. My

education was in nursing and taking care of sick people. I could work my way around a ventilator like the best of them but keep me out of the boardroom.

I took a bite of the crunchy fish and moaned when the delicious flavor burst across my taste buds. Stella put her forks down and sipped her wine. "Maybe that's why her lawyer made a comment at all. I mean, isn't information like that protected by the attorney-client privilege. I just thought he was terrible at his job."

I didn't like discussing this where others could overhear what we were saying. It would be just my luck if I gave someone the idea to try and steal her business out from under her. I would have to keep my eyes peeled and make sure Hattie was safe.

"Tell me more about these rumors about her being a witch, so I know what to look out for."

Stella laughed and nearly choked on a french fry. "They say she can hex people and that she has a black cat. Oh, and one time I heard there were wolves running around her property during the full moon. They were howling and everything."

Dunking a piece of fish into the tartar sauce, I took another bite. "Her cat's a multi-colored tabby, not black. And she's spoiled rotten." Her coat was beautiful and softer than any animal I'd ever encountered. I imagine it was thanks to expensive cat shampoo. "And wolves are native to the area, aren't they? I believe howling is something they do when they run in packs. Has anyone ever seen a ghost at her house?"

"No one's ever been inside the place. When she updated the interior a few years ago, she brought in a crew from somewhere else. I'd bet the rumors started because she's such a private person. You know how nosy people are here. Which reminds me, I heard about what your ex did. Why didn't you tell me he was such an asshole?"

I should have known I wouldn't be able to keep the affair and divorce secret. As much as I didn't want my dirty laundry aired, all I really cared about was that Stella understood the truth.

"Honestly, I was embarrassed. And I had no idea for twenty years that he was hiding an evil soul."

Stella reached across the table and squeezed my hands. "Did he really leave you for a twenty-five-year-old model?"

I had to take a deep breath and focus on the soothing sea breeze to keep my anger from rising. "She wasn't a model. She worked for the hospital where we both worked. I was clueless that he was slipping it to her right under my nose. Not my finest. I should have known. Maybe then I wouldn't have lost everything, including my career, when he left me."

Stella growled and bared her teeth. "I'd like to say I will help you get back at him and get your job back, but I'm glad you're home. Hey, maybe if Hattie really is a witch, she can curse him with erectile dysfunction or something."

I laughed at the idea. I'd considered it more than once. "She's offered, but I declined. I refuse to stoop to his level. Life isn't fair. Vengeance for me will be taking my midlife makeover and making it something he will envy."

Stella held up her glass. "Here, here."

I clinked my lemonade with her glass and took a sip. It had never been in my plan to return home and become the nurse for a filthy rich hermitess. I spent twenty years working hard to establish myself as the best nurse in North Carolina, next to Fiona. Regardless, I meant what I said. I was going to rock this makeover.

CHAPTER 3

"What made you bring me some fish and chips?" Hattie cocked her head and gave me a look I couldn't decipher.

I stopped short at the question. Hattie Silva was difficult to read on her best days, but she had been even weirder lately. She moved from irritated to confused to touched to pissed-off faster than I was hit with hot flashes. I got them every five minutes, it seemed, so that was saying something.

"I know I left you a sandwich, but I thought you might enjoy something different. I was only trying to do something nice for you. I know you can't get out much. Next time I'll grab something you prefer." Honestly, I rarely ever only thought only of myself.

Turning around, I headed back to her bedside to grab the tray when she took a bite and held a piece out to Tarja. "No one has done something for me without expecting something from me. Thank you. This is wonderful."

A vice tightened around my chest, making me feel like the worst nurse ever. I'd been here for her and had done everything I could to help her. I had been so wrapped up in the unfairness of my divorce and the odd things happening around her house that I didn't notice much beneath the surface.

Hattie used sarcasm and insanity to keep others at bay. Anger, as well. It had to be hard when you assumed everyone you encountered was using you and trying to take advantage of you.

"I'm glad you like it. I ate so much at lunch I can hardly move." I patted my distended belly.

Hattie covered her mouth and laughed. Food splattered behind her hand as she bent forward, coughing. Eating was a challenge for her at times. I had assumed she would be okay with the soft fish.

Rushing to her side, I pushed the rolling table away, grabbed the suction from the wall, and pushed her against the pillow. She fought me for several minutes. "Let me get the pieces from your throat. It'll help."

Her eyes were wide as she opened her mouth, coughing openly on me. I didn't have gloves on and didn't hesitate to stick the plastic tube down her throat. The suction gurgled as chewed-up fish traveled up and into the canister.

Once her airway was clear, I sat her up and rubbed her back until she stopped hacking up a lung. Grabbing her water, I gave her a drink and waited a few more minutes until she settled.

"Would you like to eat anymore?" In the hospital, a doctor would have had me withhold food until her esophagus stopped spasming. I knew it was a risk, but Hattie was in enough pain. She didn't need to add hunger to the list. She nodded and covered her mouth while she coughed again.

"Alright. Small bites. I don't want you asphyxiating on my watch. That wouldn't look good on my resume."

Scratchy laughter filled the room before she broke off a

small bite. I thought she was going to choke again when she cleared her throat. "You took all the candles from the house?"

The change of topic was abrupt but not difficult to follow. "I did. I think someone used it to try and harm you. I have no idea how they got inside the house. You don't think your cleaning lady would have let them in, do you?" That was the only explanation that made any sense.

Her green eyes shifted from me to the window across the way, and her hand went to her chest. She was still coughing. "There is no way she allowed danger inside this house. The attack came from outside the house. I need you to keep the candles safe. They contain elements of my power."

Did she have safe deposit box keys inside them? She was talking crazy again, but I thought it was more of a code than anything else. "They are safe in my bedroom at home. My grandmother won't let anyone get close to them. Neither will my mom."

A smile broke over Hattie's face even as she did this weird throat clearing-cough combo. "Amelia is a bulldog. They'll be safe in her house. Your mother, Mollie, is there with her, right?"

I nodded my head. "Yes. They're both there. Mom takes care of Nana, but they both keep an eye on the neighborhood. I don't think Mr. Carson likes that very much. They constantly gripe at him for leaving his trash can at the curb."

Hattie finished one piece of fish, set the plate in front of Tarja on the bed, and then looked at me. "I can imagine. Amelia has always been a stickler for the rules. How would you feel about going for a drive?"

I watched her closely. No one placed restrictions on her, but it made me nervous just thinking about taking her out of the house. Especially when she was still coughing. "What did you have in mind?"

She leaned over and pulled the drawer on the side table

while clearing her throat loudly for the tenth time. "There's a store about forty miles from here, and I need some supplies from there."

I brought the stool closer to the bed and sat down. "I'm happy to get whatever you need. Let me check your heart and lungs before I go." She'd been coughing less, but I could tell there was still something stuck in there because she continued hacking.

"Can you take me to the bathroom, as well? I haven't wet myself since I was a baby and have no desire to do so now."

Grabbing my stethoscope, I stuffed the ends in my ears and put the drum on her chest. "I am more than happy to take you. You can use the bedside commode or a bedpan. Whatever you feel up to."

Her heart was surprisingly strong for a woman with her conditions. Her lungs were gunky, so I'd have to keep an eye on them. If some of the fluid didn't clear soon, she might need surgery to have them cleared.

"I prefer using the bathroom. I have no choice but to use the bedside commode overnight. I don't want to use it during the day, as well. It's not a fun experience." Her chin went in the air, and her fingers fussed with her pink top. She was dressed in a silk button-up and soft dress pants.

One of the first things I noticed about her was that she insisted on being dressed daily. I was beginning to understand that she was proud, and insisting on getting out of her pajamas every day, did many things for her. It improved her self-esteem and reminded her of who she was.

"Do you want me to stay here overnight, as well? If you need help, I can make arrangements with my mom and grandmother." I had advised her to hire someone else for the night shifts, but she declined, saying she slept while I was gone. She insisted that she wanted to keep things the way they were until she had no other choice.

MAGICAL MAKEOVER

Her head shook gently side to side, sending her silver hair flying across her face. Her skin was thin and wrinkled, like most her age, but there was an underlying glow that made her stunning.

"No. There is no need for that. Now, let's get this list together."

I put the stethoscope down, then picked up the plate and took it downstairs to clean while she wrote out what she needed. Movement caught the corner of my eye when I reached the landing.

I looked out the porthole, expecting to see the dragon. There was nothing but a dark patch of grass with withering flowers in the distance. I was glad my mind had stopped playing tricks on me.

* * *

LOOKING up from the paper in my hands, I double-checked the store name. It was the place. What on earth was *The Last Spell*? If the sign and windows were any indications, this was a place to purchase accoutrement for doing witchcraft.

The name of the shop was bracketed by pentagrams. There was a tall stool with a massive pink crystal sitting on top of a dark pink cloth. A table below the crystal had an array of tarot cards. In the other window, there was a cauldron, some jewelry, and knives. What use did they have for weapons?

Regardless, the whole place screamed 'woo-woo' to me. That's what my mother called anything having to do with magic. Turning off the ignition, I climbed out of the car and looked around the street.

I hadn't been to the town over from ours in decades. It wasn't a place I spent much time in throughout my life, so I couldn't say if the quaint little street had changed at all over the years.

The town reminded me of Boone. A small area in the mountains of North Carolina. Both sides of the streets were lined with brick buildings and shops that sold a variety of knickknacks, treats, and antiques. There was also a yoga studio and law offices. It was the feel of the place that I loved so much.

I headed for the door and pushed it open. The gentle tinkle of a bell chimed when I entered the store. The scent of flowers and herbs greeted me. It was overpowering and immediately gave me a headache. Strong odors always did that to me.

My attention was driven in a hundred different directions at once. For several seconds, I felt like I had the worst case of ADHD ever reported. The walls were purple, and there were tables and bookshelves throughout the shop. One section even had skirts and shirts hanging from a circular rack.

There was a tall woman with braids throughout her red hair and bangles on each arm up to her elbows standing behind a counter. I could clearly see her billowy blue top above the counter. Through the glass display case below, I could make out the colorful skirt she had on.

"Welcome to 'The Last Spell.' How can I help you?" Her smile was warm and welcoming. I didn't fit in this place with my medical scrubs and scientific mind, but she didn't look down her nose at me, which was a relief. I was out of my element and would need her help.

I walked down the aisle toward her and lifted the list to scan the ingredients. Yep, they were still just as odd as before. Too many things had me questioning how this was my life now. I wasn't going to waste more time thinking about it.

MAGICAL MAKEOVER

The bottom line was that this was my life, and I was making the best of it.

Plastering a smile on my face, I set the list on the counter and sneezed as all the scents tickled my nose. Crap, had I just peed myself a little? I didn't feel like I was wet but couldn't be sure without going to the restroom. Getting older sucked sometimes.

Wanting to get this over with more than I wanted to check for leakage, I focused on why I was in the shop. "I take care of an older woman, and she sent me to pick up these items for her."

The woman lowered her brown eyes to the list I put in front of her. "This is quite the list. What spells are you using these for?"

I cocked my head to the side and tried to hide my shock. "What do you mean spells? Aren't these just for decoration?" When I saw the list, I assumed Hattie was trying to create an atmosphere that proved the rumors were true. I knew she sensed her time was close, and I could see her giving the busybodies around town something to talk about even after she'd gone.

"These items are designed for potent spells. They aren't something any witch can perform. Even if you discovered your family's grimoire and have explicit directions, you will want to rethink trying to cast something you read."

I shook my head. "These aren't for me. My patient asked me to pick these up. She didn't mention why she wanted them, but she's very ill and not able to move around on her own."

"Exactly who is this for? I won't give such powerful items to just anyone. It would be irresponsible of me if I did."

I could respect that. More people needed to be this cautious. "It's for Hattie Silva. I know she's not really a witch, and she might not be someone you want to give these items to, but I promise I won't let her misuse them."

The clerk's head snapped up, and her brown eyes went wide, then she practically bounced in place. "Hattie Silva? I've waited years for her to come back to my shop. I've been worried about her. How has she been doing? Are there are still vultures hanging around trying to curry her favor?"

I swallowed and wondered if this had been a good idea after all. It didn't seem like this woman was after Hattie, but that didn't mean I would let my guard down. "She's sick. It's why she hired me to care for her."

The clerk eyed me as she tapped her fingers on the countertop, making the bangles jangle with each movement. She nodded. "I'm Clara. My family has owned The Last Spell since the late seventeen hundreds. I'm not after anything from Hattie. I'm not Tainted."

That was reassuring to a point. I doubt I would ever blindly trust anyone again. Miles had burned me too severely. "I'm Phoebe. I'm not sure why Hattie wants this stuff. It would make more sense to install cameras and a security system with round-the-clock monitoring. Someone is after her money."

Clara hmphed and came out from behind the counter carrying the list. "A security system won't help against those stalking her."

"What do you mean?" Of course, it would. Especially if it was connected to a system that was monitored. Police had responded to my old neighbor's house before they even knew someone had broken into their house.

"Witches and Fae can work their way around electronic systems. She needs powerful protections, and from the looks of it, she is reinforcing what she's likely had in place for centuries."

"You can't be serious. Witches and Fae don't exist."

One of Clara's eyebrows rose to her hairline as she looked down at my necklace then back up at me. "Yes, they do. Normally, I wouldn't tell a mundie anything. However, I can see you're already familiar with someone who has magic, and I don't want any of the Tainted to steal what belongs to Hattie." There was that term again.

My mind skipped over that, and in reflex, my hand wrapped around the dragonfly and thought back to what Hattie had said about it. It was too much to consider at the moment. And frankly, I didn't believe these two.

My mind kept returning to her comment about people trying to steal from Hattie. My anger rose for the hundredth time, and I was suddenly eager to return and make sure she was alright. The last thing we needed was to have someone else break in and start a fire while I was gone.

"I will never let anyone hurt Hattie. She's my patient and my responsibility. If this stuff helps make her feel secure, then I'm all for it, but I will be taking steps of my own to ensure she is safe from harm."

Clara nodded her head as she focused on grabbing the candles, crystals, and herbs on the list. When she reached for a jar of what looked like tiny eyeballs, I almost threw up. These people took this witchcraft seriously.

"Some of the witches aren't abominations. Many believe that they should be able to court her since she has no heir. Others see her as fair game. I'm adding a few ingredients she might find useful, as well."

My head was pounding more the longer I was in the shop, and I had to force myself to remain in place and nod in response. "I'm sure she will appreciate that."

I headed over to the display of cauldrons and looked them over. I'd seen pictures of the pots in posts online and in movies, but I'd never seen them in person. They were surprisingly heavy when I picked one up. They had to be cast iron.

I approached the counter when Clara told me she had everything. I retrieved the money Hattie had given me from my purse and set it down, then watched. At the same time, Clara carefully wrapped each crystal and set them into separate bags.

There was no way I was asking about that. I had reached my limit of crazy for the year. My midlife makeover was going swimmingly so far. There wasn't one aspect of my day to day that resembled what it had been like before Miles flushed me down the toilet. I spent decades scrubbing after finishing twelve to fourteen-hour shifts.

I had gone from caring for an entire surgical floor of patients to being responsible for one older woman that believed she was a witch. And I was shopping for magical gear for her while wondering if I'd seen ghosts and a dragon. Was my patient the crazy one, or was I?

The only thing that mattered in all this crazy was that Hattie is as healthy as possible with her condition and, most importantly, that she isn't taken advantage of.

CHAPTER 4

"What did you do, Phe?" My mother was whispering, but the condemnation in her tone was crystal clear.

The voice message I had been listening to was coming to an end when she walked into the kitchen. It had to be disturbing for her to hear Doctor Wilson talk about Hattie's latest neurological exam. Or perhaps she was upset because he agreed to do an MRI if Hattie's function had significantly declined.

I felt like I had to explain myself while at the same time I shouldn't say anything because of patient-doctor privilege. "Just following up on my patient. Nothing to worry about."

The scowl my mother shot me took me right back to when I was fifteen years old and tried to sneak out of the house to meet Stella at the park. "I can't tell you anything about the healthcare of my patient, mom. You know that."

She sighed in response and walked to the fridge, and grabbed the creamer. "At least tell me you didn't tell that man she is losing her marbles. She's suffering enough without having to deal with more tests and scrutiny."

I shook my head. "All I can say is that I was following up on test results."

"Has something new happened?" I turned to see my grandmother shuffling into the kitchen. I greeted her and gave her a kiss on the cheek, then did the same for my mom.

I poured coffee into my travel tumbler and added enough cream to turn it light brown, then added sugar. "Nothing new. Yesterday was surprisingly calm enough that I managed to meet Stella for lunch and ran an errand for Hattie. Alright, I've got to head out. You two stay out of trouble and tell Nina I love her."

"Will do," my mom and Nana promised. I grabbed my bags and the supplies I bought for Hattie yesterday. As I was leaving, I heard my mom telling Nana about the message she overheard. I prayed something else occupied their minds today, or I was going to hear about that tonight.

The drive across town to Nimaha house was busier this morning, and there was fog as I got closer to the coast that wasn't typical for this time of year. We didn't usually see this until October, and it was barely August. Plus, it usually extended much further inland. My drive had been clear enough that I saw the sky lighten and the horizon turn a gorgeous ombre of pinks and oranges.

I slowed my speed when I turned off on the road leading to Hattie's house. My headlights came on and reflected off an animal's eyes. They flashed yellowish green. It had to be a cat up in a tree because they were at my eye level. I prayed it wasn't Tarja. I didn't feel like hunting her down in the forest. I was not precisely outdoorsy.

Pulling into the driveway, I parked where I usually did. Off to the side of the house and out of the circular drive in front. It was dark on this side of the house, and the fog made it feel like I was surrounded. It was not a fun feeling. Particularly when there was an unusual chill in the air. I practically ran up the steps and to the front door.

To my relief, Tarja greeted me when I made it inside. "Morning, Tarja. How are you this morning?"

Setting my bags down in the office at the front of the house, I climbed the wood stairs. The place was quiet. Hattie must still be sleeping. I didn't hear her television playing the news in the background.

With no sun shining through the windows, the house was eerie. My clogs echoed loudly as I headed for the stairs. The house felt lonely and sad. It was probably me projecting how I would feel if I were at the end of my life and I wasn't surrounded by those I loved.

The painting opposite the porthole window on the landing even looked foggy. I finally understood seasonal affective disorder. It was no joke. This gloom was infecting me.

Shaking that off, I climbed the rest of the stairs and was surprised to see Hattie sitting up in bed, reading a book. "Morning, Phoebe. How was your evening?" And where the heck had she gotten the book? I hadn't left anything with her before leaving for the shop the day before.

"It was quiet. I watched another episode of Charmed. That show has so much wrong, but it's oddly addictive."

I chuckled. Perhaps that's where she got her ideas from. "I have your supplies downstairs, but let's get you showered before we dive into them."

I helped her from the spare bedroom where her medical bed had been set up and into the master bathroom. After sitting her on the shower seat, I turned on the water. The stall was big enough for us to disrobe on one side before moving her to the other and washing her hair. Handing her the soaped-up loofa, I stepped out to grab a towel for her while she washed up. I had her rinsed, dried, and in her robe in no time.

"What would you like to wear today?" I asked the same thing every day, and she always had an answer and the outfit of her choice hanging in the front of her closet. I bet she asked Mythia to do that for her when she came in.

Hattie sat down on the bench in her restroom and braced herself on her stick-thin arms. She waved one hand toward the closet before saying, "There's a teal top and black pants. Be sure to grab the tank top sitting on the chest in the middle."

Entering her closet was like entering an entirely different world. The space was bigger than my entire bedroom suite had been at my old house. One side had bars for shirts with alcoves above that. There were countless cubbies along the back wall for her shoes, and the remaining wall had bars for dresses and a combination of lower bars and storage on top.

The chest in the middle wasn't a dresser at all. It was larger than the island in the kitchen. It had drawers above it with jewelry and various clothes in the ones below the top. There were even those stairs you found in libraries to reach the top levels and a couch. The extravagance was mind-boggling. Exactly what I always imagined a rich person would have in their home.

Grabbing the clothes, I walked back into the restroom to find Hattie staring out the window next to the massive claw-foot tub. I followed her gaze and was surprised to see a car driving down the road.

"Are you expecting someone?"

She averted her gaze and sighed. "Yes. I hoped it would take her longer to get here. Help me into my pants, and I will get the rest on while you show Myrna into the parlor."

"Alright." I slipped her underwear onto her legs, followed by her pants, then stood her up and finished pulling them on. "I will be back for you soon. Don't try to get up on your own. We don't need you to break a hip or worse."

Tarja followed me down the stairs. I reached the entrance right as the doorbell rang. Smoothing my dark blue scrub top, I opened the door. "Good morning. May I help you?"

The older woman lifted one perfectly manicured light brown eyebrow as she looked me over. She had on a maroon skirt suit with a cream top under the jacket. With her cream heels, she stood well over my five-foot-six inches. "I'm here to see Hattie Silva."

I inclined my head. "She asked me to show you to the parlor." I stood aside and gestured to the open entrance.

Myrna entered the house and glanced up at the crystal chandelier before continuing to the hall on the right. She'd definitely been here before. I followed, wondering why she was here.

"Can I get you some coffee? Or tea?" I asked as she entered the parlor and turned in a circle.

She shook her head, and her shoulder-length blonde hair swayed with the movement. Her blue eyes narrowed as she noticed Tarja sitting at my feet. "Tarja. Nice to see you again." My eyes widened, and I shifted my gaze from her to Tarja. I swear the cat snarled at the woman.

"I'll go retrieve Ms. Silva." I never used the formality with Hattie. She'd asked me to call her by her name, but something told me to be more formal with this woman. I took my leave and noticed Tarja standing sentry in the middle of the entrance to the parlor.

Climbing the stairs for the second time, I returned to the bathroom and found Hattie with her hair done and her makeup on. She was setting a mirror down on the counter when I entered.

"Did you get up and grab this stuff on your own?"

Hattie scoffed. "I didn't have far to go. Let's get this over with."

I sensed her irritation and imagined this woman was here to either deliver some bad news or try to manipulate her in some way. I would stay close and intervene if their conversation went sideways. No way was anyone taking advantage of Hattie Silva on my watch.

We made our way slowly down the stairs and through the house. Typically when we reached the bottom, Hattie grabbed a walker to help her move around. This time she bypassed the closet saying, "Not this time."

"I'm here to help. Lean on me." She paused and looked up at me, then nodded and slid her arm through my offered elbow. I was glad she used me for support as we took our time making our way to the parlor.

"Myrna. Nice of you to stop by," Hattie said as we entered, and I helped her to the loveseat on the right. "Would you excuse us, Phoebe?"

I hated the idea of leaving her alone, but I nodded. "I will fix breakfast. Call out if you need me for *anything*."

"I will. Go with her, Tarja." The cat hissed at that but followed me out of the room and to the kitchen, where I made some instant oatmeal and cut up fresh fruit.

Unable to stand it, I tried to tiptoe back down the hall to listen to what was being said. All I could hear were indistinct murmurs. When I moved that way, Tarja swiped my leg and moved toward the back door.

There was a window in the parlor that looked out on the back deck and yard beyond. Figuring it was worth a shot, I hurried out into the gloomy fog. The sun had come up, but it barely made it through the thick mist.

I plastered myself against the house next to the window. My heart was pounding so hard I couldn't hear what was said. I had to take several deep breaths before it slowed enough to catch their conversation.

"Time to stop being stubborn and give me your power." Myrna was trying to get something from Hattie. I was about to say fuck it and rush into the room when I heard Hattie.

"I will never give you an ounce of my power. You claim you aren't Tainted, but I know better. You've somehow managed to hide it with a glamour." The command in Hattie's voice was a relief. She'd seen through the woman's façade.

I returned to the kitchen to put the food on the tray and headed for the parlor. Hattie had turned Myrna down. It was time for her to leave. Myrna scowled at me when I entered and set the platter on the coffee table.

"I trust you're done here. Ms. Silva needs to eat so she can take her morning medications. I can show you out."

Hattie lifted a hand to her mouth to cover her chuckle. That only pissed Myrna off more. "I can show myself out."

I followed her as she left the room. She cursed under her breath but otherwise didn't acknowledge me. Tarja was on the porch when we reached it. Myrna got into her car and took off without a word.

"Are you coming in?" I asked the cat. She shook her head and ran after the vehicle: oddity number one thousand and one at Nimaha house.

* * *

I JUMPED when I heard a voice. It sounded like someone grunting from exertion. My hand flew to my chest, and I looked around the yard. I had to be hearing things. Ever since Hattie's visitor a few hours earlier, I had been on edge. There was something about the woman that didn't sit well with me.

I crept forward slowly. There was very little on this side of the house. The grass led to the forest. I could see one of the outbuildings in the distance. I was reasonably certain it was the pool house. My eyesight wasn't what it once was, so I couldn't be sure it wasn't the gardner's shed.

Ever since Myrna had shown up earlier that day, my nerves had been jittery. I crossed the pavement to the grass and headed toward the pool. It seemed like the noise had come from that direction. I didn't trust Myrna not to return after I left.

I wasn't leaving until I was sure Hattie wasn't in danger. I was a nurse, not a cop. I should call Stella's husband and ask him to come and check it out. Deciding there was no basis to involve him yet, I continued to move through the yard.

Something was glowing on the beach. Initially, I thought perhaps she placed a bomb there, but it was human-shaped. My eyes were no longer what they used to be, so I couldn't see clearly. Crouching down, despite the protest in my thighs, I made my way down the terraced yard to the beach.

Blonde hair blew in a non-existent breeze as she stood on the pebbled shore with her arms out at her sides. I noted she wasn't on Hattie's beach but several feet from the property line. She was definitely up to something.

Yanking my cell from my purse, I stood up straight. "You need to leave now. I'm calling the police."

Myrna turned to face me. Her face looked much older now, and she wore no makeup. The glow around her was grey and reminded me of the fog earlier that day. "You should have kept your mundie nose out of my business."

My heart was in my throat when honest-to-god lightning left Myrna's hands. What the hell was going on here?

CHAPTER 5

A scream left my throat, and I dove to the side like I was a pro-ball player stealing home plate. My phone flew from my hand, and my purse dropped off my shoulder in the process, making me curse.

The air crackled inches from my face as the energy passed me. It even smelled like ozone. My mind was struggling to figure out what the heck was going on while devising a way to escape at the same time.

Magic didn't exist. The most logical explanation was that she had some kind of supercharged taser. *Sure, and I suppose she ate some comb jellyfish, and that's why she's glowing.* Okay, so I couldn't explain that one so easily. And I didn't have time to worry about it.

I needed to get the heck out of there. I scrambled to my feet, backing away. I stopped when water soaked my shoes. Unable to walk on water, I tried to move toward the house.

"You really should have kept to yourself, mundie. Now you're going to pay for interfering." Myrna's countenance was a twisted version of the well-groomed beautiful woman that had visited a few hours earlier. Even her clothes were a tattered, dirty mess. It was the maroon suit, only the jacket was shredded in places, and her skirt was ripped up one side. Her heels were gone, and her feet looked like they ended in claws.

"I'm doing my job. I won't let you steal from Hattie. Leave now, and you won't be arrested." I thrust my shaking hands on my hips to hide how terrified I was and show my bravado.

Myrna's body shook as a crackling noise erupted from her throat. It took me a minute to realize she was laughing. I was so shocked by the sound that I didn't see her lift one of her hands.

When fire slammed into my shoulder, it sent me flying backward. I saw the moonlit sky and heard the energy arcing through the air right before it was replaced by the sizzle of flesh.

For several nauseating seconds, I didn't know anything except pain. Myrna had hit me with some kind of energy blast. My heart stuttered and sped up while my lungs seized from the current running through my body.

I landed with a splash in what felt like freezing cold water. It numbed my entire body. Relief flooded me, and it took the pain from kill-me-now to I-only-wish-I-was-dead. For the second time in as many minutes, I was crawling. I would pay for that later.

For the moment, I scanned the beach for my cell. I needed to call for help, or she was going to kill me. It never occurred to me that I could be murdered. The concept was as foreign to me as magic. Murder was something that happened in movies and the slums. Not in a middle-class neighborhood in Maine.

A black streak flew toward Myrna. I couldn't catch what it was but was certain I heard a snarl. Myrna sounded like a dying cat when the animal passed her, moving so fast I didn't realize it had hurt her until I saw the blood spread across her chest. Oddly, it was so dark it almost looked black.

That couldn't be right, and it wasn't something I was going to worry about. I spotted my phone and dashed from the water, splashing my way to the shore. It took a second for my feet to adjust once the resistance was gone, and I fell on my phone rather ungracefully.

Reaching for it, I winced when Myrna's objection pierced my eardrums. Where was the wolf? I grabbed a fistful of the small rocks on the beach and got to my feet. Myrna was barely ten feet from me now.

She was panting, and her chest now resembled a loaf of butter top bread. The slide down the top of those loaves was smoother than the ragged edges of her wound. And the smell was worse than durian fruit. Fiona and I had bought one in college and made the mistake of cutting it open in our dorm. We couldn't clear the smell for weeks.

Lightning was shooting from Myrna's hands while she frantically clawed at her chest. I hopped around like frog legs in a frying pan and tried to flip my phone on. It used facial recognition, and between the dark and me dancing around, it didn't open.

In my frantic attempt to avoid the blasts, I saw wolves further back in the trees. The black wolf must have run back to them. I tried to take off toward the house and had given up calling anyone. I hadn't made it more than five steps when a bolt made me windmill to keep from falling on my ass.

The tire around my mid-section overbalanced me, and I landed hard enough to make me worry about breaking my butt. That, coupled with the shoulder injury were so painful I saw stars.

Rubbing my eyes, I realized it wasn't stars at all. It was the fireflies I'd seen most nights I was at the house at dark. Myrna was stalking toward me. Her chest was a naked mess, and dark blood dripped on the pebbles where it started smoking.

"Enough playtime. It's past time I take over the East coast, and you're standing in my way."

"What the hell are you?" Aside from a nutcase? Those questions I had about what was going on before vanished. After what I'd seen, I was ninety percent sure magic existed, and somehow this woman had harnessed it.

Her clothes had fallen from her body, leaving her chest bare and bleeding. There was no device strapped to her, and I knew there was no other explanation for why she was glowing.

"I'm the witch that's going to steal every drop of power from Hattie. I'm the one that discovered how to extend our lives. It's fitting I should be the one to claim the magic from the most powerful witch line in the United States." She lifted her hands, palms up, and tossed a black fireball between them.

I had taken small steps toward the house and stopped when she shifted her blue eyes to me. Only they were no longer blue. She'd look like a shark if her skin wasn't a wrinkled bag of peach.

"What are you? You aren't the mundie you pretend to be, are you?" She had tilted her head to the side and lost the look of hatred for a split second. She saw me as a puzzle to figure out.

Sweat poured down, mixing with the saltwater to create eau de toilette. Between that and the stench she was giving off, it was a surprise I kept my dinner down. My hand tightened around my phone. There was a way to call emergency services without opening the phone. Unfortunately, I had a case of *terrornesia*. Fear-induced amnesia was no joke. My mind couldn't form any sentence aside from 'get the hell out of here.'

MAGICAL MAKEOVER

"I'm a middle-aged divorcee and nurse that Ms. Silva hired to take care of her. The most exciting thing about me is the fact that my ex-husband is a cliché who left me for a woman half my age."

Her forehead furrowed, and she threw the black fire at me. I jumped to the side and twisted my ankle. Thankfully, I didn't fall over again. Her attention never wavered from me for a second, so she never saw the black wolf prowl closer to her from the back.

I needed to distract her so the wolf could attack. The animal must know she wanted to hurt Hattie. Given that she gave them sanctuary, I had to believe they felt a sense of loyalty to her. Not sure where that odd thought came from, but it felt right.

"A human has an item of Power. Who do you know? Maybe I'll keep you alive to lead me to the maker. I'll need a new power source after I finish off Hattie's line." Hattie said something similar the other day.

My hand closed over my necklace reflexively. "I found it at an estate sale. I had no idea there was anything special about it. I chose it as a symbol for my midlife makeover."

The wolf growled as it launched itself into the air. Far faster than I thought possible, Myrna swiveled around, and her hand shot into the air. I didn't waste time. I took off running toward the house. It was harder to force myself to move as fast as possible with my hurt ankle. Books and movies make it seem easy to use sheer determination to move even when hurt.

I was trying to open my phone again when the wolf yelped painfully. My heart stuttered and squeezed in my chest. Without stopping to reconsider, I backtracked. I still had the rocks in my hand.

Using all the anger simmering in my core that this woman wanted to destroy people and take their power, I lifted my hand and tossed the rocks I was holding. It wasn't much and might not even phase her, but I needed to get her attention off the wolf.

Her eyes followed the pebbles, and that was all it took for the wolf to wiggle out of her hold. One second, Myrna was holding a black wolf, and the next, there was a flash of skin before the wolf landed on its paws and raced toward me.

The line of wolves advanced behind Myrna, but they didn't attack. The black canine stopped at my side and reached my hips. I'd never seen an animal so big. It was the size of a small horse. And energy vibrated off it.

"Join me, Layla. It's time to return to the fold. You and Tsekani both need to return where you belong. Together we will be unstoppable."

The black wolf lowered her head and snarled in response. That was one terrifying 'hell no' if you asked me. Of course, Myrna's reaction was just as scary. She called up another ball of black flames and tossed it at us. It hit the ground between Layla and me.

The flames scorched the ground and burned my leg. With the fire spreading up my body, I rushed for the ocean. Getting the fire out occupied my mind. The water sizzled when it hit the flames. At first, they continued to burn. When I started to sit down, they finally disappeared.

Layla hit the water next to me, and steam surrounded us. Myrna was distracted by the wolves attacking her from behind. "We need to get out of here and to the house. I have no idea if you can understand me, but that crazy witch is going to kill us."

The wolf yipped and wagged her head. I stood up, regretting that I once again lost my phone. The quick scan of the shore didn't reveal it anywhere. If we were lucky, Mythia would show up and call the cops for us.

When Layla fell into the waves, I reached down to try and

pick her up. We ended up walking with me supporting her mid-section as I was bent at the waist. Her attention was pulled to her packmates when one of them yelped.

I couldn't stop her as she ran for Myrna. I continued toward the house and thought I was going to make it until I stopped short. I pounded on an invisible wall in front of us. That degree of certainty rose to ninety-nine percent at that moment.

Nothing on this planet would have created a barrier that couldn't be seen. Not even my palms left any impressions on the air. There was no substance to it, and I couldn't see anything, so it was oddly disorienting to hit something when I expected my fists to go right through.

The sound of snarls and yells was so loud that I anticipated the fight had moved with me and was shocked to see they were barely right at the edge of Hattie's property. I took a step, forgetting about my twisted ankle, and went down like a rock.

My knees hit first on the side of me that had been burned. It felt like sandpaper debriding my wounds. I'd seen more than my share of patients on the burn unit and grit my teeth to keep from crying out. Something clasped my foot and started pulling me toward the fight.

My vision wavered as my burns were scraped raw. I tried to find something to grab onto and got handfuls of ammunition better suited for my son's slingshot. I wasn't going to make it out of this, and thinking of my kids closed a vice around my heart. I didn't want to leave them or my mom and Nana like this.

The worst part was I risked myself for nothing. She was going to get away with hurting Hattie. As a witch, I had no doubt that she could hide her trail from law enforcement so there would be no one to warn her.

The hold on me released several feet from the border and

Myrna. This close, I could see several wolves bleeding out. The amount of blood leaking from their injuries told me they weren't likely to survive this battle.

Guilt stole my breath for several seconds as I wondered if I was the reason they were going to be killed. There was a reason Myrna hadn't crossed onto Hattie's property, and I had to guess that she couldn't.

I should have kept my freakin' nosy face out of the whole thing. A lightning bolt flew past me and slammed into one of the walls supporting one level of the yard. Bricks and dust went flying, and I slumped in relief. It was the stupidest thing to be worried about at that moment. My thoughts splintered when a piece of wood landed by my head.

I didn't want to be responsible for the deaths of wolves because they came to defend me. "Layla," I whispered. She was jumping and snarling at Myrna, who had lost her skirt at some point, while somehow managing to keep her cloak in pristine condition and had cuts all over her legs. I needed her help to distract Myrna, or I would end up dead for sure.

As if she could read my mind, the wolf stopped and looked back at me. Her gaze zeroed in on my hand then she nodded. Figuring I would think about that oddity later, I wrapped my hand around the stick and jumped to my feet, bracing myself. Adrenaline gave me the boost needed to surge to my feet and kept the pain of the movement at bay.

I wasn't dumb enough to think there was no pain. I had a hole in my shoulder. I had been burned, had twisted my ankle, and I was covered in cuts and bruises. I lost my crocs when I entered the water, so all I had on my feet were socks, and yet somehow, I found the energy to pull my arm back and let the stick fly.

I prayed it would land with the pointy end in Myrna's chest. Given my luck lately, it was going to rebound back at me. Turned out the stick wasn't what came at me. Myrna's hands were lifted in the air, and energy sizzled across her fingertips. Three wolves latched onto her legs while a fourth hung from one of her biceps.

Chunks of flesh flew, and simultaneously, Layla lunged for me, then green lightning shot in a straight line right at my skull. My feet were too slow on the reaction time, and the green energy slammed right into my chest.

It felt like I was shot as something sizzled on my breastbone, and I went airborne. Because I had the house at my back, I landed on one of the remaining brick walls with a loud crack. Pain was all I knew.

My head lolled forward. I heard the wolves howling and snarling but was distracted by how the dragonfly amulet of my necklace glowed bright green. It looked like a green apple lollipop. That was why I felt like I'd been shot. Black dots blurred my vision. I tried to shake my head and clear it.

Dizziness turned my stomach, and it felt like acid burning me from the inside out. Layla's black head nudged my chin. The spots grew, and I felt more than saw her lick my chest. Had the dragonfly Fiona's boyfriend made for me been shoved into my body? It was the last thought I had as darkness swallowed me whole.

CHAPTER 6

Loud pops and snarling startled me awake. Before I had even opened my eyes, pain besieged me. More agony than I had ever experienced in my life. What had happened? Was I in a car accident? I listened for the sounds of the ER department but only heard crackling and booms. *Fireworks.*

That made no sense with the agony stealing my ability to breathe. My back hurt like a bitch. Something was pressing against the middle of it, and my chest felt like an elephant was sitting on it. I tried to roll, and my body screamed hell-to-the-no.

Growling in my ear brought back thoughts of Myrna attacking me and wolves coming to my rescue. I cracked one eye open to see the black wolf. Layla. She nosed me and whimpered, then she latched onto my scrub top and pulled.

That tore a scream from me when my back raked over the terrace wall. I had no control over my head, and it rolled as she continued dragging me toward the house. I noticed Myrna was batting green flames from her body right before

MAGICAL MAKEOVER

she disappeared. The wolves shifted from fight mode to rescue.

Right before Layla let go of me, I saw them grab their injured or dead friends by the scruff of the neck and pull them toward us. The next thing I knew, a dragon was barreling through the forest. A dragon was living on the property! Jean-Marc would love that.

"You're a little late to the party, Tsekani."

My heart jumped out of my chest, and my head finally obeyed my command as it turned toward the female voice. A naked woman stood behind me. She had long black hair and brown eyes with a slim, muscular figure. There was something primal about her that told me she was the wolf, Layla. Before I could open my mouth to ask, the shock of fear wore off, and the pain flooded back in.

My back arched, and I screamed as acid ate through my body inch by inch. I could feel the life getting sucked out of every cell in my body—little by little. I was going to die after all. Whatever Myrna had hit me with was still working its way through my system.

She bent to pick me up. "It's okay, Phoebe. I'm going to take you to Hattie. She will know what to do."

"Nhnn." There was no way I could form words. After everything that had happened that night, I was most surprised by the direction my thoughts had gone regarding Layla, the wolf. Wolves couldn't transform into women. Could they? My mind disagreed. I'd seen it happen.

The woman shifted me in her hold and opened the backdoor. "Don't try to talk. I can't take the pain, but Hattie will be able to help. I'm Layla, in case you were wondering. What you did out there was brave, mundie. I've never met anyone with more courage."

Warmth enveloped me, making me realize I'd been freezing and shivering. That relief was quickly overwhelmed by the pain. Every step she took sent a jolt through every nerve ending.

Gritting my teeth did nothing to help the agony. Middle age had acquainted me with aches and pains, so there was a degree that I could bear. Unfortunately, this was so far above that level it was an entirely different universe.

My heart should be racing. That would make sense to me after everything that had happened. Instead, the slow thumping frightened me more than anything. My lungs constricted, and I couldn't get enough O2 into my system.

Whatever that bitch had done was going to kill me. Now that I wasn't battling something that shouldn't exist, reality crashed into me like a train going a hundred miles an hour.

Emotion choked off what little air I could manage to suck into my starved lungs. I would never see my kids again. My mom would have no one to help her with Nana, and I wouldn't get to say goodbye to Nana, either. My death would hurt them, but I hoped they would be proud of me for keeping Hattie safe. That was the only thing that made this the least bit bearable.

"I've got her, Tarja. Can Hattie help her?"

I blinked and looked up at Layla as she spoke with the cat. I would miss her as well. She was snobby and spoiled, but she'd grown on me as much as Hattie had. The world shifted, and I saw a lightning bug as we passed through the kitchen. Only it wasn't a firefly at all. It looked like a cartoon character.

No, she's dressed in pants and a tight top, not a leaf dress like Tinkerbell. That couldn't be right. The spell must be making me see things.

The tiny fairy flew closer. She was holding a rag and wringing her hands. "Oh, gods. I should have called the colony and come out to help. I'm sorry, Layla."

Nope. She was real and talking. Layla shook her head. "It

MAGICAL MAKEOVER

all happened so fast. I'm not sure they could have responded in time, Mythia. Tsekani didn't arrive until it was all over."

This was the maid? The idea of a fairy cleaning Hattie's house made me want to laugh despite the agony I was experiencing. My mind had shut down from the pain, so I filed this away with the other items I wouldn't live long enough to decipher.

"Maybe I never woke up outside, and I'm in a coma."

Layla's brown eyes focused on me as she moved through the house. The tiny fairy flew to Layla's shoulder and stood on top of the black fabric now covering Layla. When had the wolf-turned woman gotten dressed? The question blew away like a dandelion seed when I noticed Mythia's pinched teal eyes.

"Thank the gods you can speak. I was worried you were too far gone." Layla's relief was palpable and snagged my attention. My mind ping-ponged all over the place, unable to remain on one thought for more than a fraction of a second.

"What's happening?" Hattie's voice boomed throughout the house.

"Myrna attacked, and Phoebe was hurt. A pestiaris *spell hit her."*

"Was that voice in my head?"

"That was Tarja. She's Hattie's familiar, and yes, she spoke inside our heads. Where should I take her?" Layla's gaze shifted from me to the ground as she spoke, so I assumed she was asking Tarja.

Of course, the cat was telepathic. I was definitely in a coma and having the oddest dream of my life. I prayed that was true because then maybe I wouldn't die. *You aren't in a coma, dummy. You don't feel pain in dreams.*

"Take her to the workroom." Tarja's voice was calm and soothing while adding to the pain at the same time.

The throbbing in my skull had reached nuclear levels, and

so had the pressure. Any second now, brains would squirt out my nose and ears. The ceiling shifted as Layla continued moving. I turned my head in time to see Mythia open the door to the pantry. The pantry was massive, but it didn't have a workroom hidden inside it.

Layla remained by the door, and I saw Tarja's head and front paws as she stood on her back legs and pressed the back wall. Light exploded, making me blink to clear the stabbing pain.

When I was able to keep them open, there was a door where there had once been a wall, and we were moving through the area. The second we passed through the new entry, the walls shifted from plaster to stone, and lanterns replaced light fixtures. The pain might muddle my mind, but I no longer had any doubt that Hattie was a witch.

My body started shaking as the air turned cold once again. At the bottom of the stairs, we entered a large room. One side of the space had a comfy recliner and a side table with a lamp. There was a bookcase nearby with some books.

My view changed, and I saw more bookshelves along with cabinets hung on the stone walls. It was an odd sight. The shelves had jars, crystals, and candles on them. Dried herbs hung from various locations, and candles lighted the room. The area reminded me of The Last Spell.

"Put her on the table, please, Layla." My head moved slowly, and I was shocked to see Hattie standing there with a good-looking guy. Who was the tall, dark, and handsome guy? And how did he get here? For one blissful second, I was looking into stunning dark green eyes before my gaze dipped to a deep bronze, rippled abdomen. Was he naked?

A soft hand cupped my cheek and moved my head before I could get a look below his belt until I was looking up into Hattie's blue eyes. She picked up my necklace then held it in her fingers. "This saved your life, Phoebe."

Bees buzzed around my skull, vying for my attention. I simply stared at her. After I don't know how long, I finally found my voice. "What do you mean?"

She placed the necklace down on my chest and laid her palm over it. "Myrna cast a *pestiaris* enchantment. It's a death spell. It hit you in the chest. You should be dead right now. Layla tells me you were defending me."

I knew that last one was bad. I felt the difference when it hit me. "I wasn't about to let her take what didn't belong to her. It's yours, and you aren't dead yet. I'm sorry I won't be here to make sure you're around for years to come."

She chuckled and released my face. The pain stole my breath and stopped my heart for several seconds. I had no idea what she had done to take the pain away for those few seconds, but I wished she would do it again. I'd rather not die in agony.

"I won't live long if I can't manage to counter the spell. Myrna will return. She is determined to take my magic."

My eyes shifted to Layla, then the man that had helped Hattie to the workroom. He had more muscles than a Greek statue and short dark blonde hair. Was he like Layla? Could he shift from an animal to a man? The idea that people could change forms was fascinating, and I had a million questions about that, but what I wanted to know was if he could change into an animal. The pupils in his green eyes changed from round to slit and back again. There was no doubt about it. He was something magical. I couldn't believe I even thought that was a possibility.

"Tsekani and Layla are both made shifters different than born shifters. And you will not die today if Hattie and I have anything to say about it."

"Tarja is right. But I will need help from you both," Hattie said, looking at Layla and Tsekani. "I don't move like I used to, and I want to reserve all my power for saving Phoebe."

"Anything you need." I didn't know Layla, yet she was willing to jump right in to help. After my cliché of a divorce and the encounter with Myrna, it was nice to see there were decent humans left in the world. *They aren't humans.* Oh, right.

Tsekani brushed strands of my messy brown hair out of my eyes. In a small act of rebellion, I cut my long locks off after Miles left me. One I didn't regret for one second. I had fallen in love with the short style. It was edgy and fun. And super easy to style. I imagined that I looked like a drowned rat at the moment.

"Tsekani, move that smaller table over here and grab the cauldron, please." The man lifted his hand from my forehead and moved to do as Hattie had asked. I wondered what kind of animal he was. His eyes tickled my mind, but I couldn't pinpoint why. And then all I could think was how good he looked without a shirt.

The only bare chest I had spent any amount of time appreciating was my ex-husband. Miles was slim and relatively fit, but he didn't have much in the way of muscles.

The bees were in a frenzy by that point, and white spots danced around the edges of my vision while my heartbeat slowed to dangerous levels. I didn't have the muscle control anymore to take my pulse, but it was only a matter of time before I passed out.

"Hold on, Phoebe. Let Hattie do her magic."

I turned my head to find Tarja but couldn't see her. Hattie grabbed my hand, and the pain eased enough I was able to suck in several breaths. My cardiac function increased, as well. "Save your energy," I told Hattie through gritted teeth.

She nodded her head and lifted her hand. This time I was prepared for the floodgates to open. I closed my eyes and focused on my breathing. That made things worse. All I could think about was how slow my heart rate was and how

MAGICAL MAKEOVER

bad the pain had gotten. My eyes snapped open and focused on an eight-pack—Tsekani's abs. At least my view is nice.

Hattie moved, filling my line of sight. "Layla. I need some turmeric, comfrey, lavender, and dragon's blood. And grab a rose quartz while you're at it. The one on the top shelf is fully charged."

Tsekani set an iron stand down then hung a small black cauldron from it. Hattie muttered something under her breath then snapped her fingers. Kinda. Her fingers were gnarled, and it was more like she rubbed her fingers together. While she didn't make a popping noise, her pointer finger acted like a lighter, and a small flame ignited on the tip.

If I wasn't still experiencing blinding pain, I would once again question if I was dreaming. My chest constricted and rattled as I exhaled. My eyes were tired, and I wasn't able to see much anymore.

This time when my eyes slipped closed, it wasn't so bad. I was so tired. A nap sounded good right now.

"No!" The voice in my head shouted the order, and energy shot into me. My eyelids got a workout lifting the twenty pounds they now weighed.

Layla set an armful of items on the table. I watched, fascinated as Hattie dropped them in bit by bit. She picked up a wooden spoon and dropped it in the pot. She moved it in a circle above the cauldron with one finger, sending the spoon into action. It stirred the mixture while Hattie then added more ingredients.

I couldn't see inside, but I heard bubbling as if the potion was boiling. I was a little disappointed it didn't glow green like Winnie's large cauldron did in Hocus Pocus. That was one of my favorite movies.

The soothing scent of lavender filled the room, and when Hattie lifted a vial to pour it into the cauldron, Tsekani stopped her. "Use mine. It has more magic. That's got to be better, right?"

Hattie nodded and handed him an intricate knife. The blade was double-sided, and the handle looked like it was bone and had symbols engraved into it. Tsekani sliced his thumb then held the open wound over the pot, squeezing several drops into the mixture. Hattie circled her finger, and the wooden spoon stopped. Now, red steam rose from the cauldron.

Hattie scooped the liquid into a cup and gave it to Tsekani, who set it next to me on the table. His palm cradled the top of my shoulders. I couldn't help but focus on how big his hand was and the fact that it spanned the width of both shoulder blades as he lifted me so I could drink the potion. The concoction smelled foul and turned my stomach. Wanting to live, I stopped breathing through my nose and took a big gulp from the cup Tsekani held to my lips.

I coughed as I choked it down, which made Tsekani rub my back. He smiled down at me, then settled me on the hard surface and took a step back. My body thrashed when the pain centered on my gut. I curled in on myself and looked to Hattie.

She stared back at me, and her face was crestfallen. It told me everything I needed to know. The potion hadn't worked. I was going to die. As if to echo that sentiment, my heart stuttered. My life was slipping away.

My mind did a quick calculation, and I realized Fiona had been right when she said the divorce was exactly what I needed and that I should embrace my midlife makeover. It was that description that prompted me to cut my hair. I wanted to makeover my life and create something that was all me. No more answering to someone that didn't even like me. And no catering to his stringent needs.

I suddenly regretted not doing more with my new beginning. I had barely begun my makeover. The hair was done, but I hadn't toned my middle-aged body as I wanted. Or tried every flavor of margarita like I had promised myself. *But you were a hero to Hattie and saved her from Myrna. At least I had done something good in the end.*

"It's all right. You've done everything. Tsekani, Layla, please protect Hattie and don't let that bitch get to her. And tell my kids I love them. Mom and Nana, too." My eyes slipped closed. I was so tired. I just needed some sleep.

Something soft landed on my chest. "She doesn't deserve to die. She's a mundie and put her life on the line for one of us." Given the tinkling tone of voice, I thought that was Mythia.

"I know," Hattie replied. She laid her hand on my arm, and the pain suddenly eased. That was much better. I'd rather not die in that much pain.

CHAPTER 7

"There's a way I can save her."

My eyes flew open when I heard those words slide from Hattie's mouth. "What? Why haven't you done it already? I want to live." I wasn't done yet. There was so much more I had to do. I hadn't even put down a complete layer of foundation on the new me yet. My makeover still needed shading, highlighting, blush, eyeshadow, eyeliner, and mascara.

"You can't," Layla objected. That stung. Not that I could feel much beyond the unbearable pain. But I thought we'd made a connection out there. In the least, I didn't think she'd want me dead.

Tsekani crossed his arms over his chest. "There has to be another way. A way for both of you to live."

"I can use pixie magic," Mythia offered. She hovered above me, her iridescent wings fluttering faster than a hummingbird's. Her tiny braids flapped in the breeze she created, and I swear I felt glitter fall from her to my cheek. It might be nothing more than a pain-induced hallucination.

However, the area seemed to warm when it connected with my skin.

Hattie smiled at her. "You and I both know pixie magic isn't capable of healing the damage. There isn't another way. The strongest healing potion in existence didn't even heal her bruises."

"Is this truly what you want?" When I turned my head this time, I noticed Tarja was on the table next to me, and her paw was on my shoulder. The telepathy was a real mind trip. Of course, that paled compared to the fact that my mind and body felt like I was on a roller coaster.

Magic moved into my reality like an unwanted house guest that never leaves. It slammed into me with so much force it started eating at my insides, and now my organs were on the verge of shutting down. And here Tarja and Hattie were offering me a multi-organ transplant so I could survive after all. I held my breath to hear what Hattie's response would be to the question.

I could read between the lines. This was something big. Perhaps something that their world forbade. Hattie gazed down at me. I could see the strain so much activity had on her as the lines around her eyes and mouth had quadrupled, and sweat dotted her forehead. Her cancer was in an advanced stage and caused enough discomfort when she took it easy. Traveling down to the basement and trying to save me had taken its toll.

Hattie's gaze shifted to Tarja. "Yes. I have searched a lifetime for someone to succeed me. Phoebe is the first person I have even considered. She has stood up for me time and again. And she walked into danger to ensure Myrna couldn't attack me and take my power by force. She's the best person to inherit my power."

I opened my mouth to ask what she meant and ended up spraying Mythia with blood as she hovered above me. That wasn't a good sign. And prompted Hattie to act. She clasped my hands in hers.

"We need to move quickly. Do you take my powers as yours?"

Tarja's voice in my head interrupted Hattie from saying more. *"And do you promise to be mindful of the choices you make and how they impact the good of all?"*

"She will have you to keep her on the straight and narrow, Tarja. Answer quickly, Phoebe. We are running out of time." Hattie's grip on my hands was surprisingly firm.

"Will it hurt you?" I needed confirmation for what my gut was telling me. "I don't want anything that will cause you any harm."

"I told you she was the right choice. I will face the fate I should have for some time now. Nothing more, nothing less."

"She is the only choice. I see that now. I wondered why Fate allowed you to lose your ability to produce an heir so young, but now I see what she had in mind." I couldn't follow Tarja's response and didn't even try. My eyes slipped closed.

"I will take anything you want to give me. I would like to live." I spoke without opening my eyes because I had ten-pound dumbbells instead of eyelids now.

Hattie's hands heated where she clasped mine, and energy started buzzing beneath her skin. It reminded me of what it felt like to use a belt sander on rough wood. The warmth sunk into me like a bomb striking a target. The second it hit my barely beating heart, it detonated.

Magical shrapnel blew through every cell, breaking me apart before sucking the pieces back in. The low-level vibrations followed in the wake of the explosion, agitating the blood in my veins. My heart rate went from I'm-close-to-v-fib to I-just-had-the-best-orgasm-of-my-life.

Light made it seem like daylight behind my closed lids. That illumination seemed to sink into me along with the

MAGICAL MAKEOVER

heat. My lungs strengthened along with my heart, and I swear my kidneys started working again. I just hoped I didn't pee myself while her magic healed me. I didn't have reasonable bladder control at the best of times.

This was better than a shot of epinephrine straight to the heart. Hattie's magic yanked me back from the edge and shot life and vitality into me. There were no words for the energy buzzing through me. It went beyond even what a quad shot of espresso would do to me. My muscles jumped beneath my skin.

The itch to move translated to me blinking my eyes open. It seemed like all the energy suddenly coursing through me was focused on shedding those ten-pound weights holding my lids down. The room was dim, and I saw the rough stone ceiling above me. Turning my head to the side, I saw Hattie smiling down at me. She cupped my cheek, and for a second, I saw a bright green glow surround her. Between one blink and the next, it had disappeared.

Tarja moved around my head to approach Hattie. She was her familiar. I had no idea what that meant, but I could now sense the connection between the woman and the cat. Except Tarja felt more like I had wrapped my fingers around a transmission line between two massive power poles.

Wait. Did I feel her? Another scan confirmed that I did, indeed, have some awareness of her presence and energy. It had to be because Hattie's magic saved me. I gingerly sat up and rubbed my chest. There was a scar where the dragonfly had embedded in my skin.

Branded like a side of beef. "I wish that vile excuse for a woman…"

"Witch," Layla interjected. "Myrna is a witch."

I chuckled. "Thanks for liberating me. I had hoped to keep my head in the sand for a few more minutes. Back to my point. She marked me and polluted what the charm stood for to me."

Hattie laid her hand over mine, where it covered the dragonfly between my breasts. "Think about how much your friend loves you to have given you such a valuable gift. The charm saved your life and has a vessel for you to inherit magic. Without it binding to your DNA, you would never have been able to inherit my power."

I liked thinking of it that way. The mark was a symbol of Fiona's love for me, not Myrna at all. I jumped to my feet when Hattie's upper body fell toward the table where I'd been lying.

My scrubs were stiff and scratchy against me as I caught her and pulled her into my side. "What's wrong?"

Tarja shared a look with Hattie, but neither of them said a thing. I looked from them to Mythia, Layla, and Tsekani. "Someone say something, dammit."

"Let's get her up to her room."

Tsekani moved toward us at Layla's suggestion. He picked Hattie up and cradled her gently in his arms as he ascended the stairs. I followed closely behind him. "Mythia would you make some tea, please," Hattie asked. Her voice was wispy and weaker than usual.

My heart thudded in my chest as I climbed, placing one foot in front of the other. When we entered the kitchen, I noticed several men and women milling around the yard without clothes. It reminded me that Layla had been naked.

When I glanced back over my shoulder, she was dressed in dark clothes. Something tickled at my mind, but I didn't chase it when she grabbed my hand and squeezed it. As I turned toward the woman that shifted to a wolf, the stars in the sky caught my attention, and one particular cluster caught my eye. It spoke to me on a visceral level.

MAGICAL MAKEOVER

Layla's voice made that thought scatter like the wind, as well. "It's a lot to take in, I imagine. Don't worry. I will be here to help you adjust and learn all about this life." The promise meant the world to me. Questions whirled through my head like debris in a tornado. They were fast and furious, and I couldn't grab hold of any before something else passed by and took center stage.

"I will, too." Tsekani's promise stopped the winds, and all thoughts vanished. It hit me right then that I had not only been in a loveless marriage without passion for more years than I cared to think about, but my body had gone into a kind of hibernation.

"Thank you. You both might regret that soon. Especially when the questions last long after the magic wears off." Although at the moment, it was difficult to imagine losing the power infiltrating my cells.

I was wide awake, and so was my body. My much-vaunted control over my emotions and libido scoffed at me as I was hit with twin desires to run my hands over the planes of Tsekani's chest and get Hattie to her bed and make sure she was alright. My gaze scanned the muscles of Tsekani's back.

The vice around my chest returned with a vengeance. Hattie didn't look good. The slice of her face that I could see over Tsekani's shoulder was paler than usual. My head was a ping-pong ball batted across the table at warp speed. Hypoxia. My brain must have gone without oxygen for far too long, and that was why I couldn't focus on anything for more than a second.

We were in the room, and Tarja had jumped up onto the bed next to Hattie. Crossing the room, I sat on the rolling stool I brought with me to make treating her easier. "Alright, someone needs to tell me what is going on."

The atmosphere in the room became heavy and oppressive. *"Hattie has passed the Pleiades power to you, and without that power, she is dying."*

I couldn't draw in a full breath. "What?! I said I didn't want to cause you any harm. Oh my God. How do I give it back? You can't die."

Hattie reached out to me. "There is no going back now. I have needed to pass this magic onto an heir for more than a decade."

I grabbed her hand gently. "I don't understand."

"I have been sick most of my life. The cancer was first discovered in my youth and should have killed me. Fate stepped in and gave my doctor the idea to take out the source of my disease. That's how doctors came up with surgeries like the hysterectomy. My magic has kept me alive until I was able to pass on my line. It's beyond my time."

"Chaos would reign if Hattie didn't pass on her powerful lineage." Tarja must have seen the confusion on my face and responded to that. *"The balance would be upset, and chaos would ensue. We're talking Armageddon type pandemonium."*

Tears gathered in the back of my eyes. "Let me try to help you." I had no idea what the hell I was doing. But I couldn't sit there and do nothing.

Following Hattie's example, I stood up and took both of her hands in mine, and laid them gently on her chest. Now what, genius? After several minutes of staring at Hattie's tired face, I decided to resort to what I knew best.

Releasing her hands, I grabbed my bag from the desk off to the side of the big bedroom. Mythia flew into the room at that minute with a teapot five times bigger than she was in one hand and a teacup that was twice her size in the other. Layla rushed forward to help her pour a cup while I returned with my stethoscope and blood pressure cuff.

My head fell when the numbers confirmed what Hattie had said. I was surprised she was coherent and talking with a systolic pressure of seventy-two and a diastolic of a mere forty.

There was nothing medically I could do. Listening to her slow heartbeat only confirmed my suspicions. "I can call for help. Just hang on."

Tarja laid her paw on my arm when I went to stand up again. *"There is nothing a doctor can do."*

I looked into Tarja's green cat eyes and nodded. My throat ached with repressed emotion as I retook Hattie's hands. Not sure how this magic worked, I imagined it sinking into her frail body and making her better.

"Thank you," she sighed.

"I didn't do anything. I don't know how to help you." My mind refused to believe this was the end for her. I had helped patients pass countless times over the years. I was a firm believer in people passing on their terms. For some reason, I couldn't let Hattie go.

"Because you blame yourself. She gave you her magic to save you. It is what she had to do, and she doesn't regret it for one second. You can't beat yourself up about it." I was startled when Tarja's words hit close enough to home for me to question if she could read minds. *"Yes, I can hear what you are thinking. We are bonded now."*

I would need to be careful and watch what thoughts crossed my mind. Hattie's soft voice had me leaning closer so I could hear what she was saying. "This is the natural order for a Pleiades witch. Usually, we pass our power onto our daughters. However, for those without daughters, or children of their own like myself, we must find an appropriate heir to inherit the power."

"What happens if one of you dies before you locate someone? Or what if one of you passes without their children close by?" It seemed impossible for them to be able to pass their magic along consistently.

Hattie's chest slowly rose and fell, and it took so long for her to respond I wasn't sure she was going to. "There have been instances where a Pleiades witch died without a daughter, and her power has traveled to her son who will give it to his daughter when she is conceived. Chaos remains at bay because the gods sense the power hasn't been corrupted or lost."

Tarja took over the explanation. *"There has only been one witch that died without any children at all. She was young and hunted by Tainted. They tried to steal her power, but it automatically went to her best friend and cousin. This is the first time it has been passed outside the bloodline entirely."*

"I picked you because you have a pure heart. Without the bloodline to choose from, I knew I had to be careful with where it went." Tarja must have been speaking to everyone at once because not only had Hattie expounded on what the familiar had been saying, but Layla and Mythia were watching with rapt attention while Tsekani was scanning outside the window.

"Not to mention she bonded to a powerful Fae," Mythia added.

My eyes widened. "What do you mean?"

The pixie flew down to my eye level and picked up the necklace hanging on my chest. "The charm."

"Hattie said something about someone powerful making it. I should have known that, but honestly, I'm an unmoored boat drifting out at sea right now. A tumbleweed is probably a better analogy. I can't tell which way is up as I roll head over heels—speaking of my necklace. I can call Fiona. She might know of some way to help you," I said.

It went against every fiber of my being to simply throw up my arms and say all hope was lost. They hadn't even tried to do something to help Hattie yet. Who knows what was possible? It might be feasible to heal her enough she could live for many months.

"You might want to call your house while you're at it. Your mom is likely worried." There was little chance Nina was concerned. She was used to me being late at the hospital when emergencies came up, but my mom and grandmother had no experience with it.

Resolved to call home before I called Fiona, I went in search of my cell phone. I had jumped down the rabbit hole and got lost in wonderland. Thankfully, there was hope. Fiona could guide me through the worst of it.

CHAPTER 8

"Where the hell is my cell phone? It should be out here." My body didn't hurt at all as I bent to push the pebbles out of the way. We were on the shore of Hattie's private beach.

I needed to find the damn thing and call home, then reach out to Fiona. A time clock was ticking in the front of my mind. It was loud enough that it was making me cranky. That might be my worry for a woman that had become a friend over the last month.

Layla looked up from her crouch on the lawn a few feet from me. "I didn't see where you lost it, but I already told you that you could use mine."

"I don't have Fiona's phone number memorized. I don't have many phone numbers memorized anymore. Cell phones made me lazy where that is concerned. Hell, the only reason I know the number to my house is that my mom and grandmother have had the same house number since I was a teenager."

My gaze stuck on the sight of where Myrna had stood when she attacked me earlier. There were bloody spots, paw prints, and scuff marks from shoes. The shoes were confined to a small space while the wolf paws scattered over a ten-foot section.

Images of wolf after wolf lunging at Myrna flashed through my mind like one of those viewfinders I loved as a kid. I had to admit I preferred looking at the Rocky Mountains or Grand Canyon instead of the fight's gruesome scenes. Recalling what had happened had my heart racing like the green flag was waving through the air, and I was trying to win the Indy 500.

Tsekani straightened from across the beach, holding a black object about six inches high. "I found it. But, the screen has cracks in it."

"Crap. Does it turn on? Gah. I lost my manners along with my mind. Thank you for your help."

Our fingers touched when he handed me the phone, and it sent a zap of electricity to travel through my veins. My mouth watered, and I was focused on his lips when I gazed up at him. Forcing my eyes up, they landed on his green orbs.

"You should call. Hattie won't have much time." His words weren't harsh, and yet, they lashed me.

My cheeks heated when I considered how I was mooning over a guy that couldn't care less about me. I took note and pressed the button on my phone. "Yes!" I practically fist-pumped the air when the screen lit up.

I thumbed it on and called up the phone app. My kids had no idea what life was without smartphones to run their lives. They had everything at the tip of their fingers, whereas, at their age, I had to scour the yellow pages and master the Dewey decimal system to find something as simple as a cake recipe.

The cold breeze sent a chill through me, making me shiver. I called up Fiona's contact as I made my way up the path to the house. Lights blinked in the forest on both sides, and the wind whistled through trees. Otherwise, the night was quiet.

The lights were on in every room, which lit the entire house up against the dark backdrop. Heat blew across my body when I entered the back door to the kitchen. Mythia looked even smaller as she buzzed around the massive room.

The stainless appliances and dark wood cabinets offset the grey marble countertops and light grey walls. There was a large platter of fresh fruit on the island in the middle of the space.

"Did you make that for everyone?" My mouth watered as I looked at the fresh berries.

One corner of Mythia's mouth curved up. Her iridescent wings and her miniature stature automatically conjured images of sweet Tinkerbell. Mythia was no Tink. She had braids throughout her red-streaked hair, and she wore leather pants with tiny biker boots. "I did. It was hard to miss the growling of your stomach."

"It's best to feed the beast when it starts talking. Thank you for this." I popped a piece of strawberry into my mouth and pressed the call button for Fiona. I chewed while the line rang. "You'll need to teach me how you get all your cuts so uniform."

"I will if you teach me how to make that soup from the other day."

"Deal. Oh, hey, Fiona. It's Phoebe."

"Hey, Phoebe. How are you doing? How's Maine? Cold yet?" Fiona's excited voice made me smile.

I grabbed a diet soda from the fridge and sat down at the island on one of the stools. It was coincidental that I sat right in front of the platter of fruit. "Maine is exactly like I remember. Well, that's not entirely true. But it is cold here. Nina likes the school here so far, and she loves living with my mom and grandmother. On the other hand, I have struggled to adjust to the idea of being under their roof again. I feel like I'm back in high school again."

Fiona laughed. "I know what you mean. Do you miss the hospital?"

Popping a blueberry into my mouth, I savored the sweet flavor as it burst over my tongue. It seemed so much better now. "At first, I missed OR 2 and the hustle. I thought I would go crazy from too much time to think. Now, I don't miss it at all. So much has happened here in the last week that I can barely remember my name."

"What's going on? What do you mean?" I could hear the concern in Fiona's voice, and it brought more tears to my eyes. I missed having a close friend nearby to confide in and have for support.

How did I break this to her? What if she had no idea what her boyfriend was? There was no guarantee Fiona was aware of all this. "Well, after seeing ghosts and a dragon, I discovered that magic is real last night and almost died in the process."

When Fiona gasped, I reconsidered my plan of blurting it all out. "Okay. You have to tell me more. Starting with how you almost died. Did the dragon do something to you?" I heard a deep, masculine voice say dragons in the background before there was a rustling noise, and Fiona told whoever it was to be patient while she got more information.

"You might want to put me on speakerphone, Fi. It'll be easier if he can hear me too." I looked up at Layla, who was mouthing 'you, too' to me. Nodding, I set the phone down on the island and hit the speaker button.

"I have you on speaker. Hold on a sec. We're going up to join Hattie and her familiar Tarja."

I didn't have to tell the others to join me. Layla grabbed the platter while Mythia flew past me and Tsekani brought up the rear of our little group. When we entered the room, I had second thoughts. Hattie's breathing rattled in her chest, and her eyes were barely open. Tarja curled in a ball in the crook of her arm.

"I have my friend Fiona on the line. The one that had her boyfriend make me the necklace. I was going to add you guys to the conversation. Should I take it to another room? We don't want to disturb you." I set the phone on the rolling table and checked her pulse. It hadn't gotten any slower. I'd take that as a win.

Hattie drew in a ragged breath. "Stay. I'd like to hear... what is said."

I nodded, then moved closer to the phone. "Alright, Fi. You there?"

"I'm here along with Sebastian and Gr...my Grams." I could hardly believe what I was hearing.

"What do you mean along with your Grams? Is she a ghost or something? Didn't she die?" That was the whole reason Fiona moved across the world.

"I'll give you the abbreviated version of events because I want to get back to the reason you called. I can tell it's more important. My Grams did die, and I discovered I was a Fae-witch hybrid and Guardian of the portal here in Cottlehill Wilds. Evil Fae started hunting me, and I had to learn my magic under pressure. During the process, I brought Grams' ghost back. Then I brought her back to life a few months ago before I went to Eidothea to fight a war there."

I cradled my head in my hands as I tried to wrap my mind around this new information. My head immediately started pounding. Strong fingers pressed into my temples, and I looked up at the sexy dragon as he rubbed my skull.

"Thank you," I told him as the pounding lessened right away. Turning my attention back to Fiona, I said, "That sounds like my day yesterday. First off. Why the hell didn't you tell me you were a witch?"

"That's not exactly a conversation you have over the phone."

I found myself nodding in agreement before I realized she couldn't see me. "You're right. I wouldn't be calling you now if Hattie hadn't assured me you were in the magical world. Or at least your boyfriend is. The charm he made me saved my life last night and is the reason I now have magic."

"I gave her my Pleiades magic to save her life," Hattie interjected.

"What?" The sharp tone had to be her Grams. There was a distinct grandmotherly tone to it. "Hattie Silva? Did you coerce her? If you did, I will hunt you to the ends of the Earth and make sure you pay for what you did."

I threw my hands up in the air. "I promise you I did no such thing. I would never hurt Hattie. She's the reason I'm calling."

"You'd better tell us what happened last night." Fiona sounded like she had her face right over the speaker compared to previous comments.

I gave them a brief rundown of what happened when I left the house and how Hattie had saved me. "That's why I called to see if you can help me in any way with how to save her. I can't just let her die. She saved me. And what did you do to the charm to make it help me."

"I infuse all of my items with my magic as I create them. It's a natural part of the process, which is why Fae items fetch more money. And why I rarely sell or give away what I create." Hearing Sebastian say he rarely sold or gave them away made the item mean so much more to me.

"I couldn't be happier that I followed my gut and had him make the necklace for you. But to answer your question, I have no idea how you can save her. I'm way too new to this whole thing." Fiona's disappointment reached through the phone. I knew my friend well enough to know this was killing her as much as it was me. We might have been quick to jump on board with helping a patient pass peacefully, but we hated when we couldn't do anything to help them.

"There is nothing you can do, Phoebe." Fiona's grandmother squished any hope I held in my soul. "When a Pleiades witch passes her magic, she loses the energy tying her to this life."

"Can I give it back to her?" I didn't want to die, but keeping her power felt like I was killing her myself. And that didn't sit well with me.

"No." I was shocked by the way Fiona's Grams snapped at me through the phone. "Hattie is old. It's her time to pass on, and she chose to give her magic to you. There is no way to give that back. Isn't her familiar there to give you this information."

I looked at Tarja, who was watching me with an unreadable expression. Not because she was hiding something from me but because she was a cat. "I am here. I told her there was no way to save Hattie. And I have allowed her to do what she needs to so she knows she did everything she could. Living with the guilt of not trying would only cause her unnecessary grief."

"Did you also tell her she needs to help Hattie pass from this world peacefully so she can complete the transfer? And if she doesn't, she won't survive, and neither will Hattie? Not to mention that as a result, countless humans and paras alike will die?"

My gaze narrowed on the familiar. "No, she left that part out."

Tarja licked her paw and ran it over her head, cleaning herself while she spoke. "I didn't have a chance. She raced from the room to call Fiona. But you need to know, Phoebe, that once a witch starts the process, there is no going back."

Grams sighed into the phone. "I understand. I know how

impulsive my Fiona is. I am sorry to hear about your situation, Hattie. I should have had Fiona checking in with you. I didn't have much time to prepare before my death, and I focused on a way she could bring my spirit back to help her adjust."

Hattie smiled. "It's alright, old friend. It has all worked out. And, in a way, your death was part of Fate finding a way for me to pass my magic along. Without Fiona returning and meeting Sebastian, Phoebe never would have had the charm that saved her from being killed instantly."

My brain hurt at all the twists and turns and pieces that needed to fall in place to ensure this day happened. The seriousness of passing this magic on had finally sunk through my thick skull.

"What exactly is a Pleiades witch?" Fiona interjected.

"A Pleiades witch is a descendent from the Greek gods. A different line of witches from the common ones. They're considered royalty in the witching world. Ensuring their line continues keeps the gods from interfering as they did in ancient Greek times. No one wanted to see another Atlantis, so the witches' pleas were heard by the gods, and the Pleiades were born," Grams explained.

"Does Violet know all of this? I can't believe this is the first I'm hearing about this. Right when I thought I was more like Hermione, it turns out I'm Ron."

I chuckled at Fiona's description and missed what her grandmother told her when Hattie fell into a coughing fit.

"Help her through the process, Phoebe. Don't be afraid. She's going to be with her ancestors," Grams told me.

"Call me if you need anything. Take care, Pheebs. And it was nice to meet you through the phone, Hattie. I consider it an honor."

"I see why Isidora hid you from the world. Your magical aura is unmistakable," Hattie replied to Fiona.

I lifted one eyebrow. *"She can sense it through my connection to her and the fact that I have established a link to the three of them through the cell phone. You can too if you paid attention. You've inherited me too, after all,"* Tarja informed me.

I tried to pick up on what she was saying. There were only about a million and one things running through my mind. I didn't bother trying too hard. Hattie was looking worse and worse by the second. "Thank you, Fiona." And Tarja, I thought to the familiar. "I look forward to meeting you one day, Isidora. You saved my life, Sebastian. I owe you a debt I can never fully repay."

The others said their goodbyes, with Mythia referring to Fiona and Sebastian as Eidothea's heroes. I hung up the phone and turned to find Tarja standing next to Hattie on the bed, nodding her head. I didn't want to interrupt the moment between them. It had been clear to me, even before I knew about magic, that they shared a special bond.

The fruit sat untouched on the desk where I kept my medical supplies. Layla stood across from me, and Mythia was hovering to my right. The tiny pixie was vibrating with energy, and it looked like she wanted to say something. I filed it in the Rolodex with the million and one other cards containing my questions.

Now was the time to focus on Hattie. I sat on the mattress next to her and clasped her hand between mine. Tarja jumped down and hurried from the room. Tsekani started to follow her, then paused and looked over his shoulder. "Where's she going?"

"To take care of the paperwork transferring the house, bank accounts, and business into Phoebe's name." Hattie's voice was even softer than it had been before.

I didn't think any more surprises could hit me. "What? I can't let you do that."

Hattie squeezed my fingers. "You can, and you will. It

comes with my powers. Inside my safe, you will find the contracts I have with all the creatures I have given sanctuary to here at Nimaha. It ensures their safety from the Tainted. Tsekani can help you deal with the CEO handling the day-to-day operations of the business."

Tarja returned at that moment and jumped into my lap. It was the first time we had contact beyond me, scratching her behind the ears. I felt bad for treating her like a nuisance and thinking she was nothing more than a spoiled house cat.

"Do not worry about that now. We need to focus on Hattie at the moment." I nodded my understanding to Tarja.

"The paperwork has been filed and dated a week ago. All of the bank records are changed, and everything is in order."

I gaped at Tarja. "How? It shouldn't be possible for any of that to occur so fast."

"Magic," Layla replied. "Hattie, can I get you anything?"

Tsekani knelt at the head of the bed closest to me, and Layla was on the other side. Mythia landed on Layla's shoulder, and we all focused our energy on Hattie. Emotion choked me. I couldn't say anything, or the waterworks would start.

"No, thank you. Having you all close has been the highlight of my life," She told her friends, then focused her attention on me. "Trust Tarja. She will guide you through this turbulent world. Thank you for coming to my rescue."

I should be the one saying that to her. I remained silent when her glassy eyes slipped closed a second later. Her breaths rattled in her chest, and I knew she was close. Tarja remained in my lap but laid her head on Hattie's stomach.

Tears blinded me. I didn't bother holding them back when I saw Hattie's chest rise and fall for the last time. This extraordinary woman had given me so many unique gifts. She'd become an unexpected friend, and it hurt to think about her being gone. I was going to miss her terribly.

With tears blinding my eyes, I hugged her one last time then set Tarja next to her so I could make arrangements for her body. I had no idea who to call or what to do. I stood there in the room, turning in circles as if that would give me the answers I needed.

"The answers are in a letter on the desk. And before you ask, Hattie drafted it and the other legal papers when she first had the inclination to pass her power to you. I did the rest with magic."

I looked back at Tarja and smiled. "Thank you." This had been the longest day I'd ever experienced. It felt like I'd lived an entire life in the past twenty-four hours, and all I wanted to do was go to sleep.

CHAPTER 9

Hattie had considered giving me her magic before tonight? I had no idea. She was fussy and high maintenance, but I liked working for her and getting to know her. She had grown on me, especially over the last week, and now it was time to say goodbye to her.

My chest ached with a loss I shouldn't be feeling. I may have come to like Hattie, and we'd gotten close with me caring for her twelve plus hours every day. But in the end, I wasn't her family.

"Do not dismiss your grief. There doesn't need to be decades or years spent with someone for them to make an impact on you."

I met Tarja's amber gaze and nodded. The day weighed on me like a heavy blanket. My body begged for a respite I had to ignore at the moment. There was too much work to be done before I could rest.

I crossed to the desk and found the letter Tarja mentioned in the desk drawer and was relieved there was a name and number to call. Before calling this Lilith La Croix, I dialed my house.

I nearly choked out a sob when I heard my mom's voice.

"Phoebe. Everything alright? Your grandmother had one of her bad feelings when you didn't come home."

I took a deep breath and wiped the tear tracks from my cheeks. "It's a long story, mom. One that I will tell you later. I wanted to call and let you know Hattie passed on, and I won't be home anytime soon. I need to take care of things here."

My mom's gasp was overridden by my grandmother asking what was wrong in the background. "Oh no. That's just too bad to hear. She seemed like she was doing so much better with you around. You let us know if you need anything, and we will be there."

Knowing they were there to support me was the only way I'd gotten through the past six months and the divorce from Miles. It meant everything. "Just make sure Nina gets to school in the morning and tell her to pack her clothes. Hattie left me the house."

"Phoebe Margaret Dieudonné, you better not have manipulated Hattie to give you her house." I hadn't heard that angry tone from my mother since I ditched biology class in high school. I thrust my hand on one hip, ready to give her a piece of my mind for even believing I was capable of such a thing.

There was a rustling noise before I could respond, and my nana interrupted. Someone had put me on speaker. I followed suit, needing my new friends to back me up. "Based on what I heard of your mother's side of the conversation, poor Hattie has left this world. Why is she accusing you of manipulating her?"

"I'm sorry, sweetie. I should never have said that. I know you would never do such a thing."

I sucked in a breath to respond, but Layla cut me off. "It's been a long night, and before Hattie passed away tonight, she let us all know that she left the business and house to

Phoebe. None of us were surprised because in the weeks since Phoebe started caring for Ms. Silva, the two developed a close relationship."

"It was an odd one, that's for sure. But Phoebe proved how much she cared about Hattie's well-being, or each of us would have questioned the choice and voiced an objection. We would never have let her pass on that amount of magical power without being sure the person wouldn't abuse it." Tsekani had just outed me to my family. They had no idea witches existed or that there was this hidden world right under their noses.

"Okay," my mother drawled. I knew the uncertainty in her voice all too well. I had never mentioned anyone, and I was certain she was wondering if they were insane. "Thank you for clearing that up. Have you all eaten dinner yet? I could whip something up and bring it over." That was my mom's way of trying to get here so she could see what was going on over here.

Taking a deep breath, I gave them a brief rundown of what had happened. Nina found her voice first when I finished giving them the details of my frantic night. "Oh my God, mom. I almost lost you. After Nana said something was wrong, my heart jolted, and I assumed her crazy was rubbing off on me. I wasn't sure what to think when it persisted then started fizzing like I was a bottle of soda someone shook too much."

I shifted my glance from Tarja, who was still lying next to Hattie. If anyone had the answers, it would be her. "Do you know what this means?"

As your heir, she is connected to the magic, as well. She won't be capable of spells at your level until she matures. There will be time to learn all that later.

Nina's gasp echoed through the tiny speaker on my phone. "Who was that talking in my head?"

"What? What have you gotten into, Phoebe? This is beginning to sound crazier than when you saw dragons and ghosts in that house."

I wanted to respond to my Nana and work through this but now wasn't the time. "I don't know what all of this means, Nana. But I promise we will all sit down together sometime tomorrow or the next day. Right now, I need to take care of Hattie."

"You do what you need to, and we will be there soon with some food and a change of clothes for you, sweetie."

I wanted to tell my mother not to come, but I desperately needed to shower and change the stiff scrubs. They were scratchy and covered in dried saltwater. "Thank you, mom. Be careful when you approach the house. I have no idea if Myrna is out there or not."

"Perhaps we should wait until morning," Nana suggested in a shaky tone of voice. I wanted to reach through the phone and hug her.

"You guys can wai…"

Tsekani cut me off. "There's no need to wait. There will be shifters and pixies in the forest as soon as you leave the highway. You need to come tonight. I will have to scrub my nostrils if I have to smell Phoebe in these scrubs much longer."

I gaped at the dragon. What the hell? My cheeks filled with heat, and I took back every lust-filled thought I had about the guy. If I'd known he was so rude, I would have never allowed my mind down that road. Being a dick made the hottest guy uglier than a turd covered in flies.

I told my family I would see them soon and hung up before they experienced any more of my humiliation. Layla punched Tsekani in the shoulder while I scanned the letter on the desk. "That was uncalled for. First, her night was rough. No thanks to you. And second, not even your boyfriend would smell so good if he had fought with a Tainted witch, been burned, hit with a death spell, and dunked in the ocean."

Boyfriend? Well, if I hadn't already lost my attraction to the man, that would have done it. Tsekani crossed to me and wrapped one arm around my shoulders. "I didn't mean any offense. You do smell, and you are filthy, but that doesn't mean I don't like you. You're quickly becoming one of my favorite people. Also, you should learn now that I have no filter."

That helped, but honestly, I was over the initial gut reaction of being hurt and upset. The best part of reaching my forties meant that I no longer let the little things upset me. And his comment was minor compared to the rest of my day. It would have been different if I was falling for him and cared greatly if he found me attractive.

I nodded to him without responding and dialed the number for Lilith. Butterflies took flight in my stomach when it started ringing. It was just after nine at night, so I wasn't calling too late. Perhaps she wasn't home. I started going over what I would say in a message before moving onto the next person on the list. Someone had to respond today.

"Hello."

My heart ricocheted around my chest as it went into overdrive. "Hi Lilith. Um, you don't know me, but I have been taking care of Hattie Silva for the past month, and I have instructions to call you when she passed to make arrangements for her."

"That's terrible news. We were hoping we had more time. Someone will be right over. We need to deal with the transfer of her power. We can't leave it, or it will attract the vultures."

"There is no need to worry about that. Hattie gave her magic to

Phoebe before she passed." The line was silent after Tarja's mental voice jumped into my head. Based on previous conversations, I realized she could talk to other witches and paranormals or just one person and that she had more than likely spoken to us both.

Lilith cleared her throat. "That's unexpected. What coven are you from?"

"I'm not from any coven. I didn't even know witches existed until I tried to stop Myrna from attacking Hattie tonight."

"Sounds like there is a longer conversation to be had. We will be there shortly to prepare her for the ceremony."

My heart settled, and I was able to take a deep breath finally. The black hole of grief still ached in my chest. "That's the second-best news I've gotten tonight. Can I do anything to help?"

"Not right now. I'm sure Hattie has everything we will need for the service. I'll call Bridget so she can prepare the death certificate. See you soon." Lilith hung up the phone before I could say anything else.

I looked at Tarja, who was lying with her head next to Hattie. Someone had pulled a sheet up to her chin. It looked like she was sleeping. Not wanting to interrupt her mourning, I shifted my focus to Layla, Mythia, and Tsekani.

"Who are Lilith and Bridget? Won't it be suspicious if Lilith calls Bridget and says Hattie died from her disease or whatever, so you can fill out the death certificate and send it to her lawyer?" I had dealt with death many times, but I was never the one to handle the details or any of the arrangements. This was more than slightly uncomfortable for me. It had images of me being thrown in jail for killing Hattie or something because it didn't pass through appropriate channels.

Layla pushed the rolling table to the side while Mythia

picked up some of the medical supplies and placed them in a pile along the wall next to the door. "Bridget works for the coroner's office and is a member of their coven. They've had a plan in place for how to handle any death of a supernatural of standing in the city for decades now."

I started gathering the gauze, ointments, and other dressings and replaced them in the drawers of my organizer. When I took this job, I put together a large rolling cart to have everything in one place. "I've only been part of this world for half an hour, and I'm already overwhelmed."

"No one expects you to know everything right now. The members of Mystic Circle will understand, as will those for whom you are now responsible. And we won't let you face someone outside of that without one of us." I was surprised by Tsekani's offer. And realized I hadn't precisely forgotten what he'd said.

"That's reassuring, and it brings up a million new questions. I'll settle for starting with who I'm now responsible for. I don't recall being told I had to take care of others now." Given that I had inherited Hattie's business and house, I couldn't imagine I would have the time.

Tsekani shook his head as he moved the commode from the bedside. "I didn't explain that very well. You don't have to feed or house anyone. Just provide them with a safe place to live here on your property."

Mythia stopped what she was doing and hovered close to me. "That means you renew the protection spells and contracts when they come due."

"Do not let the list of duties overwhelm you. I will walk you through things as they come up." That was reassuring. I had an idea based on books I'd read and movies I'd seen about what a familiar was to a witch. Not that I took it all as truth, but I knew the most important fact was Tarja was here to help me with my magic. It helped to know I wasn't in this alone.

"Are all the wolves that live here shifters?"

Layla nodded. "There are about a dozen of us in my pack. Not that we are anything like other packs. You are our alpha."

"Does anyone live here in the house with me? And are there any creatures that will scare me to death if I come across them?"

"We don't have any Dark Fae living here. Only pixie mounds," Mythia explained, "and most find our forms appealing."

Tsekani laughed. "I don't know. Some of the wolves are pretty frightening. They have no sense of taste. Plaid is not a color."

I couldn't help but laugh at that. "No, it's not, but I wouldn't trust any man that's too well dressed." Miles rarely wore anything but Armani. It was far too pretentious for me. I had no desire to get into a discussion about fashion at the moment, so I changed the subject. "Why didn't Fiona or her Grams seem to know much about the Tainted anyway."

Mythia paused with a pack of blue pads that was even bigger than the teapot had been. "Things are different in the United States. My colony crossed over through Pymm's Pondside a long time ago and was surprised how much more independent things were when we crossed the pond, as they call it. In England, a council governs paranormals, and a supernatural police force ensures no one goes rogue. There's nothing like that here."

Layla nodded her head from where she was organizing something in the piles. "That lack of oversight is how the Tainted came to be. Some greedy witches discovered that stealing power from others gave her more magic and prolonged her life. The first time they take a life like that, it corrupts them forever."

"Hattie had a suspicion a demon instigated the first witch to turn, but she never got proof. What's important to know is that the

wards you will take over tomorrow night keep the Tainted out." I doubted I would ever get used to having Tarja's voice pop into my head at random moments.

"Then how was Myrna able to visit? She shouldn't have been able to come here today."

"Hattie didn't know she was Tainted when she asked for an audience. She's from New Orleans and had been after her power for years. Hattie assumed she wanted to visit to plead her case once again. She gave her a thirty-minute window to convince Hattie."

My head was throbbing. "Makes sense. I'm going to take a shower before my mom arrives. Can someone let them in when they get here?" I needed a break to absorb the information I'd gotten so far. If I tried to stuff anything else in there, it would simply spill out the other side.

CHAPTER 10

I raced to the door and worked hard to hide my disappointment when it wasn't my family on the other side. "Hello. Can I help you?"

The guy standing on the porch was slim and fit with dark blonde hair and brown eyes with wire-rimmed glasses. He wore jeans with loafers and a tweed jacket with leather patches on the elbows. Everything about him screamed, professor.

"I hope so. I need your help locating my Aunt Sarah's ghost and her sewing machine. They're both missing. In the wrong hands, my aunt can make Tainted and Dark Ones nearly unstoppable. We have to find them both." The guy was wringing his hands and kept biting his bottom lip.

I tilted my head to the side. I had no idea who he was or why he would be coming here for help finding a sewing machine. And a ghost? Was he kidding? And this wasn't even the weirdest thing that happened to me in the last week.

"Um, I'm sorry. Who are you? And why are you asking me?"

"You took over for Hattie. You're the one we go to for

MAGICAL MAKEOVER

help now. I drove two hours and took the ferry to get to you. I was hoping to get this resolved quickly. I'm Harold Peterson, by the way. What you need to know is that if the wrong person contains my Aunt Sarah, it will create big problems."

Everything in this world meant big problems. A lost shoe could be catastrophic. It was exhausting. "I'm Phoebe Dieudonné. Hattie gave me her power last night, so technically, you're right. I did take over for her. Unfortunately, I'm not in a position to do anything at the moment. I'm still adjusting and have to take care of her right now."

Mr. Peterson shook his head from side to side and persisted. "This is very important. It might seem inconsequential, but my Aunt Sarah being is a big deal. She created the sewing machine and enchanted it to imbue fabrics with magical shields. She was a seamstress for the Fae King's guards and can be compelled to inform others how to use it and maybe even make another one. This can't fall into the wrong hands."

I took a deep breath as I listened to what he was saying. I could see how that was a problem. I even felt bad that someone had kidnapped his aunt. But it wasn't a priority in my world. There were too many other catastrophic events hurtling at me.

"Hattie was known as the local leader for more than just the coven. She *helped with various problems. Most often hunting down ghosts. She called herself a Grim Reaper when she took on these jobs. She saw it as her duty.*" The cat speaking in my head was the weirdest part of what had happened the last twelve hours. It would take time to adjust to it.

"I didn't realize it was so recent. A notice went out about the change in guard, and I came right away."

I grimaced. I hated turning him away, but there was just too much on my plate at the moment. "I will get back to you as soon as possible. There are other life and death matters I have to address first.

Mr. Peterson inclined his head and pulled a card from the inner pocket of his jacket. "I look forward to your call."

A car pulling up interrupted my reply. Mr. Peterson took it as a sign he needed to leave and was walking away while watching my mother pull in front of the house. I descended the stairs and opened Nana's door.

"Why was there a line of wolves running alongside our car as we drove in?" Trust Nana to skip pleasantries and get right to the point.

"Those were your sentries, making sure you guys didn't encounter any problems." I gestured towards the front door.

Nina climbed out, holding a bag, and gave me a quick hug before heading for the house. My mom joined Nana and me a second later. It took Nana longer to move, so I had started escorting her to the porch stairs.

"It's good to see you, sweetie," My mom said as she leaned her head towards me and air-kissed my cheek.

We entered the house, and I considered changing into my clothes but decided to sate my hunger. The flannel robe I was wearing was fine for now. "I see you brought food. Let's talk in the kitchen. Lilith will be here soon enough to take care of Hattie, so now might be the only chance I get for a while to catch you guys up."

"We live here now?" Nina's eyes stopped bugging out of her head, and she was walking beside me down the hall. I missed hearing and seeing her excitement. The divorce had taken a toll on us all.

"Yes, we live here now." I wrapped my arm around her shoulders as we entered the kitchen.

"Is that a...a fairy?" My mom's question had all eyes in the room turning to her.

Nana strode past her and took the pan she'd been

carrying from her hands. "Looks like it to me. I suppose we shouldn't be all that shocked, given what Phoebe has already told us. It seems like you have one helluva story to tell, child."

I released Nina and crossed to the fridge, and retrieved the pitcher of iced tea. "Mythia is a pixie, not a fairy, and this is Layla. She's a werewolf." I cast her a questioning gaze, and she nodded her head. "And this is Tsekani. He's a dragon."

My mom's gaze scanned him from head to foot. Tsekani had put on a green silk top that matched his eyes. It was no surprise that it made him look fantastic. "A sexy dragon."

I smacked her shoulder. "Mom!"

She shrugged her shoulders. "What? I'm not dead yet. I can appreciate a good-looking guy when I see one."

Tsekani chuckled. "So, can I. I wish they would just show up at the door. I don't leave the property much."

Layla rolled her eyes. "I'm not sure Brody would be too happy to hear you want to find another man."

Tsekani waved his hand through the air. "I'm only thinking of Phoebe's mom. She could use a wingman. I'd merely be an appreciative bystander. Brody is all I want."

"It's Mollie. And I'm afraid I'm too old to go on the prowl. No one wants a woman whose breasts double as a black run. No one wants to run down the powdered slopes when they're getting intimate."

Nana had set the dish down and was opening and closing drawers in the kitchen. Mythia watched her for a second and then flew to the cabinets and grabbed plates. "Speak for yourself. I'd like more orgasms before I die. I prefer they come from a hunky man's fingers rather than mine."

My cheeks heated, and my mouth dropped open. Leave it to my mom and Nana to give me the biggest shock of the day. Nina was horrified as she gasped and covered her face with her hands. "Would you please stop it? Oh my God." I chuckled at my daughter's clear mortification. No doubt she wanted to be swallowed and disappear. I could add to her horror but decided to spare her.

"Orgasms later. Food now." Well, I had planned on not adding to the situation, but based on Nina's groan, I failed. I don't miss the days when I was a teenager and cared more about image than anything else.

Nana removed the foil to reveal my mom's green chile chicken enchiladas. My stomach rumbled, and I grabbed forks and a spatula. After loading a plate full of cheesy goodness, I took a seat at the island.

Nana was already sitting on one of the stools, and my mom sat on the other side of me. "Alright. Fill us in. First, you told us Hattie was a witch, and you had inherited her magic, and we arrive to find a pixie, a dragon, and a werewolf. What the hell is going on out here? What kind of magic was Hattie doing?"

Mythia poured me a glass of iced tea. Nina gaped as the tiny pixie picked up the heavy glass pitcher. I could relate. She had some strength to pull off the feats she did. The pixie handed me the drink. "Unlike most shifters, Layla and Tsekani were created by a witch, except it wasn't Hattie. I come from Eidothea. Witches from your realm are not capable of the magic needed to create my kind, let alone any of the other Fae."

Nina extended her hand, palm up, and caught the glittery dust that fell off Mythia. "You're like a badass Tinkerbell. Will this make me fly, too?"

Mythia narrowed her eyes and thrust her hands on her hips as she glared at my daughter. "Do you have wings?"

"Uh," Nina's head moved around, searching for help from one of us. "No. I don't. Do you have to be rude? I didn't mean to offend you." I cringed when Nina stood up for herself rather than becoming a victim. I taught her that, and usually,

I would be proud of her, but we were dealing with beings capable of god only knew what.

Mythia's head jerked in response, and Layla burst out laughing. "She's got you there, Thia. We need to understand there will be a learning curve. And someday she will be your mistress, and you will be relying on her for sanctuary, so you might want to watch it."

"What's this?" Nina asked with a smile.

I shook my head and gave them an abbreviated version of events leading up to their arrival. My mom was shaking when she grabbed my hand while Nana had a scowl on her face.

"I have magic? That's so cool. The kids at school will have to like me now."

I opened my mouth to correct her, but Nana beat me to it. "You will not mention one word of this to anyone. Given that I now know the rumors are true about Hattie, I can guarantee it will do the opposite for you."

"Besides, you don't have magic yet. It will take time for your transition to occur, and even then, you won't come into your powers until you mature. We don't have to worry about your issues until much later. Right now, your mother needs your support. She has a rough road ahead of her." Tarja had to tell my daughter she had magic. Nina's wide-eyed gaze met mine, and I wanted to erase the uncertainty with assurances she would be alright.

My thoughts scattered a heartbeat later when my mom gasped, and her head did a rendition of the exorcist while Nana glanced around with narrowed eyes. "Who's speaking to us?"

"And why is she talking inside our heads?" My mom's voice rose an octave with every word until she was screeching.

"That's Tarja." I stood up then scooped her into my arms. "She was Hattie's familiar."

"And now I am yours. I have been the familiar for the Silva Pleiades witch line for as long as it has existed. I suppose we will need to rename it to Dieudonné."

Nana nodded her head. "That would be right. I appreciate Hattie saving my Phoebe and will thank her personally when I see her again, but this is Phoebe's now, and she needs to own it. I can see she's got a whole slew of magical beings to handle. One thing I've learned in life is you have to start on solid footing."

The doorbell rang, making me jump. My hand flew to my chest. Layla placed her hand on my shoulder. "Looks like it's time to put your grandmother's advice to work. Lilith and the coven are here."

My heart was suddenly racing, and my palms started sweating. Why the heck hadn't I changed into clothes earlier? "What do I do? I'm not even dressed."

Tsekani grabbed me by the shoulders and held me in place. "You duck into the bathroom and jump into some clothes. Preferably a nice black dress if you have one. And we will lead Lilith to Hattie. She will be the one handling arrangements given the situation."

I hurried behind him, then snagged the duffle bag Nina had dropped by the staircase. They'd packed more scrubs and jeans. Not a black dress in sight. I considered raiding Hattie's closet for something. *It's yours now, Phe. You can wear whatever you want.* No freaking way was I going there yet.

Without other options, I shoved my legs into my jeans and tugged a grey sweater over my head. There were no shoes in the bag. Crap. I couldn't go out there barefoot. That was far too casual for me.

A yelp escaped me when a pair of tennis shoes popped

into existence on the edge of the sink. "Does this house grant wishes?" I'd rather have had a black dress. It would make me feel less out of place at the funeral.

"Call me your Fairy Godmother." I smiled when I heard Tarja's voice in my head.

"Thanks," I called out as I tied the laces.

Nina was hovering outside the bathroom, shooting glances toward the kitchen while biting her thumbnail. I followed her gaze and saw Nana and my mom with their backs to us. "What's going on?"

Nana turned around with a frown on her face. "Lilith, Alexandra, Clio, and Bridget just carried Hattie out to the yard. There are about a dozen of them altogether."

I grabbed Nina's hand, and we headed toward them. "Who are the other women?" I hadn't been back in town long enough to get to know anyone.

"They're witches. Bridget works at the county coroner's office. How many people in town are witches? I can hardly believe there are so many of them." Nana was walking toward the backdoor as fast as her little body would carry her.

I shrugged my shoulders. "I have no idea." My familiar was on the patio when we exited the house. I looked down at her. "Can you tell us?"

Tarja was sitting on her hind legs, watching the women stand around Hattie, who had been wrapped in white cloth and laid on the lawn. *"Camden is a hotspot in the US for paranormal creatures to gather. Supernaturals are drawn to any location where there is a Pleiades witch or Fae portal in Fiona's case. Your kind are a particular draw for the Tainted."*

Mom leaned toward Nana. "That didn't tell us anything. What is the cat's role, anyway?"

Nana never responded because Tsekani approached us at

that moment. "What is this?" He plucked at the sleeve of my sweater.

"They didn't bring me a dress or anything. They had no idea this was happening tonight. Besides, I'm not dressed all that different from them." I gestured to the twelve women gathered around the yard.

As if to mock me, they each held a hand-out, and a dark blue cloak appeared in it a second later. "I don't own a cloak," I told Tsekani when he glanced at me with one raised brow.

Layla walked out of the house with Mythia following suit. The pixie had a dark teal cloak in one tiny fist. "This was Hattie's, and now it's yours." Layla took it and held it open for me.

My entire body erupted with tingles. The vibrations weren't entirely electric, but they gave me a jolt like I'd mainlined caffeine. Remembering what Tarja had said about renaming the line, I stood straight and held my head high. Time to say goodbye to Hattie.

I wanted to figure out how to recognize Hattie and what she meant to the others and me. And not just because she had saved my life. She had established this sanctuary and worked her ass off to grow a company that would support so much more than herself. Everyone that said she was selfish was so far from wrong it was ridiculous. Knowing how others had vilified her made me angry on her behalf.

Something soft brushed against my leg. When I looked down, I nodded at Tarja. Now was not the time. The cloak fell around me and hid the clothes underneath, making what I had on irrelevant.

"How can I help?"

A woman that looked to be around my mom's age stared down her nose at me with piercing hazel eyes. I hadn't expected them to embrace me initially, but I never expected to have them look down their nose at me. It might just be

MAGICAL MAKEOVER

this woman's personality, though, given the tight bun on her head. It highlighted the greys in her brown hair.

"Hattie gave you her magic? Why I never…" I recognized her voice. That was the woman named Lilith that I had talked to earlier on the phone.

A thirty-something redhead stepped up beside the woman. "Lilith. Hattie chose her for a reason. She's our new High Priestess whether you like it or not. We need to show her the respect Hattie would demand. I'm Alexandra, but everyone calls me Lexie."

I returned her smile and continued approaching the group. "It's nice to meet you. I'm Phoebe. This is all new to me, so I appreciate the support. I'm sure Hattie would have preferred that I command respect and zap anyone that refuses to follow suit. That's not who I am. But that doesn't mean I will tolerate disrespect. I'm sure those who work for me wouldn't want to be kicked out of the coven and lose their jobs on the same day. Now, what can I help with."

Issuing threats went against who I was. I realized it was necessary to adopt some of Hattie's cantankerous personality, or they would run right over me. Seeing the looks of disapproval vanish before me told me how right I had been and explained a lot about why Hattie was the way she was.

All but three of the women paled after my announcement. I had taken a chance that they worked for Hattie's, now my, company, and it seemed I was right. From the looks of it, most of them worked for me, including Lilith.

Lilith sniffed and turned back to the table set close to Hattie. Tears immediately blurred my vision when my gaze skipped in her direction. I didn't bother wiping them away. I refused to hide my grief from anyone.

"You can light the candles on the altar." Lilith gestured to the three candles on the top, along with an ornate silver chalice and a twisted silver cord.

"Alright." There was a problem with my agreement. There were no lighter or matches to accomplish the task. My heart started pounding even faster, and my breathing started getting constricted.

"They expect you to know how to conjure flame." My wide-eyed gaze flew to Tarja. I couldn't do that. I was about to run inside and grab a lighter, but I suddenly couldn't move. Oh crap. Was one of these women Tainted and trying to take my power?

A hiss echoed through my head before Tarja continued talking to me. *"Your fellow witches can be trusted. None have taken a step down the darkest path. What you need to do right now is trust me and act like you are lighting the candles. I will do the magic for you this one time."*

Sweat was now sliding down my spine and into my clean underwear. And this time, it wasn't even from a hot flash. I was able to move by the time I took my next deep breath. My heart refused to slow down. At this rate, I'd need a shot of adenosine to stop it so it could resume an average pace. I didn't even know how long it had been beating more than two hundred beats per minute.

Unsure what I was supposed to do, I snapped my fingers, and the first candle flared to life a second later. The hacking in my mind was a cross between the sound a cat made when it coughed up a hairball and the hiss I heard moments ago. It had to be Tarja's version of laughter. I repeated the process at the other two candles.

I took a step back and joined Lexie to the side. Lilith stood at the table with her gaze on Hattie. There were tears in her eyes, making me see her gruffness in a different light. She'd lost her friend tonight. It had to be challenging to see her friend's magic in someone else.

"This witch belongs to air and has returned to the East. The wheel turns, and spring is over. This witch belongs to fire and has returned to the South. The wheel turns, and summer has flown. This witch belongs to water and has returned to the west. The wheel turns, and autumn passes. This witch belongs to Earth and has returned to the North. The wheel turns, and the winter has ended.

"This witch belongs to spirit and has returned to the old ones. The wheel turns, and the cauldron awaits. This witch belongs to fellowship and love. This witch belongs to the circle and remains with us. We bid you farewell, Hattie, as you await a new destiny."

Lilith untied the cord and placed it in the chalice, then blew out the candles. The twelve witches all gathered around Hattie and left a spot for me at her head. Tears were streaming down my face by now, and I hoped they didn't ask me to talk because I wouldn't be able to utter a word.

Tarja wound herself around my legs as we all joined hands. Energy filled the space around us and pulsed like a heartbeat. It grew and grew for several seconds until I wondered if it was going to ignite like kerosine. When I looked down, I saw Hattie's form was now lit up. I watched in awe as Tsekani approached in his dragon form.

The witches at her feet parted, and he picked Hattie up in his claws and carried her toward the forest. The witches released each other and followed the dragon. Nana, my mother, Nina, and I followed at a slower pace. By the time we reached them, I had noticed what looked like hundreds of pixies hovering around what looked like a burial site. Only the sides and top of this one were covered in grass and flowers.

"It's to protect her while she returns to the Earth," Mythia explained. The tiny pixie was close to my family and me. I wondered why she didn't join her friends. A question for later. Individuals started approaching Hattie and lying flowers around her body.

We were each handed one by a pixie. My chest felt like it would implode while at the same time ached with a gnawing emptiness. Moving back to Camden had been fraught with turmoil for me. I never thought I would get the makeover I wanted when I left North Carolina. Yet here I was in the beginnings of a magical makeover. Unexpected, but I would take it with gratitude.

Thank you, Hattie. You saved my life in more ways than one. I hope I live up to your example.

CHAPTER 11

What the hell was that? I was clutching my chest as I sat in bed, wondering what had woken me up. It sounded as if someone was moaning painfully from another location in the house. *Haunted.* This place was haunted. Hattie had confirmed there were ghosts living there previously. I just thought she was senile at the time.

Now, I realized I should have listened closer. And done an exorcism before moving into the place. It had been such a long day that I had fallen asleep the second my head hit the pillow after the funeral had ended.

My mom and Nana were asleep in one of the rooms. It had been too late for them to return home. Not to mention I was terrified for them to leave the property at night. The noise stopped, and I glanced over to make sure Nina was still asleep on the other side of the king-sized bed we had fallen into together.

She wanted to claim the room as hers the moment she laid eyes on the closet, but I refused to give her the luxury. I wouldn't be able to fill a third of the space. That wasn't going to stop me from trying.

There was a chill in the air, and I grabbed the robe I had worn earlier. It was one of the softest things I'd ever felt next to my skin, and I had fallen in love with the fluffy pink thing. I made a mental note to get my slippers later that day. My piggies were in danger of becoming frozen sausages as I crossed to the partially open double doors.

By the time I made it to the hall, I was convinced I had heard things. I was heading down a hallway I had only been down on my tour the day I started working there. The home had six bedrooms and was massive.

My skin started tingling, and the chill intensified as I approached the bedrooms at the end of this hall. The doors were open, and all I saw were large spaces that were tastefully furnished in varying shades of greys, blues, and white. It was precisely how all the magazines depicted beach houses and completely empty.

I was ready to give up my search when my neck prickled with a warning. The last room drew me. I was next to the bed before my vision opened, and I found myself surrounded by ghosts. Honest to god, spirits were hovering around me.

They were exactly like I had seen in movies and read about in books. The air around them was several degrees colder than usual, and their forms were a bluish color. And they were all women. I would find that odd if my brain wasn't behaving more like a TV with a bad antenna. And my ears were filled with a loud buzzing sound.

One of them stepped forward from the group. She had grey-streaked black hair pulled into a bun at the back of her head and a dress that placed her from a time at least a century and a half before. The bottom layer was topped with an apron and flowed to the floor.

She opened her mouth, and a keening moaning sound came out. I hunched and covered my ears with my hands. I turned my head and looked up at her. She tried to talk to me, but I couldn't hear anything aside from the awful noise.

When soft fur wound around my calves, the sound receded, and I picked up my familiar before standing upright. "I can hear her now. I assume this is your doing."

"You have much to learn about your magic. We will discuss more later. For now, you need to focus on why they have come."

I nodded my head and met the stern brown eyes of the woman I considered the leader of the ghosts. "I'm sorry. What were you saying?"

"You're new to witchcraft. I don't know how it's possible. We came for help. Someone is hunting us."

I bit my lip to keep from gaping at her. "Someone is hunting you? How is that possible. You're already dead. How are they able to hunt you, and why would they even bother?"

She rolled her eyes and sighed in exasperation. I was ready to give her a piece of my mind. I'd had a very long night and didn't need this shit. "We are witches. Even in death, we carry magic. Someone out there is trying to trap us and harness that magic for their use."

I gasped then and looked down at Tarja. "Can ghosts be used like witches that are alive? Could stealing their power extend their lives and give them more power?"

"This is a new and dangerous development. Ghosts would give a witch an even bigger boost than a live witch. The soul is the seat of power and cannot be accessed until they have crossed over."

I had to rub my temples in an attempt to stop the animated hammers trying to break free from behind my eyelids. "Crap on a stick. Okay. I will do what I can to look into this issue. I make no promises, but you are safe here at Nimaha. You can stay as long as you will not haunt the house or me or my family. The attic or the forest are good places to hang out."

"You have just made an ally no other witch has ever managed."

My chin lifted, and I wanted to preen at Tarja's praise. I wasn't a complete liability. That hiss-cough was back. Tarja laughing at me again. She really could read my mind. That was good to know. And gave me even more incentive to learn my magic so I could block her.

The sky outside was turning pink. So much for getting any more sleep. The adrenaline coursing through my veins had already made it unlikely. Now it was going to be impossible.

Setting Tarja down, I decided to put on some coffee and make breakfast. Tarja followed in silence. I checked on my mom and Nana and found them both sleeping. Nana was restless and would be up soon. Nina, on the other hand, was drooling like a basset hound. She wouldn't be up until noon. Good thing it was Saturday, and she didn't have school.

I startled when I ran into Layla and Mythia in the kitchen. "Oh, hi. I didn't expect to find anyone in here so early."

Layla, who was leaning against the counter next to the coffee pot, poured some nectar of the gods into a nearby mug and handed it to me. "Thanks," I told her as I grabbed the creamer from the fridge.

"I heard you get up and was about to investigate when Tarja passed me. I left her to it and decided to put on a pot. I found her here cutting up fresh fruit." Layla jerked her thumb in Mythia's direction.

Mythia paused with a butcher knife in her hand. "I hope you don't mind, Madam. I wanted to prepare a meal for you and your family, and I forgot to ask when you wake up."

"You don't have to do that, you know. I can handle it. But I would like you to continue helping clean the house until I can look at the finances and see if I can afford to hire someone. I have no desire to do all this by myself."

Mythia's head fell. "Did I upset you?" Seeing this tiny

version of Buffy broken like this was wrong. She should be smiling as she drove wooden stakes through a vampire's heart. Or fileting vegetables.

"Oh no! I just don't want to take advantage of your kindness. And I certainly don't want you to feel obligated."

"But she is," Layla interjected. "It's part of the agreement her clan's leader has with Hattie."

I inhaled the hazelnut aroma and took a sip. I needed a moment before I betrayed my anger that I had judged Hattie so wrong. It was appalling to think she would take advantage of frightened creatures like that. "Well, it won't be like that under my watch. What do I need to do to change this?"

"Watch yourself, Phoebe. You are dancing across a delicate rope right now. The pixies are a proud people that must give back in return for being given asylum. They are the ones that suggested they care for the land and home for Hattie. And Mythia volunteered to clean the house and feed Hattie. It has been hard enough for her to lose some of those privileges when you came on board. She felt Hattie should have let her do it all. Only now do we all understand what Fate had in mind."

"That makes more sense. Forget I said that. I don't need to reinvent the wheel. Will you both promise me that if you think there is a way to improve our contract, you will let me know?"

Mythia moved her head up and down, and the large knife started slipping from her grip. She squeaked and wrapped both hands around it before setting it on the counter. "You don't have to worry about me. Now, what does your family like for breakfast?"

"Biscuits and gravy," Nana announced as she shuffled into the room. I couldn't help but chuckle.

I wrapped my arms around her neck, then told her to have a seat and got her a cup of coffee. "Even though it's not a very healthy choice, it does sound delicious. How did you sleep?"

I noticed the circles under Nana's eyes weren't as dark as she added cream and sugar to her coffee. "I haven't slept that well since I was peri-menopausal. The energy in this house is soothing."

An image of the witches popped in my head. I wouldn't necessarily say it was calming. I wasn't to share that with her, so I did what any smart woman would. I nodded my head then changed the subject. "Have either of you heard anything about Myrna?"

I had offered a room to the three of them the night before. Yeah, I fully admit I wanted those that had fought beside me close while I was unconscious. It was like having a security blanket. All of them had said they would return after they went out to learn what they could about Myrna.

"The pack had been running the border when Clio returned with news someone had seen Myrna fleeing across the state line. She was burned and bleeding at the time. Tsekani managed to hit her with his dragon fire as she took off. There's nothing that burns quite like it. It continues to do damage even after the flames disappear."

Mythia stopped stirring some mixture and buzzed in place. It almost looked like she was hopping in place only with wings. "She's in bad shape. We poisoned her wounds, hoping they wouldn't heal. Daethie brewed the potion herself. I don't think we will see her again."

I nodded absently. It seemed far too easy for her to be eliminated like that. She was beyond powerful, and I saw the vengeance in her eyes. Not to mention she was bound and determined to grab whatever power she could for herself. I had no doubt she was the one hunting witches, which told me she had accessed powers none of them had even considered.

* * *

THE HOUSE WAS SO different today than it had been in the weeks prior. The house itself was no longer holding its breath, waiting for its mistress to pass away. There was a sense of relief and hope in the air.

Tarja jumped onto my lap and prodded my stomach. It was enough to jolt me out of my wandering thoughts. I was more than a little distracted. Hattie's attorney sat on the loveseat across from me and went over the details of what I had inherited. After he mentioned the house and the business, he went on to list other properties around the world as well as vehicles.

My mind fritzed when he mentioned how much I was now worth. I was a gazillionaire or something. He was looking at me and waiting for me to answer. Little help here, I sent to my familiar.

"He asked if you want to keep your personal account in a trust set up like Hattie had hers. You had better pay attention. You need to handle this transfer right away."

I nodded my head to both her and him. "Yes. That sounds like it's the best approach." Honestly, I had no idea whether it was or not. I trusted Hattie's judgment where that was concerned. She ran a successful business and created this massive conglomerate.

At least the kids won't have to rely on their dad to pay for college. Given what his little tart had already convinced him to do, it was entirely possible she would have him cut them off completely, too.

"Wonderful. If you'll just sign where indicated, please." He slid a stack of papers my way. I wasn't even halfway through the signatures when the doorbell rang. I was about to get up and get that when my mom called out.

"I've got it, sweetie. You finish up in there."

My heart made an impression of the Road Runner inside my chest while I debated if that was the right choice. Thoughts of what Myrna could do, ran like a peep show inside my grey matter, making me shake my head in denial. She couldn't cross the protections. Tarja had assured me no one could breach them even if I still needed to renew them.

I got through the rest of the papers quickly then pushed them back to him. "Is there anything else?"

He shook his head and put everything in his briefcase. "Not at this time. The board will be calling a meeting soon to go over the change in ownership. I'll send you a message when that is scheduled to take place."

I got up and followed him to the door. My throat dried up, and my girl parts stood at attention when we passed by the sexiest guy I'd ever laid eyes on. He was well over six feet tall with short black hair that was artfully messy. His sapphire eyes burned right through to my soul.

I thanked the attorney and turned to face the group standing in the entryway. My mother was shamelessly flirting with the guy while Nana was openly leering at him. Layla stood off to the side with narrowed eyes.

It was apparent the shifter saw something suspicious in him, so I worked hard to shove every lustful thought aside before it could take hold and distract me. Extending my hand, I greeted him. "Sorry about the delay. I'm Phoebe. How can I help you?"

"I think you should be asking how he can help you," Nana whisper yelled.

My cheeks heated, and he laughed. "I'm Aidoneus with UIS, Underworld Investigative Services, and I'm here to inspect a disturbance in the veil."

So, he was some kind of supernatural. And from the Underworld. Good to know. That made things much easier. I didn't need to worry about hiding anything from him. "I'm new to this world, so I'm not sure how much I will be able to tell you."

"Perhaps we should have a seat."

Aidoneus's gaze shifted from me to the cat at my feet. "That's probably wise."

My mother gestured to the room to our right. "The front room should work for you guys. Can I get you anything to drink, Aidoneus?"

"Do you have any grape Fanta? I tried it recently for the first time and am addicted."

Everyone laughed at that. "I'm afraid not. But I do have some purple energy drinks. I need the caffeine boost during long shifts." Except I no longer had to take care of Hattie. Tears built in my eyes once again as emotion choked me.

"I'll try one of those, thanks. I'm afraid the day is going to be a long one."

I gathered myself while we made our way into the front room. I took a seat on one of the armchairs while Nana sat on the love seat. Aidoneus took the seat closest to mine. "Now, what exactly can I help you with."

"My team was alerted when a ritual was performed on or near your property last night. This spell perforated the veil between this one and the Underworld. And, well, let's just say some undesirable creatures managed to slip through." There was more he wasn't saying.

My instincts had me biting my tongue to keep from snapping at him and demanding answers. I couldn't take out my trust issues on this complete stranger. Thanks to Miles, I lost trust at the first sign of a lie, or in this case, withholding information.

Focus on the issue. Right. Something from hell was here! Fear blinded me for a split second, then my breaths hitched, and my eyes flew wide. Before I knew what I was doing, energy sizzled through me and shot out of my fingertips.

Aidoneus's eyes flared, and he had jumped from his seat in the blink of an eye.

Tarja was in my lap, helping stabilize my magic, when my mom returned with a tray and some snacks. "What's wrong?" My mom asked as her gaze flew around the space before landing back on me.

I cleared my throat. "I just lost control of myself for a second. The thought of demons running around out there is terrifying."

"She shot fireworks from her fingertips," Nana added unhelpfully.

I ran my hand over Tarja's soft fur. There was no reason to panic or be embarrassed. It wasn't my fault. I had no idea what I was doing yet. "I have been a witch for less than twenty-four hours now, so I don't know how to control anything. But I promise you I didn't do anything last night. We held a funeral for Hattie Silva, the woman I used to take care of. She gave me her magic to save my life." To avoid further confusion, I gave Aidoneus a rundown of the events from the previous evening.

"You've had quite the evening. And you're handling this extremely well for everything that was thrown at you. I don't sense any demons nearby at the moment. But someone on this property cast a Dark spell and, in doing so, weakened the veil. We don't have an exact count of how many demons ended up crossing through before Hades managed to secure it once again."

"It could have been Myrna before she took off. She might have been trying to heal herself after her injuries," Layla suggested.

Aidoneus inclined his head at her. For some reason, I didn't think he believed Myrna was responsible. There was a calculating gleam in his gorgeous eyes. "I will look into that

MAGICAL MAKEOVER

possibility. First, I'd like to take a look at the area where this occurred."

I nodded my head and led the way to the backyard. Everyone followed behind us in a long and awkward silent train. The crisp morning air soothed me, and I took a deep breath. "We held the funeral there," I pointed out the section of the yard where the coven met last night, "and buried her in the forest. The fight happened closer to the shore and along the opposite border."

"And it was just the thirteen of you?" Aidoneus walked around the lawn where the initial ceremony had been held.

"Yes. We were the only ones involved in the ritual. Layla, Tsekani, and Mythia watched from a distance. Others joined us in the forest."

Aidoneus knelt on the grass and withdrew what looked like a wand, only it was glass. I stifled a laugh as he waved it through the air. The power that burst from him in a dark orange flare sobered me and reminded me this was all very real. The magical object in his hand had dark purple lightning shooting through it that shifted to a dark green color.

He muttered something under his breath, and sparks shot from his hands this time. Static electricity traveled along my skin. Nana gasped next to me and rubbed at her arms. "I never expected to encounter something so fascinating at my age. I'm so glad Miles left you, and you moved home, Phoebe."

A growl left me, and I glared at Nana. She was oblivious to my embarrassment. My face heated, and I quickly averted my gaze when I noticed Aidoneus watching me. "Would you like to see the area where I encountered Myrna?"

Aidoneus inclined his head and started for the beach without waiting for me. He walked to the spot I hit my back, then where I landed on the pebbled beach. I followed as he headed right for the place Myrna had been standing and threatening me. Two days ago, I would have asked how he knew where to go. Now my world had been expanded, and my eyes opened. Magic was real! My grey matter still grappled with all I had learned.

I knelt next to him when he did. He still had his wand out, and I noticed the glass now looked like a cloudy sky at night. Flashes resembling black shooting stars appeared when he waved it over the area while muttering under his breath. There was nothing purple or green in it this time.

"I'm going to scout the area around the house if that's alright—both on and off, your property. I appreciate you letting me inside your wards and granting me an audience. Here's my information in the event you discover any information that might be helpful."

Aidoneus had turned his head when he addressed me, and our faces were much closer than I had realized. I nodded my head, unable to speak at the moment. My skin burned where it made contact with his when I accepted the card. Apparently, since Tsekani broke through the daze I had been living in for months my body had become a live wire. Hell, it'd been more like years. Things were terrible long before Miles left.

Finding my voice, I smiled. "I'm more than happy to help in any way I can."

"Would you like to stay for lunch?" I shot my mother a glare and stood up.

Aidoneus laughed and shook his head while he climbed to his feet, as well. "Raincheck. I want to get through the property, then I have another lead to follow up." He was responding to my mom while his eyes remained glued to mine. If he turned out to be gay, as well, I was going to scream at the unfairness of life.

"We will be around if you have questions," I assured him.

"I know how to find you if I need anything."

My cheeks turned pink as I imagined his words carried a

double meaning. I watched him cross the way and my imagination went wild. When I turned around, I discovered everyone else watching him just as raptly. Even Tsekani.

"C'mon. I'm hungry," I blurted, trying to grab everyone's attention.

There was no denying Aidoneus's appeal. He was attractive in a rugged, undeniable way. Not that this was an appropriate time to be thinking about such a thing. In my defense, perimenopause was akin to your body being on a roller coaster ride. I went from one extreme to the next. And at the moment, the hormones coursing through me were winning.

I have to admit part of it was that it had been far too long since I'd had an orgasm, and my body was trying to make up for lost time. One thing was certain, I needed to get control of myself before he showed back up. Given his goodbye, I was convinced he would be back sooner rather than later. And I was determined to be prepared to handle my attraction to him next time.

Aside from being incredibly good-looking, I would bet my net worth that he would be another ally I wanted at my side. I hadn't been thinking in those terms before Tarja mentioned it. Now, it was always in the back of my mind. In nursing, it was essential to have skilled people around you in the event of a crisis.

He was precisely the kind of man I wanted on my side should shit hit the figurative fan again. I was new to this world, and I wasn't a twenty-something without experience to guide me. I knew enough to know I needed solid people I could call on.

CHAPTER 12

I needed to call Mr. Peterson. Between Myrna still being out there and Aidoneus showing up unexpectedly, I was overwhelmed. I didn't have the mental capacity to handle his investigation right now. However, I needed to communicate with him.

There was no such thing as too many friends. As a new person on the scene, I needed all the paranormals in my corner that I could get. Besides, I wanted to keep the lines open and let him know that I would look into it when I had time. Part of me was tempted to tell him I wasn't going to pick up those pieces from Hattie. When I thought about it, I got excited about the idea.

Helping find a ghost wasn't life and death emergent like the other stuff I was facing. It was far more appealing. I'd bet a hundred bucks I would be less likely to get my ass kicked, or worse while searching for his Aunt Sarah.

Another bonus of taking on this role would be getting to know the various supernaturals in the area. Not only would I develop valuable relationships, but it would also educate me quicker than almost anything else.

I dialed his number and listened while it rang. "Hello." Mr. Peterson's professional demeanor came through the phone line.

"Mr. Peterson. It's Phoebe Dieudonné. We spoke the other day about me helping you find your Aunt Sarah."

"Ah, yes. Please call me Harry. I am glad you called. I've got some ideas of where we can start. I kept some debris from the living room the night I heard her call out. Whoever kidnapped her spirit disappeared in a flash of smoke. When it cleared, the dirt and leaves were left behind. You can do a tracking spell. I also took pictures of the room in case you can get anything from them."

God, this guy was desperate to find his aunt. The fact that he had collected evidence and taken pictures twisted my gut because I was calling to deny his request. *It's only for a little while. Demons are a bigger problem.*

"I know you are anxious for me to get started, but I'm afraid I can't at the moment. I have a Tainted witch-hunting in the area, and someone breached the veil to the Underworld. Needless to say, those issues must be resolved right away. Your missing aunt is important, and I will help. Just not right now."

His sigh hit me like a knife to the gut. "Oh, dear. If demons are running around Camden, that does pose a problem to us all. Tainted witches are even worse. I understand. Keep your eyes peeled when you deal with the Tainted. They could use a ghost like my aunt. I hope you can address these issues quickly. In the meantime, I will continue to look for her. If you ever need the help of an elf, please call me. I'm happy to return the favor."

I thanked him and promised I would keep him apprised of the situation, especially if I encounter any ghosts. I wanted to pat myself on the back. Turned out life had prepared me more than I thought for this new development.

I was ready for the magical makeover. Welcomed it even. I'd already made an ally and was building relations with others. I still had a long road ahead of me. First things first. Learn how to wield my magic.

* * *

"You look like you're constipated."

I huffed and flopped onto the mat we'd brought into the room on the third floor. Technically it was an attic, but Hattie had the space finished and windows installed to make it feel open and inviting. Layla thought it would be safer to practice casting spells here, where I couldn't damage anything vital in the house.

It took about five seconds for Layla to put a halt to the practice when one of my sparks hit a support pylon in the basement. I agreed immediately. We were about to remove the furniture from one of the many rooms when Nina informed us the attic would be perfect.

My daughter had taken to this life like a fish to water. Not much fazed her, and she adjusted her thinking quickly. She spent Saturday exploring the house with my mom while Nana and I went through Hattie's closet.

We discovered some great clothes and jewelry. The shoes weren't my style, but mom and Nana would put them to good use. They'd each gotten a makeover and new wardrobe by the time they returned home last night.

I sat up and wiped the sweat from my brow. "Why is this so hard?"

Tarja looked up from grooming herself. *"Because you're fighting instinct. You are at a distinct disadvantage not having grown up with power. Now you have to relearn how you think about everything. That knot in your stomach is your gut trying to tell you you're in danger. It's wrong."*

MAGICAL MAKEOVER

I leaned my elbows on my knees and slowed my breathing. It felt like I had been working out when all I had been doing was trying to conjure a witch light. It's supposed to be a basic spell that most master by the time they're Nina's age.

Layla extended her hand and hauled me to my feet. "You've got this. Just push your fear aside."

Bobbing my head, I lifted my hand and felt the energy buzzing through my body. My heart started racing, and my breathing once again increased. It reminded me of my college days when I drank two and a half pots of coffee the day before my practicals. I needed to stay up and cram all night, and that was the only way I could think to do it.

Intent. I had to hone my purpose and keep it at the forefront of my mind. I pictured a light hovering above my palm and willed it to come to fruition. Come on, come on, come on. The tendons on my neck stood out as I tried to push my magic that way. It was hard because I wasn't entirely certain which of the million things that I was experiencing at the moment was my power.

"Stop rationalizing," Layla warned.

Shit. I was getting lost in thought. This time I took a deep breath, closed my eyes, and called up a picture of a baseball-sized orb of light hovering a few inches above my palm. I went back to looking at the light every time my mind started to stray. My entire body hummed as I remained focused.

"You did it, Phoebe. Look!"

My eyes snapped open when I heard Layla's excited voice. "Holy shit!" The light flickered, and I refocused solely on it. It took a couple seconds before it stabilized and got brighter.

"Woah." Mythia's musical voice was followed by the sound of heavy objects hitting the wood floor.

I glance toward the stairs and felt the magic sizzle then pop. The hum was gone, and the energy had receded. I didn't need to look to know my light had disappeared. "What's that?"

Mythia shook herself then dove to pick up the mesh bag she'd dropped. I knew what she had brought in. Just not why. The bag was see-through, and I could see the gold, silver, and what looked like gemstones.

"They're gifts from the colony to welcome you."

Layla slapped me on the shoulder. "Close your mouth. You're not a fish."

"Shut up. I can't help it if I'm shocked about being given gold and jewels. This is too much. I can't accept this."

"Technically, it belongs to you. The pixies mine the area when they dig the tunnels for their mound. Hattie instructed them to keep them and ensure no one got their hands on them. Metals and gems can be infused with Fae magic and therefore be used as talismans."

"Or cursed objects. It's easier and more effective if a witch uses Fae infused objects to combine her hex with."

I gaped at Layla. "How do you know so much about this?"

"My creator was a bitch, but a powerful one. It was a powerful object that fused my cells with that of a wolf. She did the same thing to Tsekani."

My gut clenched with her announcement. "Then why did you bring it here? We can't let anyone get ahold of that."

Mythia picked up the bag and brought it closer. When she handed it to me, I could feel the buzz coming off the pieces. "Daethie thought you could use it to create protection amulets for your family. Using these, you should be able to protect against even the death spell Myrna cast on you. We all know how much you worry about them."

Powerful allies. They were going to help me keep those I loved safe, as well. I was now a target. The last thing I wanted was for any of them to come under fire. "That was very thoughtful. I was hoping I would find a way to protect them."

"This will be a good way to practice the incantations you will

need to use when you tie your own protections to the barrier around Nimaha."

"Now? I barely formed the light ball. How am I supposed to do anything with this?"

Layla sat in the armchair she brought up and steepled her fingers in front of her face. "You're a Pleiades witch. You can do this. Just give it a try."

Mythia landed on the cushioned arm next to Layla's elbows, and Tarja sat in a regal pose to their left. They all looked at me expectantly. I set the bag down and grabbed a chunk of silver.

"Can I cast the spell then have someone make a necklace with it?"

"You will want a pixie craftsman. Or your friend's mate could manage it without destroying or damaging the spell."

"Alright. What do I do? I want to keep my family safe. It's not like I can picture a bubble of armor around them and push it into the silver."

Mythia cocked her head to the side. "Why not?"

"She's right," Layla agreed. "Make sure it's bullet and spell proof when you conjure it, and nothing will reach them."

When I looked to my familiar, I swear she was looking at me with one eyebrow lifted. I shrugged my shoulders and kept my eyes on the chunk of silver. Picturing a bubble around my Nana was easy enough. I struggled to believe the rainbow-hued construct would keep her safe from a fly.

"You won't safeguard anything with that attitude. The appearance isn't what's important. It's your intent."

Taking a deep breath, I pulled up the image again and thought of how it would feel if anything happened to my Nana. Anger, fear, and anxiety immediately had my heart racing. Forget that. No one was going to hurt her. She was the kindest woman I knew and had been an excellent role model growing up.

I poured my need to keep everything out. I didn't care if it was magic, age, bullets, or knives. I extended that to include weapons of any kind. I even went so far as to incorporate anyone that meant any harm.

Once I had that all loaded in my mind and heart, I pushed it out. The metal in my hand immediately started heating to the degree that alarmed me. I refused to let go of my intent and watched as the silver melted and dripped over the sides of my hand.

"Crap!" I shook my hand, and bits of liquid silver flew off in every direction.

Mythia was on her feet and hovered nearby in a heartbeat. Layla shook her head. "I've never seen anyone with that much raw power. What the hell?"

"Phoebe is the first of her kind. We have no idea what she will become. One thing is clear. You must develop better control and fast. Otherwise, the entire planet is at risk."

I bent down and poked the silver that was hardening on the mat. There was no mistaking the buzz beneath my digits. "I don't want the fate of the world on my shoulders. Geez. Saying that isn't going to make this happen faster, you know. It just stresses me out."

Layla got up and came to my side. "Look, we're all worried. What Tarja is trying to say is that as an anomaly, you are even more of a target. And we can't let anyone like Myrna get ahold of your powers."

"You are a Pleiades. You have seven sisters out there, and together, you keep the witching world in balance. The gods created you long ago when witches first went bad. If you go down, the rest will follow. That was why it was so important for Hattie to identify her heir and why the magic kept her alive as long as it did."

Thank God, I had worked in the cardiac unit for twenty years. I was accustomed to lives being in my hand. I couldn't think of the enormity of my current situation. Like a patient

MAGICAL MAKEOVER

on ECMO, I needed to keep things stable, usually until UNOS found a heart. In my case, it was until I could wield my magic like a pro.

I picked up the silver. It was now flat and amoeba-shaped. To my surprise, I felt magic in the object. "Is the spell in here? Did I get it right? Aside from melting it, that is."

Mythia flew closer and took it from my hands, then passed it onto Layla. "There's definitely magic there. I can't identify the spell, though."

"It's more than Fae power," Layla added.

"It will protect your grandmother. However, it's not as powerful as you intended because you got distracted at the end. It's a good start. You should have something for yourself when you leave the house."

"Probably a good idea until I can be sure I'm able to defend myself against attack."

Tarja shook her furry head from side to side. *"That is not the reason. I did some reading last night after our unexpected visitor left."*

Hearing her mention, Aidoneus had the teenager in me panting and wondering when I would see him again. This middle-aged divorcee was rolling her eyes while she recited all the reasons men were a bad idea.

Miles had broken my heart into a million pieces, and I was just putting them back together. I wasn't opening myself up any time soon. I would allow myself to appreciate how attractive he was. Nothing more.

Besides, I was in the middle of my magical makeover. It wasn't time to unveil the finished product yet.

"What did you find out? And where did you get books that mentioned the veil between the Underworld and Earth?" I still couldn't quite comprehend what he had said. Even after everything I'd learned, it seemed impossible that Hades existed, and he was apparently, a decent guy that was taking steps to protect the planet and human life. Not what I'd been taught at all.

"Our library." Tarja's mental voice was dry as a dead leaf. I could guess what she thought of the fact that I hadn't spent any time there in the last three days.

"I was merely stating the obvious. And what I discovered is that Blood magic will cause the veil to rupture. I think whoever is hunting our ghosts is the culprit behind this."

"But they didn't use Blood magic. The witches are already dead. I thought that was soul magic."

Layla and Mythia laughed while Tarja simply stared at me. *"There's no such thing as soul magic. The witches shed blood to perform their spells. I found a book of the dark arts that detailed a way to call souls over from the afterlife. It involves taking a life."*

I had to swallow back my bile. "Why would someone do such a horrible thing? For a bit more power? It's not worth it."

"Not just magic. They want to become immortal. What you don't know is that witches live two lifetimes, sometimes longer. At one point, they usually become their children. If they manage what they are trying to accomplish, they will never die."

Layla made a sound of disgust. "And become a twisted evil person in the process. Not exactly something we want walking around the planet."

"No, it isn't. So, you're saying I need to master my magic. Let's try this again, shall we?" I took the amoeba for my Nana and focused on her well-being. I poured myself into perfecting this spell so I could move onto other important matters.

These witches might think I was an easy target because I was human until three days ago. I looked forward to proving them wrong. Just as soon as I finished this damn spell.

CHAPTER 13

"Thank you, sweetheart. I appreciate the necklace." Nana held up the silver heart. She looked anything but happy to have it. After melting piles of silver, Tarja felt confident I had forged charms that would protect my family.

Nina fingered my attempt at a sunflower while my mom slipped the butterfly over her head. None of them were perfect, and it didn't matter. All I cared about was that they did the job.

"It's not the prettiest, Nana, but it will keep us safe. They hum," Nina observed. "You figured out your magic. That's great, mom."

I shook my head and grimaced. "Not exactly. I practiced the protective spell. I wanted you guys safe, and I need to recast the protections around the property soon. Tarja wants me to practice some more before I try the entire property. I'm not convinced I can do it at all."

"Well, you have to." My mom was good at being blunt and had never pulled her punches. It took decades for me to appreciate it. Now, I wasn't so sure I did anymore. "Too many are relying on you to keep them safe from danger. Hattie picked you because she saw how special you are."

Layla set half of her lobster roll down and wiped her hands on a paper towel. Mythia had made the area favorite for Nana after hearing how much she loved the sandwiches. It meant the world to me that my new friends were bonding with my family. I needed them both in my life and wanted them to get along.

"Hattie did see something in Phoebe. She hired Phoebe just to see if she was a suitable match to receive her magic." Layla's announcement was met with silence.

I had known Hattie was considering giving me her power, but this shocked me. "She hired me to take care of her medical needs. She didn't bring me on to test if I was a match for her legacy."

Mythia hovered in front of me with her wings flapping rapidly. "She was running out of time and hadn't found a suitable heir in the magical world after nearly seventy years, so she decided to go to the human one. I had been caring for her for years before you arrived and would have continued."

"I had no idea that was why she hired me." Which is why it worked. If I'd known, I would have freaked out and acted differently, I'm sure. "I wish I'd had more time with her."

"Me too," Nana threw in. "Then she could have told you if the creepy sensation driving to your house is normal. I swear there were shadows in the forest."

Mom and Nina nodded their heads. "It's true, mom. I thought I saw a pair of red eyes and sharp claws rake across the bark of one of the trees."

How were they able to see anything magical? It should be impossible. Then I recalled seeing Tsekani in his dragon form and the ghost in the house. I had been doing a lot of thinking over the last week and recalled seeing pixies at my wedding. At the time, I had dismissed them as fireflies that I'd given human bodies because I'd had too much alcohol.

"We don't have a witch somewhere in our ancestry, do we, Nana? Some rumor that our great-great-great-great aunt was burned at the stake?"

Nana laughed and shook her head. "Nothing so exciting. I'm afraid we're normal humans."

"You're mundies," Layla replied helpfully. "But you guys are great." I wasn't sure what she meant by that and decided to let it go.

"Tarja, are some humans perceptive to the supernatural?"

My familiar jumped onto the counter and sniffed the platter of lobster rolls. I grabbed a plate and sliced one up for her. *"There are sensitives that can sometimes detect when there is magic close. Some of those sensitives can even see some paras. Those humans usually have a Fae or shifter or witch in their background. We can research your family history if you'd like."*

"We will handle that while you focus on learning how to protect us," my mom offered with a full mouth. Nana nodded her head as she chewed her food.

I speared a piece of watermelon and popped the sweet fruit into my mouth. "I'd love the distraction. There's only so much failure I can take before I quit entirely."

"Relinquishing your magic isn't an option. You have no choice but to step up to the plate."

"My granddaughter's not a quitter. She's just tired. It's not easy to go full out for days on end. And from the looks of it, magic isn't anything like scrubbing a floor or taking someone's blood pressure."

I couldn't help but chuckle at Nana's vehement support. "Thanks. And you're right. I'd never just stop. But I don't take failure very well, and that's all I've been doing."

"You've managed more than Hattie did this early in her studies. It took her years to make a protection amulet."

Pride swelled in my chest. It dwindled some when I looked at the lopsided heart around Nana's neck and the butterfly missing its lower set of wings. "They aren't pretty. But they are functional."

"I can teach you how to shape jewelry if you'd like," Tsekani offered. He'd been silently eating his way through a plate of five or six lobster rolls.

I gaped at him. "You know how to do this, and you didn't tell me?"

The walls shook before Tsekani could respond. The ground rolled a second later. What in the hell? There weren't earthquakes in Maine. I raced for the patio doors and looked outside. "What was that?"

"Tainted are at our borders. They're trying to break through the protections." Tarja's tone was calm but urgent.

My heart galloped into high gear. "Shit! I need a weapon."

My mom ran into the kitchen holding two swords. "Here you go, sweetie. Will this do?" Nana was right behind her with one in her hand. Nina stood behind them, trying to hide the knives in her hands.

"Where in the hell did you get those?" I took one from her and tested the weight. I had no idea what I was doing or what it should feel like. And, yet I knew that it felt right.

Nana shrugged her thin shoulders. "I found them in the closet of one of the rooms in the house." My ninety-year-old grandmother was standing there holding a sword like she was some badass warrior. She never ceased to amaze me.

The handle tingled in my grip. "Are these magical?"

"They are Fae made." Why couldn't Tarja simply say yes? Another blast shook the walls. This time I felt the impact in my gut. I hadn't been paying attention before. Now I could feel the malevolence surrounding us.

Layla lifted her top over her head and dropped it on the counter. The fact that Nana and my mom weren't fazed in the least told me how quickly they'd adjusted to our new world. They might have gone home, but they came back every morning.

"Tsekani and I will shift and find the witches trying to break through. Tarja can you track us then relay the location to Phoebe?" Layla removed the rest of her clothes and shifted in a whirlwind of power. The current made the tray of food slide across the counter, and the napkins fly into the air. The magic died as rapidly as it started, and the wind died.

"So cool," Nina whispered.

"Your turn," Nana told Tsekani. "Go ahead and get naked."

He chuckled and gave her a smile. "I'm too big to shift inside." Thankfully he walked outside before I could tell him to keep it PG for my daughter. Unfortunately, she moved quickly as a seventeen-year-old girl while the rest of us tried to get there to watch the show.

I wanted to see the transformation. I hadn't seen Tsekani turn into a dragon yet. Nana moved faster than I had seen in two decades. I saw a well-muscled chest then a tornado of magic. Leaves swirled around his form. Between one blink and the next, a green dragon was standing on the back lawn.

I almost thought Hattie would hate that, then corrected myself. She had pixies to fix the damage to the lawn. The light was blocked, so suddenly, I ducked below the counter on instinct and grabbed Nina's shirt.

Nina laughed at me. "It's his wings, mom. We aren't being attacked."

I released the breath I had been holding then stood up. "I didn't think he had wings. I've never seen them." Tsekani's dragon form hinted at his Asian heritage much like his human form. The Fu Manchu mustache over his sharp teeth fit his overall look.

"You guys stay here. Any tips on how to confront these witches, Tarja?"

The cat wound around my legs. *"Call up your personal defenses and use the blade to deflect their spells. Remember, your intent is key in casting. Layla found the Tainted along the western border. Let's go."*

"Protect your Nana and grandma. And stay inside the house. Mythia, will you be with you guys, won't you?"

Mythia's tiny chest puffed out. "I won't leave their side."

It had to be good enough. They had their necklaces. It provided more assurance than I ever expected. It allowed me to run away from them. I jumped down the short steps between the terraces and was on the beach within a minute. And I was only mildly out of breath. Score one for the middle-aged divorcee running daily on the treadmill.

I hadn't gone very far when my steps faltered. Why anyone dressed in black robes would look menacing, I wasn't sure. It wasn't the cliché of them covering themselves with black from head to toe. It was the shadows surrounding them. They radiated evil and made my skin crawl.

It was my determination to keep everyone on the land Hattie had entrusted to me that kept me moving forward. I saw the witch on the left lift her hand before I saw the spell leave it and was able to twist out of the way.

I felt like Wonder Woman or Zena Warrior Princess until electricity slammed into my left shoulder. I heard the crackle and smelled ozone but didn't think about another attack. The spell coated me in a film, and oil slithered over my body at the same time pain took my breath away. The dragonfly around my neck heated. I needed to thank Fiona for the best gift ever. It was saving my ass every time I looked around.

I thought about how much I wanted to make them regret attacking me in my new home. It offended me on more than one level. This was an affront to Hattie and her choice for an heir. And an outright display of their desire to take my new magic from me.

MAGICAL MAKEOVER

When I was certain I had my intent firmly in mind, I threw my hands out and sent it in their direction. The second it came in contact with the witch in the middle pink light exploded, and the robes turned pink. Their hoods disappeared, revealing their faces.

They were young women in their late twenties to early thirties at most. The one in the middle snarled at me, and black lightning shot from her hands. Tsekani flew between the spell and me and used his claws to slice through the enchantment, making it dissipate. His massive dragon was graceful and fast.

I could see Layla's wolf prowling toward the group from behind them. Tsekani was too far away the next time black lightning came my way. It crackled and sparked as it traveled toward me. I stopped running and brought up my sword. The spell hit the blade with a hard jolt.

The vibrations traveled up my arms and shook me. The trick worked, though, and the spell headed back to its caster. Unfortunately, the dark-haired witch caught it with a smile.

Next, I concentrated on throat punching the witch with beautiful mocha skin and green eyes. I hoped by focusing on one of them, it would work this time. I released it before I had a chance to second guess its readiness.

A yelp pierced the crackling air. Blood was dripping from a wound on Layla's side. Not that it stopped her from jumping and snapping at the witches. One of them faced her while two-faced me. Tsekani flew overhead and blew a stream of dragon fire at the scum with the gall to try and take what didn't belong to them.

Why wouldn't they just leave me alone? *That's it!* I needed to make them leave me alone. That was a spell I was reasonably certain I could manage easily. I kept my intent to make them run away firmly in mind and held it for several seconds. I poured my frustration at not being able to attack them with offensive spells, along with my need to keep my family and friends safe into the power building in my chest.

When I thought I had enough power, I let go of the magic. To my surprise, the spell exploded out of my body with so much force I was surprised I hadn't been reduced to a puddle of bone and goo.

As I watched, the witches turned tail and ran away with their pink robes flying behind their retreating figures. When Layla started running, I raced to catch her. Unfortunately, she was too fast. When I went to ask Tsekani to help her, he was gone as well.

What went wrong this time? I didn't include them in my intent. Would I ever get this right? I thought I had this one mastered. *"Your spell carried so much power it affected everyone on the property. I was able to stop it from setting into your family or the pixies and shifters nearby,"* Tarja told me.

"Oh. I have that much power?"

Tarja's scratchy laughter filled my head. *"You have more than I've ever seen. It's curious."*

I didn't want to be a curiosity. I wanted to be normal and predictable. Pushing that aside for another time, I hurried for the back door. "We need to have Mythia get Layla to the house. She's hurt."

"I've already sent her. She and Tsekani will be back soon."

"I tried to hurt them, but I couldn't. I should want to kill them for what they've done. The problem is, I don't. I blame it on the oath that I took to do no harm when I became a nurse. My entire life has been about helping others. How do I go from that to attacking people?"

"This world isn't soft or easy. It's full of danger, death, and greed. The reason Hattie picked you is that you hold none of that in your heart. It presents a challenge when dealing with those willing to do anything to take you and yours out. We will address the problems as they come. There's no reason to borrow trouble at the

moment. Just remember you're not alone in this." Tarja was still loyal to Hattie, but she had my back and was there for me, as well.

Knowing that Tarja, Layla, Tsekani, and Mythia were with me helped calm my frazzled nerves. *There's also Aidoneus. He'd like to be at your back.* I shut my inner slut up and added him to the possible column. I didn't know the rest of the residents well enough to count on them, as well. I needed to change that ASAP. Knowing there were so many there to help me changed how frightened and overwhelmed I had been.

They weren't simply taking from me or using me for safety. They were willing to lay their lives on the line to help me. Together we could do this.

CHAPTER 14

I smiled when Fiona's light brown hair and hazel eyes popped up on the screen. "Phoebe! I'm so glad you called. I haven't been able to stop thinking about you since you called last time. How are you doing?"

I sagged against the sofa in the media room and hit mute on the television. I was watching Grey's Anatomy of all things. I missed the hospital, and this was like my guilty fix now. Fiona's face and voice were a balm to my frazzled nerves.

I set the phone on the stand Nina bought me a few days ago. It made Face Timing with Jean-Marc much easier. "I've been better. I swear I will never get this right. And if I don't, so many people will be hurt or worse. There's so much pressure, and it isn't helping me learn."

Fiona chuckled and set her teacup down. "I understand that. Bas used to scowl at me and brood because I had no idea what I was doing. It takes time, but you will get it." She looked better than she had since our college days. The fine lines and wrinkles were almost invisible, and there was a glow about her.

I made a pfft sound and smoothed the rat's nest on the top of my head. "How can you be so sure? How did you learn to do magic?"

A guy that rivaled Tsekani and Aidoneus in the looks department lowered his head over Fiona's shoulder with a smirk. "Listen to your guide. They are connected to you and giving you advice because they know what you need. And for the record, I didn't scowl at her."

I laughed because I could see the scowl on his face. And the adoration he had for Fiona. I was happy for her. She deserved to have another great love. She was the best person I'd ever known.

"You must be Sebastian. Thank you for the necklace. It's saved my life more than once. I owe you more than I can ever repay."

His face softened, and his gaze shifted to Fiona then back to the phone. "I was happy to create it when Fiona asked. She shared what your ex-husband did, which is what prompted me to add some protection. I didn't want him to hurt you anymore. I could see how much you meant to Fiona. I should have known Fate had a hand in matters."

He believed in Fate? That was a concept I had heard more than once since discovering magic existed. I expected the belief in the gods. Never in a million years did I think some beings believed in a mystical force that had a hand in how lives unfolded.

"What about Fate? And if she landed me in this situation, why didn't she prepare me better?" I couldn't hide the bitter note in my voice. It pissed me off that there was no one held accountable for messing with people's lives.

"It's hard for mundies to understand the forces at work in our lives. It's not easy to shift things and create situations that help keep the balance in the universe. Just keep an open mind. I'll leave you two to it. Can I get you anything, Butterfly?"

My heart melted, and I was momentarily jealous of what she had with Sebastian. It morphed into happiness for my best friend. "Wait. I have another question before you go. Do either of you know Aidoneus with UIS?"

Bas's forehead wrinkled, and his mouth pursed. His face disappeared, and I could see his abdomen as he paced behind Fiona. She shifted her gaze from her boyfriend to the screen. "I've never heard about anything like that. Remember, I've only been in the magical world about a year."

"That's the Underworld big wigs." The woman's voice came from Fiona's side of the conversation, and I wasn't surprised when she addressed her grandmother.

"What do you mean, Grams?" Fiona was focused on something above her screen.

"I've only encountered them once when I was a little girl. The agent that came to Cottlehill Wilds back then wasn't Aidoneus but Nakir. He was investigating demons or something. He was smart as a whip. Nothing got past him. And he had all the women vying for his attention. Yeah, he was handsome and strong. No one could resist him."

Sebastian stopped pacing right before he rejoined the conversation. "That's right. He was all business until he found the supernaturals that had been possessed and dealt with them."

"What had happened? How did the demons cross over?" Maybe they could tell me something that might help Aidoneus.

Bas leaned down. "It was only one, and a dwarf summoned the demon, wanting more power and hoping having a demon under his control would elevate his position in the community."

There went that theory. Dammit.

"Why?" Fiona asked.

Bas was no longer standing behind her. "Aidoneus stopped by the morning after Hattie's funeral saying someone cast a Dark spell on my property and some demons got through. I couldn't help. I wouldn't know if someone was doing Dark magic right in front of me. That's why I called. I need your help."

Fiona nodded her head. "I'm more than happy to help, but my magic is more elemental based. One thing I can say is the key to any spell is your intent. Keep that clear in your mind, and don't get distracted. Even the slightest distraction or odd thought will veer your casting off course. But I'm not the best to help with witchcraft. I can ask Violet if she's feeling better."

I recalled Fiona talking about her bestie from childhood many times. "What's wrong with Violet? Is she alright?"

"She hasn't been the same since we returned from Eidothea. It's not like Aislinn, who has been physically ill. Violet just isn't herself."

I grabbed a grape and ate it. "I'm sorry to hear that. I would help if I could, but I'm busy trying to keep these witches from stealing the magic Hattie gave me. I keep wondering how I went from a happily married middle-aged woman that kicked ass at work to being a broke divorcee that was taking care of an elderly woman when she gave me her magical powers to save my life. Now I'm a Pleiades witch, and there are Tainted after me. It's insane!"

Fiona sipped her tea. "This is the first time I've ever heard of the Tainted. We don't have witches stealing power here in Cottlehill. You can become the first member of the Backside of Forty coven across the pond if that helps any. We'd all love to have you."

I laughed at the thought. "I inherited Hattie's coven, but I would love nothing more than to be a part of yours. I don't even know these women or what to expect from them. I know you better than I know myself. It would be reassuring knowing you're on my side."

"Well, official member of BOF or not, I will always be here for you. And I will do some research and get back to you. One thing you need to get used to is making tough decisions in this world."

My chest tightened at her warning. "What do you mean tough decisions?"

"You're like me. We've spent our lives helping people. That doesn't necessarily fit in this one. You will face situations and choices that require you to make life and death decisions with you wielding the blade, metaphorical or tangible. You have to be prepared to make those choices now, so they come easily when you're under duress." Fiona lifted one corner of her mouth.

I swallowed back the tension choking me. I had just faced a decision like this and failed. I got lucky my family and friends didn't pay for my inability to take action. "You sound like you speak from experience."

Fiona clutched the teacup to her chest and nodded her head. "I do. Not long after I discovered I was the new Guardian, I was attacked by the crazy Fae Queen. I accidentally burned her the first time I faced her and was sick to my stomach over it. Violet's kids were kidnapped shortly after because she was pissed about what I'd done. I should have killed her, but I couldn't. I didn't even burn her on purpose. The next time I faced her, I killed her. Same with her husband. He was much easier to kill. Sebastian helped me with him, and I didn't hesitate that time. He was sucking the power from every Fae that lived in his realm and killing them. He needed to die, and I was the only one that could do the job."

I gasped and put a hand over my mouth while my gag

reflex got a workout. "Holy crap. I had no idea you were going through all of that. You never mentioned anything when I called."

Fiona lifted one corner of her mouth in a wry smile. "It's not something I could blurt out to my very human best friend. Besides, you didn't need to worry about me while you were going through so much of your own turmoil."

I chuckled. "It seems like you managed to get through the fights intact. That's good. It definitely gives me hope. And you look happier than I've seen you in decades. Magic suits you."

Her smile brightened her entire face. "For the first time, I feel like myself. I was happy with Tim and the kids. I love them with all my heart, and you know I miss Tim. But there is no denying that this is where I was always meant to be."

"I'm glad to hear it. I'd better get back to practicing, or Tarja will be on me soon."

Fiona lifted one eyebrow. "Tarja?"

"My familiar. She's the tabby cat I think I told you about."

"Ah, that's right. Sebastian recently started having me practice my slice and burn spells with soda cans. Give that a try."

"I will. When you say slice and burn, what do you mean?" I asked.

"For me, it was easier to think of cutting an enemy's face or throat and pairing it with the Latin word."

I smacked my forehead. "Why didn't I think of that? I'll give it a try. Thank you so much. Let's talk soon."

"Definitely. Take care and don't hesitate to call anytime."

I nodded my head again, feeling like a bobblehead doll, and hung up the phone. Standing up, I stretched my lower back then headed for the pantry. I needed some targets.

"What are you looking for?"

I turned to see Mythia hovering in the entry. Ever since I

became lady of the manor, as she liked to say, she had claimed the kitchen as her domain, often fighting my mom for it.

"I need some of the cans in the recycling. Fiona had an idea of how to practice my magic."

"Oh," the pixie's glow brightened, and she buzzed faster. "I had Tsekani build doors to hide the containers. They're under here." She opened the doors at the center underneath the bottom shelf. I hadn't realized they weren't always there.

"Thank you," I told her and accepted the bin, then headed for the backdoor.

Layla strolled into the kitchen with sure, easy steps. I checked her every time I saw her. I needed to make sure she really was alright. The injury on her side healed within a day and a half. "Where you headed?"

"Target practice," Mythia blurted.

I sighed and glared at the tiny pixie. I didn't want an audience when I tried this. It was hard enough as it was. "It's nothing. Just something Fiona suggested. Go back to whatever it is you were doing."

"I wasn't doing anything," Layla replied as she followed me outside.

One thing being married to Miles had taught me was when not to fight a losing battle. "Just stay back. I have no idea what will happen here."

"I won't get in your way." Layla jumped up and sat on the lowest terrace wall while I set up several cans on the pebbled beach. It was the furthest I could think from the house, and there was an ocean close by should things go awry.

I stood a few feet away from the half dozen cans I aligned on the rocks. Wiping my hands on my jeans, I tried to slow my racing heart. Now was not the time to get nervous. This was practice, not life and death.

"*Frustum.*" I thought of slicing the can in half and held it before chanting the spell. When it hit, the can melted into a puddle on the beach. My shoulders slumped, and I shook it off so I could try again.

"*Surculus.*" I had intended to shoot a hole in the can, but it exploded in a hundred pieces making me shout and duck. Layla was laughing from her perch.

Glaring at her, I brushed my hand down my shirt and tried again. "*Mittite.*" The can rattled but didn't move.

"You need to find your calm center."

I swirled when I heard the seductive voice. My eyes went wide, and my heart plummeted when I saw Aidoneus standing there watching me. "Wh…what are you talking about?"

He closed the distance and approached me. I couldn't help but notice the way he moved like a predator. "Think of your power as the eye of a raging storm. In the center is where you want to be when you cast. If you do magic in the rings around that, there are a million things to send it off course."

That was surprisingly helpful advice. "I have no idea how to find the eye of the storm."

Aidoneus reached up and tapped my temple, then left his finger there. "Look for your power. You will feel everything settle when you take hold of it. Keeping that peace in mind and locking out the chaos keeps you there."

"Alright. I'll try." I closed my eyes and searched inside for the flame of my magic. It eluded me. There was nothing to grab onto. It was like a circle without edges. It unnerved me to feel his eyes on me.

Lives are counting on this. Get your shit together! I took a few deep breaths and kept trying. After several minutes I gave up and opened my eyes. "It's no use. I can't do it."

Aidoneus placed both hands on my shoulders. "Nonsense.

Latch onto the fire inside. Forget about everything outside that."

I wasn't sure this would work and was about to ask why he was there when I decided one more time couldn't hurt. "I'll try."

I closed my eyes and focused on the warmth of his hands. I had to cut off my mind before it traveled down far too distracting paths. My entire body felt like it was on fire. It had to be a hot flash. Just what I needed while being touched by the hottest guy in Camden.

Fire. I kept my senses tuned to my inner flame. It took several seconds before I saw it flickering in the middle of a dark cave. My magic was powerful. It should be brighter. As if I forced more energy into it, the fire grew and illuminated the entire cave. I grabbed hold of the flames and ignored everything else.

Opening my eyes, I focused on the can. *"Surculus."* The can popped into the air, and I assumed I had failed, but Layla jumped down laughing and hollering.

She caught the can mid-air and showed it to me with a wide grin on her face. "You did it!"

"That was a sight to see," Aidoneus relayed as he released me.

I turned to Layla and joined her in laughter when I saw the hole in the can. "I can't believe that worked."

"You're an outstanding teacher, you know that?"

He stood there with his hands in his pockets and a smile on his face. "I'm good at a lot of things. It's really all about the student."

My cheeks heated, and I wondered if he meant the double entendre or if I was misreading his comment. It was rather obvious. "Thank you for the help. Now, how can I help you?"

"I just wanted to take another look at the backyard, if you don't mind. I won't be long, and then I'll get out of your hair."

I gestured to the general area. "It's not a problem. Take all the time you need."

Aidoneus smiled then took off toward the house and yard where we held Hattie's funeral. Layla sidled up next to me and nudged my shoulder. "Bow chica wow wow. I think he wants to practice kissing next."

I shoved her shoulder. "Shut up. He does not. Help me clean this up. I don't have the time or desire for a relationship."

I ignored Layla's laughter as I wondered how true that was anymore. I liked Aidoneus, or what I knew of him. He was attractive and helpful, but I had no desire to explore anything further at the moment. I was still going through my magical makeover. It wasn't the right time. Didn't mean I couldn't enjoy flirting and looking.

CHAPTER 15

"How did practice go today, mom?"

I slid my glance to my daughter, then over to Layla, who sat at the island in the kitchen smirking. For a second, I thought she had told Nina about the sexy Aidoneus coming back and guiding me through the exercise. Tarja had been upset when she found out.

I was surprised she hadn't been out there to interject and assist me, but there was something about Aidoneus that cut off her ability to check in on me. The idea that she poked her furry little nose in my head at random times throughout the day bothered me.

I had no desire to have her lurking in the shadows of my mind. They couldn't be pleasant places to be, not to mention I didn't care for the invasion of privacy. It helped that she had assured me she never invaded when I was showering or anything like that. As if that was all there was for me to worry about.

It was apparent she could read my thoughts. I couldn't stop wondering if she had listened to the many fantasies I'd created about a certain Underworld detective. I needed to learn my magic and fast. I wanted to block Tarja from all thoughts but emergent ones.

I smiled at Nina and went back to rinsing the dishes. "Better than I expected. After several failed attempts, I was able to shoot a hole through a can with my magic."

"She had help," Layla tossed out, then walked away. I growled at her as she threw that grenade, leaving me to clean up the mess.

"Did Tarja finally give you helpful instructions? I swear when she's my familiar, she had better have improved her communication skills." The frustration I had over Layla's announcement disappeared when Nina talked about inheriting the magic.

I had been adjusting to the weight that threatened to drown me and the lives at stake if I didn't figure my magic out. The fact that I needed to reinforce the spells around the property was in the back of my mind like a ticking bomb, and I hadn't considered what this would mean for Nina's future.

My heart constricted. I didn't want this danger for my daughter. *Then it's your job to make things safer for her.* And I would. There wasn't another option.

"It wasn't me. It was that Underworld upstart."

Nina's eyebrows lifted, and she was smiling. "Oh ho, ho, mom. Sounds like you need to fill me in."

I waved my hand and returned to doing the dishes. Denial was more than a river in Egypt. "There's not much to tell. He returned to investigate the property again and saw me failing spectacularly, so he told me to identify my power as a flame inside and grab hold of it while I cast. Su…ahhh!"

I doubled over and clutched my stomach as I tried to suck in a breath. Nina was next to me in a flash. I felt her arm settle on my shoulders.

"What's wrong? Tarja, help her!" I wanted to reassure her

that everything would be okay, but nothing would come out. All I knew was a blinding pain in my gut.

"It will be alright, little one. There is no one attacking your mother directly. They are reaching her through another, and I haven't prepared her to combat it. Phoebe. Listen to me. Block the pain. It's not yours. Deep breaths. Yes, that's it."

It was difficult at first to follow what she was saying. When it registered that this wasn't my pain, I was able to push it back and take those much-needed deep breaths. My gaze landed on my familiar when I was able to lift my head.

"What's happening?" I was huddled on the floor with one arm wrapped around my stomach. The pain was better, but my insides still felt like they'd been shredded.

"Someone, likely Myrna, is using those you are closest to against you. Call your mother and grandmother."

My heart was stuck in my throat, making breathing impossible once again. Nina helped me up, and by the time I was reaching for my cell phone, my worry for my family had moved in, leaving room for nothing else in my mind.

My hands were shaking when I tried to turn the phone on and dial my mom's cell. Nina tried to help but ended up dropping the device because she was closer to a centrifuge machine with all her rattling.

One look in her eyes and my fear turned into outright terror. "I'm going to make sure they are alright." The promise gave me strength, and I managed to dial the number and put it on speaker.

"You've reached Mollie. I cannot come to the phone right now, so leave me a message at the beep, and I will get back to you. Have a great day!" My mother's voice turned the lump in my throat into a brick.

The beep made both of us jump. I took a deep breath that did nothing to calm me. "Mom. It's, uh, Phoebe. I just had an episode. I'm worried about you and Nana. Call me right away."

I dialed the house next and repeated the message when I received the machine. Nana didn't have a cell, so there were no other numbers to call. "I have to go over there."

Tarja stepped into my path when I headed for the niche where I kept my purse with my key fob in it. *"You cannot go. This could be a trap."*

"Which is exactly why I'm going. She will kill my mom and Nana if I don't show up. I can't let that happen." My voice cracked halfway through my response. "I've been practicing and will melt her into a puddle before I let her get a hold of me or harm them."

"You are the key to keeping the balance in the universe. If we lose you, all will be lost. You cannot run into danger."

Hearing that the fate of all mankind rested on my shoulders didn't change my mind in the least. These women had given me everything, and I owed them. "I'm going. You can tell Layla and Tsekani where I am headed. Nina, stay here and make sure no one gets through the wards. When I get back, we will be redoing the protections. I can't wait anymore. I don't care if I'm ready or not."

Tarja sighed in my head, and the sound was resigned. *"If you try to reinforce them when you aren't ready, it will cause them to fall entirely. Your attempt is far more likely to destroy what is already in place, leaving us completely exposed, which is why I haven't pushed you to do it yet. Keep your senses open, and don't approach the house where you will be seen."*

I gave Nina a hug, then raced through the house and out the front door and to the side where I still parked my Land Rover. Tossing my purse into the passenger seat, I hit the button and was racing down the driveway the second the engine roared to life.

My heart was racing even though it felt like an elephant sat on my chest, and I couldn't catch my breath. They had to be alright. It had only been two hours since they left my house. Surely, not enough time for her to get tired of waiting for me.

She wanted them alive to use against me. If she killed them, I would not hesitate to rip her head from her shoulders. It wasn't until that moment that I understood what Fiona meant when she said she did what she had to when she killed the Fae King and Queen.

I was so lost in thought I missed the hairs standing up on the back of my neck until loud pops like gunshots pierced the night, and the wheel in my grip swerved and wobbled.

On instinct, I slammed on the brake, and in a screech of rubber on asphalt, my Land Rover came to a stop. I was breathing heavily as I got out of the vehicle to check the damage.

It was when I was standing on the street that I finally felt menace surround me. I'd walked into a trap alright, but I wasn't anywhere near my childhood home. Ducking down, I crouched next to the flat rear tire. A quick check told me the front was also popped, as was the other side of the vehicle.

Had I run over a tack strip or something? I was still squatting so low I could see the street behind me. There was no metal strip of nails, but I did see a distinct shimmer in the air that told me it had been magic.

It was far easier to grab hold of the flame inside and hold it in my mind's fist. The first lobby of enchantments hit the car from all sides. It was only on my side that one managed to hit my shoulder while another impacted my car a few inches away.

Two cloaked people waltzed out of the trees. That was the only way I could describe it. They didn't rush as they moved toward me. Their steps were calm and their heads high.

What was with these witches and cloaks? Why hide? Maybe their magic twisted their faces into something monstrous.

Without waiting, I released the magic I had been building. I knew they wouldn't do much because I thought of a bomb at the last second. My mind was too chaotic to concentrate on my intent.

My shoulder burned right down to the bone, making it even harder to think straight. I was surprised when my spell threw them off balance. I didn't know if it would do anything. It gave me a couple seconds to pull up more power and cast a shield around me. It would be better than trying to attack them at the moment.

Snarls hitched my heart rate for the tenth time in as many seconds. My heart plummeted when the wolf and panther stopped beside the witches. I had hoped they were on my side.

I stood up and noticed three more approaching from the other side of the street. They spread out to come at me from five different directions, and each had an animal with them. I'd bet anything they were shifters.

"What do you want?"

A chorus of cackles rang out. One of them on the opposite side of the car is the one that actually responded. I couldn't tell which one thanks to their hoods, but her words were enough to tell me I was screwed. "We are here for your power, *human*."

She said that like I was filth. Taking advantage of the break I had been given, I grabbed my power and let it build. In the meantime, I thought about kicking the one closest to the passenger door in the lady balls.

"*Calcitrare in inguine.*" I looked right at her when I muttered the words to enact my intent. The woman in that position dropped, and the lion next to her roared loudly.

There was no time to think I had managed to injure one of them. Another spell hit me. This time in the leg. It made me fall onto my damaged car. When my hand went through the non-existent window, I knew they had blown them out already.

I thought of shooting the witches and started spewing, *"surculus."* I didn't have the wherewithal to aim, but I kept the intent of shooting each of them in my mind as I turned and spoke the words of power.

My stomach roiled when I caught sight of the bloody cuts on my thigh. Metal groaned, and the door frame next to my head bent inward. Not the place to be standing. I limped toward the front of the car and cast my spell. A whoop nearly left my mouth when my magical bullet hit the shifter on the side of his snout. Brain matter exploded out of the skull. The witch screamed, "No! Marge!" Her wolf hit the pavement and didn't move.

I felt the energy heading toward me before I took another step. It was enough time for me to duck. It was more of an ungraceful fall to the ground. My knees didn't bend as easily anymore. I usually didn't spend much time running or fighting for my life, so it usually didn't bother me as much.

I landed next to the driver's side door with my hands braced on the road. The enchantment hit the hood, making it fly off my SUV and into a spiral in the air. The power leaking from beneath me was electric. These witches were working up to something big.

"Tarja!" I didn't think before I called out to my familiar. Turns out it was enough for the volleys to stop. The sound of metal crashing into asphalt was followed by the ground shaking.

"I feel it. Keep your senses open. They are trying to contain you. I'm not certain how they will execute this when they haven't cast a circle."

MAGICAL MAKEOVER

I clenched my jaw and tried lobbing bombs next. The witches weren't attacking as quickly, and I was torn between wondering what they were planning and calling up the energy for a bomb. I sent the first attempt to the witch I was staring at. This would be so much easier if my joints were loose and limber, like when I was twenty-five.

She had to be older. Her back was hunched, and her knuckles seemed gnarled. The nurse in me winced when my bomb blew one of her legs off. Her hood fell back, revealing she was indeed much older. Her wrinkled face was twisted in agony, and her long grey hair was blowing in the wind.

I walled off my heart. I couldn't let this get to me right now. I had to stay alive and get to my family. "I will keep removing limbs if you don't let me go and get to my family."

"Your family will pay for what you did to Marge." The shifter got what she deserved for attacking me. "But you aren't going anywhere. Marge trained to take part in collecting your power even at death's door. You're our Donor whether you like it or not." The way she said Donor with a capital D, I knew it wasn't something pleasant. I'd ask about that later.

Right now, I was going to prove her wrong. I lobbed a bomb in her direction. I didn't know who was talking, so it hit the dirt on the side of the road, sending clumps into the air.

The animal snarls got louder, and I braced myself as I turned my back on that witch to check the others. I might be stupid to do so, but something told me she was in no shape to add her power to the spell they had been working on and attack simultaneously.

I wished Tarja saw what I managed. It was likely this was the end of the road for me, and I wanted to show her I learned something from her lessons. *"I know, child. Now concentrate on your shield. You let it slip."*

The air three feet from me shimmered right before a wall of black fire erupted, starting at the road and shooting at least five feet above my head. I couldn't see the witches anymore, and that made my mind go wild as I conjured a million different things they were going to do to me.

The flames burned before my hand made it within a foot of the inferno. I couldn't jump that high and make it over unscathed. Shit! They had me at their mercy. "Tarja. They've surrounded me with black fire."

"I can see it through your eyes. Give me a minute to try and hear what they are casting." Magic still freaked me the hell out, but it was nice to have her in my head right now.

My breaths came out in short, loud bursts while my heart tried to take flight and get the heck out of there. Unfortunately for it, my flesh and ribs were in the way.

It was likely safe for me to stand up straight, but instinct kept me hunched over on the ground like Golem from Lord of the Rings. The position made the blood from the cuts pool in the crease at my hip. My shoulder was on fire, and I lost the ability to feel the fingers on that hand.

A loud thump drew my eyes up, and I screamed when a pair of glowing yellow eyes glared down at me. Even more frightening were the sharp canines dripping drool on the top of my head.

I was on my feet and backing away. The heat stopped me before I got very far. There was nowhere for me to go except to the side. So, I skipped to the right and headed for the back end of the Land Rover.

The wolf followed along the roof, its nails scratching the surface in an ear-piercing screech that made my ears bleed. Or so I thought. When I touched my lobes, there was nothing there. It just felt like they were gushing blood.

When I stopped, so did the wolf. "Tarja, I need help now!"

"They have cast a death circle set in blood and fire. Without me

by your side, I cannot help you. If you were more practiced, you could pull me to your side, but I don't want to end up stuck in limbo. Layla and Tsekani are on their way. Hold tight they should be there any second." The presence of Tarja's voice in my head was reassuring, but her words were not.

"Shit! I need to get to my mom and Nana."

"You need to focus on yourself. There is a chance you will not survive this encounter. That means I will die. The balance will be upended, and Chaos will be given a doorway into our realm. Chaos leaves no survivors." I knew Tarja was right.

Guilt had to battle for the top position with fear for my family. I had no desire to die. And I certainly didn't want to be the cause of everything on Earth dying, but I couldn't ignore the danger to my mother and grandmother. They meant everything to me next to my kids.

The blood that had pooled in the crease of my thigh dripped off the hem onto the concrete. That was the dinner bell for the wolf, and it lunged at me. It took all of my nerves to stay still. If I moved any closer to the flames, my skin would melt into a puddle at my feet.

The wolf knocked into my shoulder as it sailed over me, making me stumble. I had to force myself to twist out of the way, so I landed on my injured shoulder. Black dots spotted my vision, and bile rose in my throat.

The wolf's jaws clamped onto my shoulder and embedded in my left breast and shoulder blade. My eyes were pointed to the sky, and I saw the green dragon soar overhead. "Tsekani," I whispered. The cavalry had come.

My heart skipped a worrying beat. Oh God, please tell me they weren't too late. The snarls returned, and screams joined them. Orange fire spewed from Tsekani's massive jaws.

A form wavered in the black flames, and my heart stopped altogether. *"Surculus."* Aidoneus ducked the second my spell left my lips with ease. He braced himself with his hands on the ground not far from me and swung his leg around—his massive black boot connected with the side of the wolf's head.

My scream was torn from me when the saber-like teeth shredded my flesh. The upside to blinding pain was Aidoneus kicked the animal into the black fire. He immediately removed his tight black shirt and pressed it over my shoulder. Wow, he was ripped.

His touch helped keep the worst of the pain at bay and allowed me to enjoy the view. "How did you get through that without being killed?"

"That spell can't touch the son of Hades. It's one of the upsides of being the Dark Lord's offspring," he said with a smile. He cupped my cheek then pressed his lips to mine in a brief kiss.

The pain vanished entirely for that blissful second. Unfortunately, it came rushing back when he stood up and turned to face the death circle. The devil's son just kissed me! I had the hots for Satan's child. Although it made sense. No normal man was that good-looking. I wanted to explore every inhuman inch of him. Wasn't that a sin or something?

What would Nana say when she found out? Nana! "We need to get out of here."

"I'm working on it." His ordinarily smooth voice was strained.

"Work faster. I think Myrna is killing them." Tears built in the back of my eyes.

He turned back to me, and his features softened. He nodded, then faced the flames once again. His hands were lifted by the sides of his head with their palms facing outward, and the muscles along his back mesmerized me as they rippled every time he moved. Blue light glowed dimly around his entire body, stopping my mind before it went all the way down the wrong street.

When his energy built, it brushed against mine in a gentle caress. It wasn't aggressive or biting like that of the Tainted witches. It was shocking after discovering he was Hades' offspring. Nothing about him spoke of evil or malevolence.

It made me wonder what his father was really like. Were the stories about the devil true? Questions for another time.

Right now, I was going to pass out, and I couldn't allow that. My vision wavered, and when the black flames died, the stench of burnt flesh reached me. There was nothing like it in the world. I worked in the burn unit from time to time and hated every second. Not necessarily because it smelled terrible, but because of the wailing and inability to help with the pain the patients suffered.

I saw Marge lying lifeless from my position on the ground, not far from where I took her leg and another one fighting off two wolves. I could see part of the other side of the road and two bodies pulled apart. A black panther was fighting the lion I saw standing with one of the Tainted. I'd bet that wasn't the corrupted panther I had seen earlier.

"Do you guys have this handled? I need to get Phoebe out of here." Aidoneus called up to Tsekani as he made another pass overhead.

Tsekani's massive reptilian snout nodded up and down. The next thing I knew, I found myself in Aidoneus's arms with my head cushioned on his bare chest. I wanted to tell him to put me down. I weighed more than I wanted.

"Hang in there, Queenie. I'll get you home and call a healer." I relaxed as much as the pain would allow. His voice soothed me, and he didn't seem to strain under my weight.

"No," I objected. "I need to get to my mom and Nana. They were hurt."

"You're injured, Phoebe. You need to get help, or you could die."

The tears fell from my eyes as I considered I might have already lost them. That didn't change my mind. I had to get to them. "I can't lose them. Please take me there."

He held my gaze for several seconds. The longer he looked at me, the closer the darkness closed in. I couldn't let it win, or he would just take me home. "Alright," he finally agreed. "What's their address?"

I told him where they lived and tried not to pass out when he settled me in his sports car. The leather seats and luxurious interior told me it was an expensive vehicle. I hated bleeding on his upholstery, but it wasn't like I could ask him to take my car. It had been ruined.

And you're distracting yourself, so you don't think about your mom and Nana. There was no comeback for the truth, but it did stop the random thoughts. A vice settled around my chest, and I watched the trees as we drove.

Please let us make it before I lose them. Whatever higher power saw fit to give me this magic had better not have taken what matters most to me in this world. Chaos might just have her chance at Earth after all.

CHAPTER 16

"Queenie, we're here. Are you sure I can't take you to a healer first? You're turning an unpleasant shade of grey."

I blinked heavy lids open and stared into Aidoneus's stunning sapphire eyes. "Grey's my color. I look fabulous. Where are we?" We weren't in front of my mother's house. I thought I recognized the tan-colored ranch style but couldn't be sure. What I did know this wasn't my mother's soft yellow Cape Cod two-story.

"We're a block or so away from their house. I didn't want to tip anyone off to our presence and make them act rashly." Aidoneus leaned over me to unbuckle my seat belt, and all of his glorious muscles pressed against my face.

He was hard as a rock, yet his skin as soft as velvet. And he was oddly hairless like the models in magazines. I wonder if he waxed like they did. Why was I even allowing myself to look? That wouldn't end well. He probably dated young, skinny, gorgeous models. Not middle-aged mothers with fifteen or forty extra pounds and more wrinkles than a pug.

My thoughts splintered a second later when I tried to

move away from him. I needed to get away from the masculine smell and perfect pectorals.

Agony stole my breath when my attempt jostled my shoulder, and I cried out. Aidoneus shook his head and let go of the buckle. All I could see was the side of his jaw twitching while he fussed with the shirt over my injury.

"I'm going to try and stop the bleeding. My talents aren't in the healing arts, so I won't be able to do much, but I might be able to help." He bit off each word as if he was pissed.

"I'll be fine. You don't owe me anything. In fact, I am already indebted to the Devil's son enough. I don't want to add to the bill."

Aidoneus jerked back and hit his head on the roof of his sports car. Not that he noticed. He sat there glaring at me. "I'm not the Devil's son. My father is Hades, and I never said you owe me anything."

He was offended. And had a right to every ounce of indignation. I had made numerous assumptions about him and his father without having one speck of accurate information. I sucked in a shaky breath and let it out. "I'm sorry. That was uncalled for, and I normally never make assumptions about people. I don't know why I did about you. I would appreciate anything you can do for me. Preferably before I throw up all over your nice Italian leather."

I took it as a good sign when his left eye stopped twitching. When he touched my shoulder again, it no longer felt the same. There was a biting edge to it. Before I could ask about him and his father, the feeling of hot pokers touching my chewed-up shoulder made speech impossible. I couldn't even scream.

"I know it hurts, but it's working. Just a few more seconds," he reassured me.

I nodded my head and fought back the tears. This was right up there with the pain of childbirth. Unlike childbirth, the pain ebbed, and then he lifted his hand. "Gah. That wasn't pleasant."

He averted his gaze and stepped out of the car. "It stopped bleeding. We should go in case it opens back up."

I swung my feet out of the door and used the top of the car to brace myself. Once outside, I got a better view and saw the garden gnomes in my mother's front yard. "We should sneak in through the back. They will see us coming through the front windows, but there's only a small window above the kitchen sink on the first floor."

He nodded and started walking without another word. I followed him silently until we reached Mrs. Harris's yard, then I grabbed his arm, stopping him. "We can sneak through her yard. There's a couple missing boards along their shared fence."

"Should we wait for your dragon? He will be here any second."

Tsekani came here? I scanned the sky but didn't see him anywhere. I was about to ask how he knew when I saw the green shape darting through the clouds. "He'll follow us. I'd rather not have a giant green dragon land in the middle of the street."

Aidoneus's lips twitched. "He could be our distraction."

"Until Mrs. Harris calls the police about a dragon. She'd be carted off to the nuthouse. Let's go."

It was wrong to be sneaking around the neighborhood. It made me feel like I was back in high school and trying to sneak back in after Trey's party. My heart raced, and I was sweating just like I had back then. If I was caught this time, I would suffer more than two weeks of being grounded.

As we entered our backyard, I realized no dogs were barking in the area. That wasn't normal. I bet they felt the danger as much as I did at the moment. Was it the dragon overhead or the evil witches in mom's house?

Tsekani shifted forms as he was descending and landed without a sound. I couldn't say the same for his family jewels. They bounced and slapped his inner thigh. "That was impressive."

My cheeks heated when Tsekani winked at me, and Aidoneus gave me glare number two of the night. "The shifting and landing, not the..." I gestured to his mid-section at a loss for words. I needed to shut my mouth. I was making it much worse.

"There are two witches inside," Aidoneus whispered in a bid to change the subject.

I went with it gratefully. "Are they in the kitchen?"

Both men shook their heads, but it was Aidoneus that spoke. "No. They're at the front of the house."

That was good. The layout wasn't an open floorplan like so many of the houses built nowadays. The formal dining room and two walls separated the living room from the kitchen.

My shoulder throbbed, and my back protested when I tried to bend and pick up the zombie gnome. Aidoneus put a hand on my shoulder. I hope he assumed my pain was all from my injuries and not because I was old. "I've got it." I nodded and rubbed my back with my uninjured arm.

"There's a house key inside."

Aidoneus's lips twitched. "I figured you had enchanted it to come alive and eat evil witches for dinner. But a key will work."

"Smartass," I muttered as he shook the spare key from the bottom and unlocked the backdoor.

I could hear voices but couldn't make out what was being said. Aidoneus entered in front of me, and I followed with far noisier steps. I didn't think Tsekani had come in yet and had to clap a hand over my mouth to stifle my yelp. He was right behind me and putting on mom's pink apron that said 'Hot Stuff Comin' Through.'

With a smile, I turned and followed Aidoneus into the formal dining room. He held up a hand, and I immediately ducked. His shoulders shook as he looked down at me. Tsekani was laughing at me, as well. They could laugh. I was new to this whole magic thing. I had no idea what I was doing. I shrugged and turned my attention to the living room. I had nothing to be embarrassed about.

Tears stung my eyes, and my heart was in my throat. Nana and mom were both tied to chairs from the table at our back, and there were two women in black cloaks yelling at them. Nana had a black eye, and my mom's nose was bleeding. Based on the little that was trickling out, I didn't think it was broken.

Seeing them like that, I forgot myself and surged to my feet. Aidoneus grabbed my shoulders and pulled me back towards the kitchen. His hand remained over my mouth. I wished he'd covered my ears. I could hear them threatening my family. I had to do something.

"You'd better hope your daughter gives us the power. Otherwise, you two won't survive the night." The witch had long red hair and grey eyes. Her skin was flawless, but when she moved, she blurred around the edges.

She was going to cast a spell. I couldn't take the chance she was going to kill them and wriggled my shoulders and broke free from his hold. My magic surged when I called, and I grabbed it with both metaphorical hands.

By the time I barreled into the living room, my hands were sparking with blue energy. I flung both fists toward the witch closest to Nana and tossed whatever magic had accumulated on my skin.

Two blue ovals of lightning careened towards the witch and impacted her stomach. I had caught her off guard. The second woman jumped behind the sofa, knocking over the chair my mother was tied to in the process.

My mom's scream stabbed my heart. "Tsekani, get them out of here!"

I saw his bare behind as he ran past me and picked my mother up, chair and all. "Are you naked?" I gaped at Nana's question. They had been beaten and held hostage by homicidal witches, and she was asking if Tsekani was naked? That's what mattered here?

I rushed to Nana but never made it. The first witch was on her knees and mumbling beneath her breath. The air around her body darkened as she spoke, and she pulled a double-sided knife from her robes and cut her palm. Aidoneus knocked me down, and the spell she released hit him in the chest.

I was underneath him and saw the hole in his sternum. His lungs spurted out blood as they inflated while his heart remained steady and blood leaked from a puncture in it. Bile surged into my throat like Old Faithful. They'd killed him. Hades was going to kill them and then me. If there was anything left when I was done.

"You have no idea who you just killed." My warning left numb lips, and my body refused to move. My family was still in danger, but I found I couldn't move. I had seen countless people die but had never seen anyone killed. And had never had someone be murdered while trying to defend me.

Thankfully, Tsekani had his wits about him and grabbed Nana. She had been aiming at me alone. No one else should be hurt because they wanted me. There was a vice around my heart, and tears blurred my eyes. It took most of my energy to force myself not to think about Aidoneus lying there.

I had a witch to defeat. And since casting wasn't like shooting a gun, I had a couple seconds to get the bitch that had killed Aidoneus. I called up my shield to minimize damage, then cried out, "*surculus*," and aimed for the coward behind the sofa.

I didn't wait to hear if she cried out while I refocused on the first one. I imagined her being held in invisible binds. I wanted them to be tight with no give whatsoever. After pressing a kiss to Aidoneus's cheek, I got to my feet.

"*Vincio*," I shouted when I met her stare.

Her grey eyes went wide, and her body jerked. Blood leaked from the hole in her stomach, but she couldn't move. Tarja would be proud I managed to execute this spell flawlessly. One of her fingers twitched, and she opened her mouth. Okay, maybe it wasn't perfect.

"I've got the other one," Tsekani announced. "She's a bit crispy. Not sure what you did to her."

"You have to bind her magic, as well, Phoebe. She can cast even though she is immobile." I could kiss Tarja for the help right then.

"Come and untie us, Tsekani. I want to give those women a piece of my mind," Nana demanded.

"Mom, there isn't much we can do to them. They have magic. That's how they were able to use us as bait for Phoebe in the first place."

I wanted to confirm what my mom said but didn't have time. I needed to keep this bitch quiet. My brain was playing a game of pinball, and I couldn't formulate a single thought longer than two seconds, so I grabbed one of Nana's doilies and stuffed it in her mouth.

When I turned around, Tsekani was coming back into the room with my mom and Nana, and the second witch was pushing herself off the floor. The dragon had been right. The side of her face was bloody and charred.

"Tarja. How are you talking to me right now?"

"I'm your familiar. We are always connected. I can't lend you

magic or help you fight at the moment, but I can give you guidance. Find out who is behind this."

Tsekani grabbed the witch by the back of the neck, but before I could open my mouth, she was foaming at the mouth, and her body started seizing. "Shit!" I dove for the first witch and grabbed the doily, yanking it out.

"You're too late," she said with a hoarse voice.

I looked down at the lace in my hand and smiled. "I don't think so." I held the tiny capsule up and released my hold on her chin. "Who put you up to this?"

I didn't like the smug gleam in her eyes. "Su..." Several things happened at once. The witch's words were cut off as blood dribbled from the side of her mouth, and the room was filled with so much energy, I thought my heart was going to stop.

"She...was...gonna cast." That couldn't be.

I swiveled and dropped to my knees next to Aidoneus. His chest was still a mess, but his heart was beating again. "Oh my God. I thought they killed you."

"I'm not that easy to take out," Aidoneus replied. The strain in his voice was evident, but he sounded stronger than a second ago.

"Is she dead?" The terror I had experienced when I thought Aidoneus was dead was gone. I wasn't upset over the fate of either of these witches. They came here intending to murder innocent people. They got what was coming to them. Fiona was right. It wasn't that difficult when it came down to it.

"She is. I didn't bother trying to subdue her. She never would have stopped trying to kill you, and you took her easy way out." There wasn't an ounce of remorse in Aidoneus's explanation. I waited for my revulsion, and it never came. I was just as attracted to him as before. And, I didn't attribute

MAGICAL MAKEOVER

it to being the son of Hades. Nor did I think of him as a heartless killer.

I inclined my head at him then assessed his situation. "Mom, grab some towels and any gauze we have. Tsekani, get rid of the bodies. We can't leave them here to be found by police. Nana, pack a bag. You guys are coming with me."

"Do you need some antiseptic, as well?" I looked up at my mom when I heard the waver in her voice. Her hands were trembling, and she had her worried face on. It was the look she had when I broke my right wrist on Easter when I was six and when the doctors told her I would need my appendix out the summer before I started high school.

"No. I'm immune to most pathogens," Aidoneus told her in a weak voice.

"It's going to be alright, mom. I'm sorry you were dragged into this mess. I never intended for any of you to be involved."

Her features hardened, and she shook her head from side to side. "Nonsense. This isn't your fault."

"I bet it's that. What did you call her, Tarja? Tainted? I bet it was her," Nana interjected. "C'mon, Mollie. Get her towels."

The two walked off, and I refocused on Aidoneus. "You need to go to a healer. Where can we find one?"

"I'll be good as new in no time."

My jaw hit my chest. "Are you kidding? You have a hole in your chest. I can see one of your lungs and part of your heart. You won't survive unless it's closed and any punctures inside your chest are closed. You will bleed out. This is so much worse than what I have from the earlier fight, and you practically insisted on taking me to one."

He reached out and clasped my hand. "I'm not human, and I heal fast."

Tsekani bent in front of me to pick up the dead witch, and I got an eyeful of his family jewels. "He's right. By the time I return from disposing of these guys, his chest will be closed."

I put a hand up, blocking some of my view. "Find some pants when you come back.

My mom laughed when she handed me the towels. "Don't tell him that. Some of us don't mind, sweetie."

The adrenaline of the incident finally faded, and my pain came rushing back all at once, and I sucked in a breath when I accepted the pile. They fell from my limp hand. The makeshift binding Aidoneus had secured around my shoulder had come off at some point, and the claw marks had torn open. It seemed like I healed faster as well. The injuries hadn't been healed entirely, but they had begun to seal along the edges.

Nana returned to the room and handed my mom the gauze. "If he's going to live, wrap Phoebe's shoulder. Tell me Layla didn't go feral with the full moon and chew on you."

My mom was gentle as she wound them around my injuries. I had to push my pain aside. Aidoneus might heal fast, but he was still bleeding. With my uninjured hand, I pressed a towel over his wound gently at first, then with more pressure.

"It wasn't Layla. There was a group of five witches that ambushed me along the road. They had shifters with them. They were feral beasts, and one of them attacked me. Aidoneus saved my life."

"You shouldn't have come," My mother told me as she tended my shoulder.

I glared at her. "How could I not? They were going to kill you guys. There was no way I was going to allow that to happen."

My mom finished wrapping the gauze and tucked one corner under a layer, then cupped my cheek. "You are part of something so much bigger now. It's not just us at stake. You cannot let evil get ahold of your powers. Besides, your charm saved us from the spells they tried to cast on us." They worked?

"She's right, Queenie. You have to consider more than just yourself."

I turned a scathing look on Aidoneus. "I will always protect myself, but I will never allow those I love to be killed. They are just as important as I am. If they die because of me, I might as well have died, too. They've earned the right to be put above everything else. Without them, I wouldn't have been worthy of receiving the magic in the first place. Mom, go pack a bag. We're leaving."

The look Aidoneus gave me made my chest constrict and my palms sweat. I didn't know exactly what it meant. We had just been through something traumatic, so I didn't think he was actually falling for me.

Besides, it was the last thing I needed at the moment. I had more than enough on my plate with the magic and being hunted. And finding Myrna. I needed to eliminate that bitch. She could not get ahold of my power. She wouldn't do anything good with it.

CHAPTER 17

"You should have seen how mad they got when they couldn't even bind us to a chair with magic. I thought the redhead was going to explode from the force of her anger." Nana chuckled as she sipped her tea.

Nina's eyes weren't gleeful or excited. They were filled with tears as she listened to my mom and Nana tell her about their ordeal. They were on the couch, and I was on a loveseat nearby with Aidoneus.

We'd been home all of ten minutes, and a dozen pixies had descended on the house along with Clio from the coven. She was the group's healer, and she had applied an ointment to the wounds on my shoulder. I wanted to go to the hospital and get stitched up, but they said it was too risky.

The pixies were checking on Aidoneus and doting on him. I didn't blame them. He was rather good-looking. Even the men were mesmerized and could hardly take their eyes off of him. It was comical the way thirteen tiny fairies flew around him, checking his wound every few seconds while dripping something onto the gauze covering his injury.

"Did they try to break the enchantment?"

I turned to my familiar. "Is that possible? I thought those were impenetrable."

"Nothing in magic is impenetrable. However, personal charms like the ones you created for them require someone of immense power to crack. Most wouldn't bother trying. It would leave them drained and vulnerable to attack."

That made me feel better. And the stress of the night was finally fading now that I had my family in my house under my protection. "I need to reinforce the protections around the property. Now. I have a feeling Myrna will try to crack Hattie's remaining wards."

Layla sat forward in the lounge chair. "If that happens, there are enough of us to slow her progress which will give you time to set some traps of your own."

"You aren't ready to cast that big of a spell yet. Besides, it's not just about an enchantment. There are potions involved, as well."

"That explains the dizziness draught coating the mushrooms," Aidoneus interjected.

Blood dotted the white of the cotton around the wound on his chest. The hole had nearly closed when Tsekani returned to follow us home, but it hadn't been sealed. A half an hour later, it still wasn't. The only reason I hadn't drug him to the nearest hospital was that he was breathing well, and his pulse was steady.

"What about wild animals? Won't that affect them?" Why would Hattie spread something that could cause innocent animals problems? I didn't worry about humans trying to sneak through the forest to reach the house. They would come down the road.

"Animals can smell the potion and know to avoid the area. Shifters and Fae can smell them, as well. And there is more than just the dizziness draught. They are secondary precautions in the event the wards go down."

I nodded my head. It made sense when I stopped thinking about it from a human perspective. This world didn't operate under the same principles. It was vastly different.

"What about the Druid runes? Does she reinforce those?"

I lifted one eyebrow. What was Aidoneus talking about? I was vaguely familiar with the Druids from folklore. They were Celtic and served kings and were said to have the gift of prophecy and other mystical abilities.

Tarja's tail twitched. *"Those are Blood runes, and the Druid priests reinforce them. Not Phoebe. It's an additional layer of wards provided to the Plaedian seven and nothing you need to concern yourself with."*

Aidoneus stared at my familiar for a couple tense seconds before he inclined his head. "Even the son of Hades would have a hard time breaking a Druidic Blood rune. That explains why Myrna attacked close to the water. The tide likely wears those runes faster than in other sections."

Knowing multiple layers were protecting my home and family was a huge relief. And confusing. I didn't understand how any of this worked. It seemed like I would be fine if Hattie's wards failed and told the group as much.

"Every potion, spell, and rune around this property is tied to the owner and her ward."

Layla was speaking before Tarja got the last word out. "Think of it as a set of dominos. Once one falls, it will trip the next until they are all down."

"I don't know if I can do it." The enormity of it hadn't gotten any better just because I managed to enchant necklaces for my family. How was I ever going to be ready for something like that? My spell had to hold up at least three additional layers.

"Since when are you afraid of a challenge? That's not the attitude of the woman who refused to let her ex-husband ruin her life and keep her from nursing," Nana told me.

My mom nodded in agreement. "Or the young woman that worked hours on end to ensure she kept up the grade point average needed on tests to remain in the nursing program. None of what you have decided to do was easy, yet you set your mind to it and did it anyway."

"You're in the middle of your magical makeover, mom. You can't stop now."

I sat back against the cushion and immediately regretted it. My shoulder screamed at me. "I'm not quitting. I needed a moment to vent. Is there a pain-reducing spell I can cast on myself?"

"Casting enchantments on yourself is tricky. You can glamour your appearance or hide your body altogether, but reducing your pain doesn't always work."

I considered Tarja's comment and why that might be. The key to magic was all about intent. She'd practically beaten that into my head. If someone didn't understand how the body worked, it would be difficult to direct their purpose, so it was effective.

"I'm going to try something. If I screw it up, can you reverse what I cast?" I asked Tarja.

I swear the corners of Tarja's lips lifted, and a smile spread over her face. *"I am here to ensure you don't harm yourself. I see what you are considering and think your perspective might have merit. No one has ever looked at the issue from that point of view. Let's see what happens."*

"What are you thinking?" Aidoneus asked before I could focus my intent.

"I'm going to block the pain receptors in my brain. I could try cutting off the nerves, but I think this is the better approach."

Tsekani looked up from his position on the floor next to where Nina was sitting on the couch. "Why do you want to?

You're home now and safe. We will protect you while you heal."

"I need to practice casting and learn all about potions. I can hardly move without wanting to throw up. There is no time to sit on my laurels."

Nina snorted. "As if you rested at all. Ever. I'm pretty sure you were issuing orders from the bed after you had me. If Aunty Fiona is to be believed."

"Phoebe is right. There is no time to waste. Myrna isn't taking time to recover."

"How is she running around causing so many problems? She was burned, wasn't she?" Witches must really have accelerated healing if she was up and planning elaborate ambushes.

A pleased smirk spread over Tsekani's handsome face. "She had a shield in place, but she was definitely injured. My dragon fire burned the clothes off her back. Her magical enchantment is the only reason she didn't become a twisted charcoal totem."

Layla tossed a licorice nib at Tsekani. "Dragon fire burns hotter than any other kind of flame, and once it starts, it takes significant magical energy to put it out."

Aidoneus lifted away from the back of the loveseat. I pulled a soccer mom arm, my limb immediately shooting out to protect him. It was the move moms did when driving a car, and their arm goes out to keep the passenger from being injured. I had no idea that a shout left me while I wondered what exactly I was trying to protect him from.

We were sitting on the couch, not driving in a car. And there was no danger nearby. He gave me a bemused look and gently pressed my hands until my arms lowered. "I'm fine. Just testing the discomfort. And for the record, hellfire burns the hottest, and no spell can put it out. Only a Lord of the Underworld can stop the flames once they start."

MAGICAL MAKEOVER

"Woah," Layla blurted at the same time Tarja spoke. *"We rarely see hellfire on Earth because only a Lord can wield it. It isn't something you need to worry about right now. Myrna cannot use it against you."*

"That is correct. Witches use Blood magic and Dark magic and believe they are accessing the Underworld's power when in fact, they are simply accessing the corrupted power Lucifer created when he was sent to rule over hell. They are different dimensions, and few are aware of that fact."

I tilted my head, allowing that information to distract from the pain that was still at a level ten. "Holy cow. That brings up a billion questions, but only one matters at the moment. Is the Dark power they wield as dangerous and difficult to combat like that of the Underworld?"

Aidoneus placed a heavy, warm palm on my shoulder. It alleviated the worst of the hot knives poking my shoulder even though our skin didn't make contact. "No. It's not. You are powerful enough that you will eventually be able to deal with Dark and Blood magic. It will always take effort, but it won't be impossible for you."

Something in the way he worded that comment struck me. "You say that like it normally isn't possible for witches."

He removed his touch, and the pain was back in full force. "That's because a witch doesn't usually have as much power as you. And it feels different. Yours registers as more than the elements to my senses."

The elements made sense. Tarja had explained that witchcraft was elemental-based magic, and we called on all of the forces to aid in our enchantments. It was why the funeral needed to be held outside with her body placed on the dirt and grass. He shouldn't feel anything else from me.

"What else is there?"

"Space. Your Pleiadian lineage comes from the stars. It's why the

Druids help protect you." Tarja had a habit of giving me bits and pieces of information when she felt it was prudent. While I appreciated learning more about my origins, I wished she'd keep non-essential details from me. At least until I had mastered my magic enough to cast the wards around the property.

My head could only hold so much and be able to sort through it when the need arises. All of this was new to me and more than a little confusing, which meant that recall wasn't swift. It was more like wading through a pool of egg drop soup. Big clouds often obstructed the view of what was needed.

Layla popped some licorice into her mouth. "That and the fact that it has been their number one mission since the gods created their race. Some say *'normal'* witches were created by the original seven Pleiades." She used air quotes when she said normal.

"They did," Aidoneus threw out there as he bowed his head to the pixies. They must have read more into the gesture than I did because they stopped treating him and flew out of the room. Only Mythia remained behind. "The Titans, Atlas, and Pleione had seven daughters, the Pleiades, whom they dedicated to Artemis. When the Olympians removed the Titans from power, the seven became mortals that contained the power of demigods. Once human, they couldn't wield it with any amount of effectiveness. That lack of control threatened to implode the universe."

"Why the hell would they do that? Seems irresponsible of them. And you guys think I can figure this out without any problems?" There was no way I would be able to get this right. I was a middle-aged divorcee and mother of two. Not a magical witch with untold knowledge of what to do.

Aidoneus threw his head back and laughed. "The gods are arrogant and irresponsible. But what it comes down to is

MAGICAL MAKEOVER

they didn't think their plan through. Many suffered as a result of their rash behavior. Although, I've been told my grandfather was an asshole, so it was likely for the best."

"Hecate stepped in and siphoned power from the original Pleiades and gave it to women she deemed worthy. It was the only way to save the planet. The Druids were created as another safety measure."

I held up my hand. "History lesson over. I'm going to see if I can numb the pain so I can start on potions."

I closed my eyes and took a few deep breaths. It helped to visually block out the rest of the world. I thought about my Anatomy and Physiology classes and recalled the brain sections that dealt with pain.

It was the parietal lobe—the middle part of the brain. I took a second to figure out how to block it. Creating a bubble around the mid-brain seemed like the best approach. I pulled up an image of the brain from the book, followed by an iridescent envelope around that.

I needed to make sure the signals from the nerves never made it through the pretty shield. If they somehow got through, it would do me no good. I lined that balloon with carbon for extra strength.

"Intersaepio." The second the word left my mouth, my pain vanished.

I opened my eyes and smiled. "It worked!"

"I knew you could do it!" my mom praised.

I lifted my arm over my head, and the skin under the bandage pulled tautly. I laughed when there was no pain. I got to my feet and clapped my hands together. "Alright. Let's get to the potions. Do we do this in the ritual room downstairs?"

"Yes. The space has been cleansed and consecrated to avoid contamination. There are plenty of herbs to get started with. Why

don't you create a potion to deal with swelling? That will help your Nana's eye."

Nana pushed herself to her feet and shuffled toward the doorway. "Sounds like a good plan to me. I'm tired of looking left because I think there is something there."

To my surprise, everyone followed me and Nana downstairs. Much to Nana's delight, Tsekani helped her descend the steep steps while Layla stuck close to my mom. I didn't see Aidoneus. That stung.

Not that I blamed him for leaving or anything. I wasn't sure I would want to stick around the Underworld while he learned how to do his job. Come to think of it. That was for the best. I had no desire for him to witness my utter failure.

"Alright, where do I start?"

"Grab the cauldron and set it on the stand on the table."

I crossed to the bookshelf, picked up the big iron pot, and then dropped it with a yelp. My spell slipped, sending the pain bouncing back through my grey matter. It stole my breath and had Old Faithful gushing again. I really hated the bitter taste of bile.

Strong arms wrapped around me and pulled me against a firm chest. The pecs were too wide to be Tsekani. And the smell was deeper, richer. Aidoneus. I turned my head and came face to face with the handsome devil.

"I'm...okay."

"No, you're not. What happened?" His warmth and touch did nothing to ease discomfort this time. Apparently, he wasn't a magical pain reducer.

"Lost my spell." I tried to straighten my spine but didn't quite get vertical. I did manage to put space between me and the hot demigod. "But it hurts worse." I shifted my gaze to my familiar.

"It's the backlash of losing your grip on your spell. Think of it like a rubber band. It had been stretched tight, and you let go of one

MAGICAL MAKEOVER

side, so not only did all of your pain return, but the enchantment also snapped you."

I brought my hands to my forehead and clutched it tight. Just when I thought I might be getting the hang of magic, it bites me in the ass. Ignoring the pain, I pushed Aidoneus away from me and stumbled up the stairs.

Mythia was hovering at the top of the stairs. "Are you okay, Phoebe? How can I help?"

"Get me a shot of vodka. That might do the trick," I said through gritted teeth and continued outside. I couldn't be in the house for another second.

The breeze was cold and the sun low in the sky when I made it to the deck. It wasn't easy climbing down the steps. I nearly fell twice before I made it to the pebbled beach and sat heavily on my ass.

"Why am I so bad at this? Countless lives are depending on me, and I keep messing it up. I've never failed more in my life."

"I didn't take you for a whiner." I jumped slightly when Aidoneus's deep voice responded. I had been speaking to my familiar who had taken a seat at my side.

I turned a glare on him. "What did you say?"

One corner of his lips lifted in a smirk, and a furrow appeared between his eyebrows. "I said you don't seem like one to complain about not doing everything right."

"That's not what I'm doing. You wouldn't understand. A couple weeks ago, I was a regular human. There was nothing special about me. I had no magic." The cool air helped with Old Faithful in the back of my throat and the hot flash that had to hit me at the worst possible moment.

"I beg to differ. You are nothing short of extraordinary, and you know it, so own it."

I opened my mouth to respond and closed it. What did I say to that? How do I own something I wasn't sure I believed? "If we were talking about being charge nurse, I would agree. Nothing in life has prepared me for this magical world, and I feel like I'm failing at every turn."

"Has Myrna managed to steal your power?"

I turned and looked into Tarja's green eyes. "No, she hasn't. But I haven't cast the wards. I couldn't even hold a pain spell long enough to pick up a cauldron."

"Do you know how many witches have ever cast a spell that blocked even a fraction of their discomfort?"

I had a feeling I knew what she was going to say, but it seemed like wishful thinking on my part. "I don't have a clue."

"No one has ever done anything of the sort. Many have attempted and not even produced the flicker of a shield. Let alone one that wrapped around their parietal lobe and allowed them to climb down a set of stairs while fighting off the virus that creates a lycanthrope."

"Most humans succumb within an hour and change for the first time," Layla called out as she and the rest of them joined me on the beach. Tsekani was helping Nana, and my mom was next to Nina.

So much for some alone time. "Shifters are created by a virus?"

"Some," Layla replied as she plopped down on the ground next to me. "Others are born with the ability. Those that are Born have an easier time shifting while the Turned struggle for control and run the risk of going feral."

"You're an A student at this like you have been everything else in life. You need to give her feedback more often, Tarja. It'll let her know where she stands and what she needs to work on. No one can go about blindly. They need guidance. Isn't that what you're here for?" Mythia set a chair down for Nana. I doubted I would ever get used to seeing the tiny pixie carry something that was over a hundred times bigger than her. Nana glared at my familiar after she sat down to punctuate her tirade.

"Noted, Amelia. I often forget she didn't grow up with knowledge of our world and how things work. She's a quick study and only needs to be told things once."

I absorbed what everyone was saying. I wasn't failing at everything. I still had my magic, and the wards around the property were still standing. I lifted my chin and smiled at Nana.

I felt like a new person entirely. My previous life seemed like a million years ago. And if it wasn't for Nina, I would have almost believed it was someone else's life. Miles was a happily forgotten piece of my past. I was a Pleiades witch now. Myrna had better watch out. I was going to kick her magical ass.

CHAPTER 18

"Are you ready to resume with the potions lessons now that you have had your moment and have been fed?"

I wiped my mouth and stood up from the stool. Walking out to the beach then taking a break to eat some clam chowder had been the best decision. My arm was far from healed, but I felt stronger. I was usually so good about balancing myself. I rarely pushed too far. This magic stuff had me in knots, and I had forced my body and mind to go further than was wise.

When I was certain I wouldn't fall on my ass, I picked up my bowl and rinsed it in the sink. Aidoneus and Nina were both on their feet, as well. My mom and Nana remained in their seats, sipping tea.

"You guys are coming down with me?" I wasn't sure I wanted an audience for this. On the other hand, I could use the help with the heavy lifting.

"Yep. I wouldn't miss this for the world. Besides, I will be getting the cauldron down for you. You are in no shape to try that again." Trust Nina to point out the obvious. She was lucky I love her.

Aidoneus didn't say a word. Just turned and headed downstairs. Okay. "Are you sure it's wise to stick around? Seems like I'm bad for your health."

Aidoneus grunted in front of Nina and me. "It's far more exciting than the Underworld. Plus, I still haven't talked to you about your coven. I was coming to ask who might have opened the veil."

"What?" I blurted and stumble-fell into his back. Both hands had come up to brace me. My shoulder was never going to heal at this rate. Crickey, this was absurd. I wasn't an athletic person with natural grace. I was fit but awkward. My mom used to say I would trip walking barefoot as a kid. That hadn't changed in forty-three years.

He steadied me then crossed to the bookshelf. "I said I need to ask you about your coven. One of them cast the spell that tore the veil. It wasn't the Tainted witch."

Tarja wound around my legs as she joined us. *"I suspected that might be the case. That would be the only reason you needed to investigate on Nimaha."*

I watched the demigod take the cauldron down as I absorbed that little bit of information. "I don't know any of them. I met them for the first time at Hattie's funeral, and we didn't spend much time together. I can't even recall most of their names, let alone tell you who might have done such a horrendous thing. Was there someone that wanted Hattie's power, Tarja?"

"Lilith was upset about Hattie choosing a human, but she has always shied away from wanting positions with more power. Lexie, on the other hand, openly asked to be Hattie's heir. And Bridget is pissed about you being the new leader of the coven when you have no experience."

I held up my hands. "Wait a minute. I'm the leader of

those twelve witches? As in, I give them orders and make sure they stay within the lines of appropriate behavior?"

"Precisely. My guess is whoever did this believed you are too ignorant to detect such a Dark spell right under your nose."

"Do they want to kill her? Or use a demon for some other nefarious purpose?" Aidoneus stood leaning against the wall without a shirt. The gauze left most of his upper chest on distracting display. It wasn't fair that he was able to sidetrack me with such ease.

Thankfully, Tarja wasn't caught up in his muscles. *"I would say they want Phoebe out of the picture, but the fact that she hasn't been attacked by a demon yet, tells me I'm wrong. I can't believe there was such a snake living amongst us. Hattie would be so angry she missed the signs."*

Hattie might have been sick with a body that no longer cooperated with her, but she was intelligent and quick-witted. Nothing got past her, and she let you know it. Her sharp tongue was one of the things I loved about her. "I wonder if she suspected something. I wish I could talk to her again. She always told me to never trust anyone further than I could toss them. I assumed she was referring to my ex-husband. Now, I'm not so sure."

"I never saw anything aside from her wariness of men and their false promises and greedy hearts. I wish I had looked further now, as well. Decades ago, she and I agreed that I would not invade her privacy, and she got good at keeping up her shields, even when she was in pain. There's no going back, and she wouldn't appreciate having her afterlife disturbed to answer questions she likely can't answer. Let's get to work. Get the alyssum, bergamot, and heather."

Nina grabbed the jars as Tarja said what was needed. I picked up the mortar and pestle and joined them at the table. "Okay. Now what? Do I just dump some in here and grind it up?"

MAGICAL MAKEOVER

"Measurements have to be precise in potions. Grab the Silva Grimoire. It has instructions."

The tome was the biggest book I'd ever seen with a leather-bound cover engraved with a wolf and runes on the surface. My fingers tingled when I picked it up. The feeling was heady. The energy connected with part of me, telling me it belonged to me while at the same time it bristled.

I withdrew my hand and rubbed the skin, trying to dispel the prickling sensation. "This isn't mine."

"What do you mean? Hattie gave you everything. Of course, it's yours." As a mother, I hated hearing the hint of fear in Nina's voice. I knew she was excited about becoming magical. It changed the game for us and gave us a new and exciting purpose. One none of us had ever dreamed was possible, and she was terrified of having it taken away.

"I mean, this is the Silva family grimoire. It's not the Dieudonné family's, yet. We need to make it ours, too."

Acting on an instinct I didn't understand, I retrieved what Tarja called an athame. It was a ceremonial knife used by witches. I wanted the magical tome to bond to my familial line as well, and I held that intent in the front of my mind—the desire to combine my blood with Hattie's family.

I sliced my thumb and held it over the open pages of the grimoire. *"Unum vinculum."* Bright white light exploded from the pages, momentarily blinding me before I was engulfed by purple sparks of magic. My skin pulled taut over my skeleton, and my heart swelled like it was ready to burst.

My chest heaved as I tried to catch my breath. The light disappeared along with the magic. Nina had her hand on my shoulder and was looking at me with wide eyes. "What was that? I thought I was going to die."

"Oh my God." I ran my hands down her arms.

She pushed them away. "Stop, mom. I'm fine. I feel great."

Aidoneus was leaning over the table, watching us intently. "What made you do that?"

I smiled. The sense of completion making me giddy. I was a freaking witch now! "A girl can't give her secrets away. We've got to keep the mystery alive. Alright, let's make a protection potion."

Aidoneus lifted one eyebrow and shook his head from side to side. "Fair enough. I need to contact another agent that was looking into something for me. I'll be in touch."

I was both relieved and disappointed the sexy demigod was leaving. "Thank you for your help. I'm not sure I would have survived that ambush if you hadn't."

He rounded the table and stepped close enough to me that all I smelled was masculine heat. "I'm glad I came when I did. It was enlightening...and painful."

"You must be a masochist if you're saying that like it was a positive part of the experience."

He laughed at me. "I never said that was a good thing or what kept me around." With that, he turned and headed up the stairs.

Rubbing my hands together, I glanced at the book and noticed it was closed, and the wolf on the front had been replaced with a dragonfly. I touched the lucky charm around my neck. My chest clenched; I hadn't wanted to replace Hattie's family.

When I turned the page, I saw the title was hyphenated with both family names. The vice loosened, and the ache eased. This was how it should be. Nina reached out and touched the page hesitantly. "This belongs to us now, too. So cool."

I nodded in agreement and flipped through the pages. "The coolest. This looks pretty straightforward. Where are the measuring spoons?" I asked while scanning the shelves. I found them next to a pair of tongs and wooden spoons.

MAGICAL MAKEOVER

The first thing I needed to do was start a fire under the cauldron. The stand it hung from had an iron platform on the bottom. According to the grimoire, I needed to conjure my witch fire and place it on the burner.

"*Ignis*," I murmured with my gaze focused on the platform. Purple flames sprang to life on the black iron. The color startled me, and the fire flickered but didn't go out. I had conjured flames before, but they never looked like this.

"You have claimed your magic fully, which means your power is fully manifested. This represents who you are," Tarja replied in response to my unspoken question.

"So, my magical makeover is complete? Do I look any different?"

"You have accepted your full power, and as soon as you cast your protections, it will be much more difficult for anyone to steal your power. That alone will deter many who want to steal the Pleiades line."

"They should be afraid. My mom's a badass. And, you look better than you have in years," Nina added.

I chuckled and measured out the ingredients, then poured them into the cauldron. Next, it called for fresh dragon's blood and a dash of pixie dust. Before I could ask where I could find it, Tsekani trudged down the stairs with Mythia flying at his side.

"You rang?" The dragon shifter called out.

"Phoebe is preparing the potion so she can cast the protections around the property, and she needs your blood, Tsekani, and your dust, Mythia."

"Thank you. I was going to ask but wasn't sure it would be appropriate." I would never take my friends for granted and assume they would help me.

Tsekani laughed. "There are plenty of pixies on the property but only one dragon, so you'd have been looking for a while."

"I don't even want to think about how hard it had to have been for witches back in the day when they had to find a dragon and pixie to help them with the ingredients," I said with a shake of my head.

A dark cloud drifted up from the cauldron in an acrid, bitter wave. It burned my eyes and started all of us coughing. My purple flames were now licking the bottom of the iron, fueling the smoke.

I waved my hand and searched for a window to open. There was a small rectangle at the top of two of the walls. It was hard to find my way over with watery eyes. Mythia beat me to it and slid one window open while Nina got the other.

"What happened? Where did I go wrong?"

"Did you read all of the directions?" Tarja's question made me realize I had looked at the first step but not beyond that.

I shook my head from side to side, suddenly feeling like an idiot. It was always good to get the big picture before focusing on the individual steps. Often future actions would impact how you handled what you were currently doing.

I snuffed my fire. "I see the mistake in not doing that now. Nina, can you wash the cauldron?"

I looked ahead and noted that the blood and dust had to be added within seconds or the herbs would burn. Once the ingredients were all added, I needed to stir it counterclockwise until it started boiling. After that, I needed to reverse directions for three minutes and add three pieces of moon-charged black tourmaline. The number made me remember Tarja telling me that the number three was significant in magic.

One of the first things Tarja had me do over a week ago was to cleanse then set the crystals I had purchased for Hattie outside during the full moon. The following day, they were done and stored on the shelves.

I picked up one of the black tourmalines and a crack rent

the air. Startled, I dropped the crystal. It landed on the table, letting everyone see the fine line running through it. "What did I do now?"

"You have no control over your power. It's leaking through your pores. Young witches learn containment early in their training. Think about establishing a netting around every cell in your body that allows magic through but not unchecked."

"That was actually very helpful. There were no riddles or half-baked explanations for me to wade through. Thank you, Tarja."

I heard her mental snort before I did as she instructed. This one was easy for me to imagine and conjure. My skin stopped tingling immediately. It wasn't until then that I realized the sensation had continued ever since I bonded with the grimoire.

Nina was back with the cauldron. The second she put it on the stand, I conjured the fire and got back to work with the herbs. "Can you guys put your donations in these vials? That way, I can be ready to add them before I scorch the herbs." The basement was never going to be clear of the stench at this rate.

"I'd be happy to," Mythia replied while Tsekani simply smiled and sliced his wrist with a clawed finger. Nina gagged as he held the glass under the dripping wound. It closed within seconds, leaving a few milliliters behind for me.

Mythia, on the other hand, picked up a stand and set the vial into it, then turned around and hovered above it. I thought she was going to drop her pants or something. Thank goodness she didn't. Her wings usually fluttered at a pace too fast for me to follow. At that moment, they went into hyperdrive as if they were the Millennium Falcon trying to do the Kessel Run in under twelve parsecs. Teal glitter floated to the table, some of it collecting in the tube.

"Magic is the best," Nina blurted. "What does pixie dust do? Can it make me fly?"

Mythia stopped, and crossed her arms over her chest then glared at my daughter. "I'm not Tinkerbell, and I don't live in Neverland."

Nina's face lost all its color while she kept her smile plastered on her face. It was obviously forced. "No, you're way better than that pixie! You're a tiny, fierce warrior pixie that can cook a mean curry. I was just curious what your dust can do." The strain had left her features, and the fine lines around her eyes disappeared.

I listened while Mythia told her how their dust has strong magic that enhances spells and potions. It also heals minor injuries, feeds vegetation, and cures brownie insanity. I tuned them out without listening to the rest so I could focus on the potion.

I added the herbs and inhaled the earthy scent before I added the dragon blood and pixie dust. The herbs turned teal, then darkened and liquified. I started stirring with a wooden spoon counterclockwise for several seconds. There was an iridescent shimmer to the potion that mesmerized me.

My heart leaped when the liquid started bubbling. I focused intently on the potion, so I didn't miss when it started boiling. My eyes started burning, and I blinked several times to relieve the dryness. When I refocused, the contents were bubbling rapidly. Cursing and praying I hadn't missed the perfect moment, I reversed directions. After the correct amount of time had passed, I picked up three black tourmalines and dropped them inside.

The liquid bubbled faster and faster, growing to the top of the cauldron. "It's going to overflow!"

Tarja laughed, the scratchy-hacking sound echoing

through my head. *"The cauldron will grow with it. It takes a lot of potion to protect this much land."*

I turned and met her distinctive cat eyes. "I did it right?"

"You were perfect. Get ready for the next step."

My chest swelled with emotion, and I couldn't stop smiling. I was getting this magic thing. I was still a novice, but I wasn't a danger to myself and those around me. It seemed like a year since Hattie passed away, yet it hadn't even been a month.

There was a traitor in my coven. I was being hunted by Tainted witches, and someone let demons through from the Underworld in my backyard. It was silly to feel so accomplished and excited because I was ready to cast the protections over the property, but I was. Without mastering the little things, you never got to the big ones. And I was ready for the next major step. It would keep my friends and family safe, along with those that had taken asylum on my land.

CHAPTER 19

One hand tightened on the *Oh Shit* bar above my head, and the other held Tarja close. Tsekani was racing through the forest on a souped-up golf cart like he was in the Baja 1000. Only this terrain had more bumps than my ass, which was never going to recover from being slammed against the unforgiving seat so many times.

"Are we almost there?" I shouted over the noise.

Tsekani's smile widened, and then the vehicle came to an abrupt halt, and I almost lost my hold on Tarja. "Yep. We are." He jumped out and nodded to the troop of pixies hovering around the area.

We were in a heavily wooded area rather than a clearing. For some reason, I expected to cast the spell where there was grass to sit on and space to stretch my arms. As it was, I touched two trees if I lifted my elbows from my sides.

Layla jumped out of the back and retrieved the cauldron where it rested on the back of the vehicle. "I'll be damned. None of it spilled. You owe Tarja a hundred bucks, Tseki."

He chuckled and shrugged. The bet he made her about spillage when I expressed concern was all for show. I'd

MAGICAL MAKEOVER

known it the second he took off at breakneck speed. Layla set the cauldron down on a natural altar created by a branch that had grown horizontal between the trunk of two trees and approached me.

"You alright? You're green."

I placed a hand over my stomach and let Tarja jump to the ground. "I've been better. You could have warned me what the trip was going to be like."

"And ruin the fun?" Layla and I had grown close over the past couple of weeks. Next to Fiona, she was my closest friend. Her snark and sass were refreshing, and she was as loyal as they came.

"Come."

My heart raced like a rabbit running from a fox as I followed Tarja to the altar. Someone had spread a purple silk cloth over the wood and placed candles and an athame next to the potion.

Tarja had explained what I needed to do on the way over. I had been working toward this for the last two weeks, and it was finally here. The fact that I was ready seemed like a miracle all its own.

Taking a deep breath, I called up an image of a dome settling over my property. The edges of Hattie's previous enchantment told me where to focus my attention. It also told me what the boundaries of my land were. It was easy for me to formulate a mental image.

Inside the shield, I imagined that protection wrapping around all of the magical creatures. I was able to feel their presence even though I hadn't met each of them. There were dozens of shifters and countless pixies. And beasts that felt similar to the Fae fairies but were different.

Like I had with the jewelry and other protective spells, I added a carbon layer to make it stronger. I picked up the athame and slashed my hand, then held my bleeding palm over the cauldron. "*Omnes in Praesidio.*"

A shock wave exploded in my chest and spread out through my pores. It was exhilarating and intoxicating. High on the power, I held my hands over the cauldron and performed the last phase of the protections. "*Terminus ad lorica.*"

The liquid lifted into the air, and I pushed out. I wanted it to go to the borders. When I released the enchantment, energy burst from me with enough power to send me crashing onto my ass. I ended up on my back, looking up at the canopy overhead.

A vice wrapped around my torso, cutting off my breathing ability and making my heart skip several beats. I stared at the leaves, watching them shake in the wind I created. The power kept me pinned in place.

I have no idea how long I lay there, trying to catch my breath while the wards set. Layla crawled to my side and helped me up. "Wow, you pack a punch, Pheebs. I've never experienced anything like it."

I looked around the area and noticed the altar was empty, and the ground was clear for fifteen feet around me in all directions. Her comment sounded more like a death knell than the compliment she intended. "Did it work? Maybe I did something wrong."

"You did everything right. Added a few extras to your spell that carried a lot of power with them." My familiar was bounding toward us through the trees. There was a slight hitch in her step, letting me know something was strained.

I screamed when Tsekani landed in front of me, buck naked. "What the hell? You can't do that."

"Sorry, love. I shifted before I was impaled on a branch. I don't think anyone's crossing those boundaries anytime soon." His laughter would have lightened the moment if Mythia hadn't fallen into my lap a second later.

One of her wings was broken, and she wasn't glowing anymore. "I should have known not to hover too close. Nothing goes as expected with you."

"You can't be mad at me. I got the spell done." I refused to apologize for something beyond my control. Although I did feel awful, they were injured.

Daethie buzzed into the area, leaving a dust trail and the formation of her warriors behind her. "What happened? Are we under attack?" I hadn't spoken to the pixie leader after the funeral. Honestly, she intimidated me more than I cared to admit. She was a couple inches tall, and I was five-foot-seven inches tall and afraid of her. If I hadn't seen countless pixies dressed in flowers and leaves with friendly expressions and smiles, I would have wondered if they were all fighters.

With Layla's help, I stood up with Mythia in my hand. "No. I redid the protections. Nimaha is now mine completely, and you are under my protection."

"It's been centuries since we felt magic ripple through a forest like that," Daethie replied. "We appreciate the continued safety of your lands. We will continue to share what we find in our mound in exchange. I will sign the new agreement."

"The document should be done soon. And, I've already put some silver to use creating charms that saved my mother's and grandmother's lives. I have some ideas about creating armor for your warriors that I have included in the contract."

Daethie's eyes brightened, and she inclined her head. "I am excited about our alliance in a way I haven't been since I was a youth. I've enjoyed a peaceful, safe life with the Silva family, and yet I look forward to the changes you will bring."

"You will always have a place here." The promise was an

easy one to make. They gave me far more than I offered them. Guilt surged when I thought about the imbalance. I didn't say anything, though. One thing I'd learned in this world was that payment was always expected. I had a feeling I would need what they gave me for reasons other than jewelry making at some point in the future.

"You created quite a show. And the shield is supercharged. I don't think there has ever been a stronger one. How did you cast something I suspect is indeed impenetrable?" Tsekani asked as he scanned something in the distance. "It's also a beautiful amethyst color that reminds me of you."

I grimaced when I noticed the golf cart turned on its side. "Seems like purple is the color of my magic. Does that still run? We should head back and make sure my mom, Nana, and Nina are alright. They might be terrified."

Tsekani shoved the vehicle over, so it rested on its wheels again. It purred to life when he cranked the engine. I thanked the pixies again and climbed onto the front seat. "Let's take it easy this time. Mythia has a broken wing, and I don't want to squeeze the other one because you're driving like a bat out of hell." Layla laughed as she scooped up Tarja and got in the back.

The return trip took twice as long, with Tsekani driving at a sedate pace. The wheels still bounced on every rock, root, and tree limb. Tsekani helped me out when we pulled up beside the house.

The vice squeezing my chest eased when I heard voices through the open kitchen window. My steps picked up when I heard a familiar masculine voice. What the heck was he doing here? He left last night and never mentioned coming back.

I walked in the back door and saw Aidoneus sitting at the island with Nana while my mom stirred something in a big pot on the stove. It smelled like her spaghetti sauce. Mythia tapped my hand. "Put me down over there. I need to help Mollie."

My mom gasped when she saw Mythia. "No, you don't. You look like you've been through a cheese grater. How can I help you?"

Mythia shook her head. "Your daughter's magic went through me. I'll be fine in no time."

"Is that what we felt twenty minutes ago?" My mom asked.

"I had to come back and investigate when I felt the disturbance," Aidoneus added. His eyes held a heat that spoke of a desire to do intimate investigations. Or maybe that was my mind filling in the blanks.

I put Mythia on the island and fanned my suddenly hot cheeks. "I added a bit too much power when I cast the enchantment."

"That's why they were after you," Aidoneus observed as if he finally understood. The look in his eyes turned from appreciative to assessing. It was more than a little disturbing. "You need to learn how to disguise your signature so outsiders cannot track you by it or identify who you are."

"I haven't quite gotten there, demigod. Or are you a god? Phoebe needs to learn basic spells before trying something so advanced."

"Did you learn anything more about whoever used Dark magic right under my nose? I still don't get how we all missed it. Every one of us was present at the funeral, and yet, no one felt a thing." That had been bothering me ever since Aidoneus told me about his investigation.

Aidoneus inclined his head as he leaned against the island a couple feet from me with his hands stuffed into his pockets. "You would have seen the black smoke and smelled the fetid winds, as well."

"Is it possible you are wrong about the location of the breach?

The veil wasn't opened during the funeral or after. Hundreds of pixies, shifters, and other magical creatures came to pay their respects to Hattie, which meant we were practically out there until dawn."

Aidoneus scowled and lost his relaxed stance. "I'm not mistaken. I was born with the ability to see and sense the veil. And our UIS agents have equipment that can detect the smallest remnant of Dark magic. You're the ones that said it happened that night."

"Can you tell us how long it's been there? Perhaps it happened months or years ago." The thought that something so egregious happened on my watch turned my stomach.

"My abilities don't give me a time frame. Neither do the devices we use," Aidoneus admitted. I was certain it hadn't happened since Hattie gave me her magic. "But my father's wards track every being bound to the Underworld, and he knows several disappeared on the last day in May."

That was the day Myrna attacked me, and I was given her magic. "It wasn't the funeral. It happened the night before when Hattie saved me."

Tsekani shook his head and cursed. "We were so busy that night anyone could have performed the spell without us noticing. The shifters and pixies were off hunting Myrna, and we were downstairs saving your life."

Layla clenched her jaw tight as fur rippled over her skin before receding entirely. "How do you know it was a member of the coven?

"After I dealt with the demons and stopped them from the killing spree they had planned, we tracked the energy signature to their gathering place up the hill—the stone cottage. I've spent the bulk of my time untangling the strands. They are twisted together and impossible to pull apart."

"There is a secret meeting place for the coven? I assumed

they met here." It was a ludicrous assumption now that I thought about it.

"Nightshadow Grove was built by the Mystic Circle coven's original members and has always been the location for sacred rituals and meetings. The funeral was held here because Hattie wanted to be laid to rest on her land so her blood and bone can help protect it."

"So, how do we root out the traitor? We can't allow her to continue using Dark magic and calling demons."

"I was hoping one of you would have an idea. I've used every device I have and even cast a few spells myself. Whatever she did to hide her trail managed to block the magic from the Underworld."

Terror gripped me. For a member of the coven to conceal themselves from the son of Hades and all of their technology and power meant something far more significant and more terrifying was at play. I couldn't imagine that was even possible. I needed to do some reading because there had to be an answer somewhere. I refused to believe we couldn't find this witch.

CHAPTER 20

My legs felt like lead as I traipsed down the porch stairs to my car. It had been three days since I cast the protections. I'd spent every second searching through my grimoire and various other magical texts that I could find. Layla helped, so did my mom. Nana's version was more of a distraction than anything, but I did learn a lot from her comments.

All that work hadn't revealed any helpful information. No spell would untangle magical threads or identify a caster weeks after the enchantment was done. Energy signatures disappeared within days. The fact that Aidoneus was able to see it still spoke volumes.

Guilt pulled me like I was taffy—first one direction, then another. I should be inside reading the tomes Layla dropped off earlier. Yet I was heading to my car with the intent of watching Nina play the part of Sandra Dee. My mom and Nana had taken Nina to her play at the high school and left me to work.

"You're a hard woman to get alone."

I held my gasp in my throat and swiveled when I heard

MAGICAL MAKEOVER

the feminine voice that I initially didn't recognize. I couldn't stop my eyes from flaring wide. They landed on the slight woman with red hair and a blue cloak on her shoulders.

"Lexie, what are you doing here? And, why do you want me alone?" Playing stupid made every cell in my body growl and spit. I hated acting as if I was a bimbo.

"I'm here to claim the Pleiades power. I know it's been too much for you. We all felt the way you lost control the other night. You can trust me. I won't misuse it like a Tainted witch would. And, don't worry, the process will be painless."

She had no idea I knew what she'd been up to. The only reason she would be in my driveway accosting me was because she was into dark shit. I could use that against her. And I wouldn't feel bad about it, either. She was lying through her teeth. The process of transferring her magic to me had killed Hattie. This woman wasn't here to *help* me.

I tilted my head and scanned her. I was beginning to see auras. Tarja had to explain it to me when it started. I hadn't learned what all the colors meant, but a dark grey seemed pretty ominous to me.

"How do I know you aren't Tainted? I'm too new to the paranormal world to have much knowledge." What I didn't ask was how the heck she got onto my property. It should have been impossible, right?

"Your protection mirrored Hattie's, and she didn't ban anyone in the coven." I nearly jumped and turned to the house when I heard Tarja's voice in my head. I didn't want to alert Lexie that anything was amiss. *"She trusted each of them. The only reason she would be kept out would be if she Turned. The ward doesn't care about your identity. No Dark soul can pass through."*

"How did the veil let the demons through?" I thought back at her.

Lexie tossed her long hair over one shoulder and laughed. "Your wards would have kept me out. By the way, Tarja did a fabulous job casting them. Now you won't have to worry about getting up to speed. I can take it from here."

"*They never crossed the boundary. I'm calling Tsekani and Layla.*"

"*No! Don't. I need to take my own stand. I will call out if I need their help.*" I needed to know I was capable of protecting myself. There would be times like before when I was on my own. Besides, I found that if I allowed others to rescue me this time, word would get around, and I would never truly be respected.

I hoped the smile I forced on my lips looked more genuine than Lexie's laugh had sounded. "That won't be necessary. I'm keeping my magic. I am glad you stopped by. I had planned on visiting soon. Hades' son paid me a visit recently looking for the witch responsible for opening the veil on my property. It must have stung that he interfered with whatever plans you had for the demons you called forth."

Lexie lost the color in her face. She recovered and sneered. "You think you can keep ahold of the power, human." She spat 'human' like it was a dirty word.

I genuinely smiled and set my purse on the hood of the BMW I'd been driving since my Land Rover was destroyed. I'd inherited four cars from Hattie, which weirded me out more than the magic now.

"Try and take it, bitch. It's mine." My skin buzzed like a hive of hornets was racing through my veins.

Lexie said something under her breath at the same time I cast my shield. The hornets immediately started jabbing me with inch-long stingers. My body reacted before I could process what was happening. My fingers tried to brush away the bugs and encountered smooth skin. I stopped myself before my nails dug through my skin.

"*Ferrum faucium*," I spat. I wanted to throat punch her.

MAGICAL MAKEOVER

Turned out I was more than a bit bloodthirsty because I had no trouble concentrating on that one.

Lexie grabbed for her throat at the same time she stumbled back. Blood dribbled out the side of her mouth, and the area over her thyroid was swollen. She countered quickly and hurled another spell at me.

She kept her voice low, so I wasn't able to hear her intent. It hit my right shoulder, but my shield kept it from causing any damage. I did have a hard time catching my breath. Apparently, the impact had done enough damage.

I opened my mouth to throw another one at her. She was faster. Whatever she did was aimed at the back of my throat because the area suddenly felt like it was being eaten away by acid.

I conjured my witch fire and let it coat my hands. The way Lexie backed away from me made me want to tell her she would regret ever crossing me and taking advantage of my attack. The pain impeded my ability to talk.

I threw the flames at her blue cloak, hoping she had weak spots in her protective bubble. As I watched the purple fire ignite the blue hem, I realized she had to have been in on Myrna's plan. There was no other explanation for how she got lucky enough to do her magic at the only moment she would get away with it.

In my research, I had discovered that the veil between the human world and the Underworld could only be pierced on land steeped in power. There were only seven locations on the planet where that could happen. The document didn't say those locations were associated with the Pleiades witches, but I was certain that was the case.

Lexie stopped screaming and removed her cape, then tossed it on my car. Dammit! Not another one. I connected to my fire and closed my hand around it, extinguishing the flames. It took great effort and several seconds to accomplish. At least her left pant leg had been burned. The blistered, blackened flesh looked painful.

At first, I attributed it to my inexperience. Then I remembered fire was the one thing I had become proficient in controlling. When Lexie started cackling like a movie villain, I knew I was in trouble.

"*Telum,*" I shouted, then ran a quick scan of my body. It was no longer only my throat that was being eaten away as if by acid. It was traveling through my entire body. I had no idea what she'd done, and my heart started racing to escape the attack.

Blood dribbled from her mouth. "*Veni ad me,*" she shouted. The second the words left her mouth, I felt a pulling sensation in my chest. It drew me toward Lexie. Only my body never moved.

"*Phoebe, get out of there. She has initiated the transfer!*" Tarja's mental voice made my blood chill on my veins. Of all that we had been through together, she had never sounded so frightened.

This vile woman was stealing from me just like Miles, and his little tart had. "I don't think so, bitch. *Virtutem meam.*"

This magic was mine. I thought of the way Miles had looked at me with such pity. The smug look on his twat of a mistress's face when she informed me I had been fired and would find it impossible to get another job in the triangle.

Worst of all, long before that time in my life, I recalled Miles telling me I would never be able to pass the MCATs, so I needed to stick to nursing. I had allowed his doubt to infect me and had followed his advice. I didn't regret it entirely because it brought Fiona and me together.

Another scene with Miles telling me I couldn't negotiate my own purchase contract on the Land Rover. Hundreds of smaller events raced through my mind, pissing me off. I was done with being bullied and manipulated.

I was a grown woman, capable of a great many things. And I wasn't going to allow anyone to stand in my way. Tarja burst through the living room window and landed next to me. The glass shattered and exploded towards us but went back to the frame before one piece touched me.

"You're done, Lexie. I hope you enjoyed your little Dark spree because this is the end." The only way to stop a spell was to kill the witch that had cast it. Every cell in my body objected. That wasn't who I was. *So, you're going to let her take your magic and kill you then?* Nope. I was keeping what was mine.

"You will never beat me. You have no idea who you're messing with. There are powerful beings behind us. One way or another, we will get your power." I wanted to ask her a thousand different questions. She would never answer one truthfully, so I didn't bother.

Instead, I focused on what I planned on doing to her. I wanted to cut her off from her magic. She didn't deserve the power she'd been born with. She abused it and used it for evil purposes. *"Indie magica falciparum."*

Lexie dissolved into a coughing fit. Blood sprayed out of her mouth. Her aura shimmered, and a blue mist separated from her and floated away on the breeze. Lexie reached for it while gasping for breath.

She fell to her knees, her face turning red then blue because she couldn't suck in any oxygen. Layla and Tsekani raced around the corner of the house. They stopped short when they saw us.

Lexie dropped to her knees then toppled over onto her side. She did a good rendition of a fish out of water for several more seconds before her mouth stopped moving, and her eyes lost that light that told me she was alive.

Bile pummeled my uvula like it was a punching bag. I had killed a witch. "Please tell me my family is alright."

Layla came to my side and wrapped an arm around my shoulders. "They're fine. I just got off the phone with your mom. She said they never went into the play because Stella, your childhood best friend, was hit by some blue mist, and she passed out. They're going to the hospital with her now."

I looked down at Tarja. "Did her magic go to Stella? Is that possible? She didn't give it to anyone."

"When a witch dies, and she is the last of her line, Hecate bestows the power on one she deems worthy. She must maintain the balance of power, or it will revert to the Pleiades line where it was originally taken."

That was one lesson I recalled. The gods had to ensure the distribution remained as it was now, or significant problems would ensue. If they allowed that, it would cause chaos and destruction.

"What happens now? Aside from me going to see Stella, I needed to help Harry find his Aunt Sarah's ghost." Hattie had been some kind of detective for the supernaturals in town. Now they looked to me to fill that role. I had a business to run, but something in me told me I would be much happier helping people like the elf. Finding a lost family member or a stolen heirloom excited me in a way I hadn't experienced since college.

I would call Harry. But not right now. I was close to collapsing. We had discovered the coven member that had Turned. Myrna was still out there. Lexie had hinted at a more significant conspiracy.

The demons were gone. What Aidoneus could find anyway. He was certain there were more. The skin with which the perpetrator had masked their presence made it impossible to be certain there weren't more.

And then there was the reason for breaching the veil. We had no idea why they breached it. All of this was enough for Aidoneus to reassign himself as the primary investigator to

Camden. He had seven special agents that served that role. Still, he indicated my property was at a greater risk because I was new and subsequently an easy target.

I'd tackle one thing at a time. I was on my way to becoming a badass witch and amateur detective. The rest could wait until I had a nice long soak to work out the kinks in my body.

"You need to buckle down and study magic more thoroughly, especially the potion-making. Myrna won't be in hiding forever. And whoever is helping her will be just as determined. You need to be as strong as possible to face anything they throw at you."

I smiled at my familiar and tossed Tsekani the keys to the car. "I will, Tarja. Starting tomorrow." I had to check on my friend and see if she really is a witch now.

Download the next book in the Mystical Midlife in Maine series, Laugh Lines & Lost Things HERE! Then turn the page for a preview.

Download the first book in the Midlife Magic series, Magical New Beginnings HERE! Then turn the page for a preview.

Download the first book in the Twisted Sisters' Midlife Maelstrom series, Packing Serious Magical Mojo HERE! Then turn the page for a preview.

Click Here to DOWNLOAD The Prime of my Magical Life, book 1 in the exciting new Supernatural Midlife Series. Then turn the page for a preview.

EXCERPT FROM LAUGH LINES & LOST THINGS BOOK #2 MYSTICAL MIDLIFE IN MAINE

I raced up the stairs from the basement before whoever was using my door as a drum broke it down. "Myrna can't get past my wards, right Tarja?"

I felt my familiar roll her eyes at me. A quick check told me she wasn't next to me, so she'd remained in the basement. *"Sure, and she's kind enough to knock on the door this time."*

I sighed as I passed my mother and Nana coming down the stairs. "Who the hell is pounding so early in the morning? Don't they have any respect for those that want to sleep?"

I smiled at Nana. The woman had no filter, and I loved her for it. I yanked the door open and gaped at my childhood best friend. "Stella!" My cheeks heated, and my chest twisted. I hadn't gone to see her over the past few days.

I wasn't sure what to say and from what Nana learned at coffee with her friends. There were two of them that met her at the Owl and Turtle a few times each week. My mom shopped for books while the three of them had coffee and talked.

"Come in. How are you feeling? My mom told me you were in the hospital."

Stella walked past me with wide, frightened eyes. "Something is happening to me. I didn't know where else to go. You're going to think I'm crazy like Todd does. He talked about having me committed.

Tarja stood in the doorway to the kitchen, wagging her tail. I could hear the reproach in the movement. At first, it was assumed Hekate passed the magic on after I killed Lexie. Turns out she initiated the transfer as was the norm when a witch died.

But instead of going to me, as the nearest Pleiades, I directed it to Stella. At least that was the theory after Tarja evaluated the magic residue before it dissipated. I had not yet gone to visit Stella to verify if she had inherited the magic.

"You'd be surprised. We need to talk," I told her.

My mom wrapped an arm around Stella's shoulders. "Let's go into the kitchen."

Stella nodded her head up and down as she took in her surroundings. "I've never been in this house. The wood floors and crown molding are original and still in pristine condition."

At least she was still herself. It was reassuring to hear Stella fall into her realtor mode naturally. I would hate myself if she lost who she was and became a different person because of what I'd inadvertently done.

"That was all Hattie's doing. She did all the hard work. I just have to keep the house and business running as well as she did. Not to mention her more clandestine activities." I needed to pay Mr. Peterson a visit, as well. His aunt and her sewing machine were still missing.

"What clandestine activities? What's going on here?"

My mom let her go and crossed to the fridge, where she took out a bowl of fruit. Nana continued to the island, and the stools set along the other side of it. Stella followed Nana while I scanned for Mythia. My pixie house manager-as I had come to think of the tiny creature-was nowhere to be seen.

Nana patted the stool next to her. "You'll want to sit down for this one. You aren't crazy. Being put in the nuthouse won't do anything for what's happening to you."

Stella's eyes went wide, and her panicked gaze landed on me. I turned to Tarja. "Can we help her anxiety before she has a heart attack?"

"Why are you talking to the cat?" Stella asked in a voice that shook.

"Because she's my familiar and guide to my magic." There was no reason to beat around the bush. "I am new to all of this, like you. In fact, I'm the reason you are a witch now."

Stella exploded off the stool and sent it clattering to the floor behind her. Mythia flew into the room, picked it up, then went to the stove and put on a kettle. My mom tilted her head to the pixie. "They're going to need Irish coffee for this conversation. Tea isn't going to cut it."

Mythia thrust her hands on her hips. "It's a special blend that will relax the human. Phoebe is right. She's one second from going into cardiac arrest, and her magic isn't strong enough to combat it."

"Th...the...that's a fairy!" Stella's voice was a screech as she pointed a wildly swinging finger at Mythia.

"I'm a pixie. Not a fairy." I expected Mythia to be offended, but her response was surprisingly gentle.

"There is much to be discussed. First, Ms. Hawkins, you have been given one of the greatest gifts. I know it's overwhelming, but you aren't alone in this. Phoebe and I will be here for you every step of the way. So will the Mystic Circle coven."

I held up my hand. Stella's jaw was on her chest as she stared at the tabby cat that sat at my feet. "We belong to the Backside of Forty coven with Fiona and her two friends.

MAGICAL MAKEOVER

They're my people. Not the band of bitches that would rather stab me in the back than help me in any way."

Stella groped behind her. Nana pushed the stool forward, and Stella dropped onto it. "The ghosts are real. I actually turned that pudding cup into a bowl of lobster bisque. How?"

I leaned on the island. "You did what with pudding?"

"I was in the hospital, and all the nurses would give me was awful tasting, bland food. They wouldn't let Todd bring in any food, and I was staring at the brown gloop wishing it was lobster bisque, and suddenly it was. I ate it before Nurse Hatchet could take it away. That was just the beginning."

How the heck was she able to make a bowl of soup when I could barely conjure a witch flame with extensive instructions, Tarja? "I didn't mean to make you a witch. Lexie was trying to kill me, and I beat her to it. I wasn't even aware of reacting when Hekate started to shift Lexie's powers to me."

"You did this to me?" It was as if Stella just realized what I'd told her a few minutes before.

"Oh boy," Nana whisper-yelled. Her whisper was always more of a shout than anything else.

I held up my hands, palms out. "I didn't mean to do that. I swear. I have no idea how to do much of anything. I can barely conjure a flame. My magic is unpredictable. Figures you'd become a natural witch from the first moment you were given the power. You always were better than me at picking up new things."

Stella snorted and waved a hand through the air. "Understanding Algebra first is not the same thing. I can't even wrap my mind around all of this. How is there a pixie in here? And, who was that talking in my mind."

Nana pointed to Tarja. "That'd be the cat. She likes freaking us mundies out. That's what they call humans. Although you aren't a mundie anymore. We get left out again, Mollie."

Layla and Nina came in from the backyard and stopped in their tracks. Nina rushed forward and tried to stand in front of Mythia and get Stella's attention. "It's so good to see you again, Mrs. Hawkins." Nina sent me a glare over her shoulder that almost made me snicker. I never thought my sixteen-year-old daughter would be the voice of reason. "What brings you to Nimaha?"

Mythia flew toward the pantry, her wings fluttering faster than my eyes could follow. She was upset at Nina trying to hide her. I put my hand on Nina's shoulder. "She's here because I did give her Lexie's magic. She's freaked out and needs my help."

Nina's shoulders dropped, and she exhaled a breath she had been holding. "Thank God. I thought you all had lost your mind, letting her see Mythia. The last thing we need is a bunch of the town gossips hunting them, thinking they're something like Leprechauns that can grant wishes."

Stella and I looked at each other, then burst out laughing. Layla grabbed an energy drink from the fridge and waved it in our direction. "I see why you picked her. We've got our work cut out for us, Tarja. And, for the record, Stella. Mythia looks nothing like a Leprechaun. Those bastards are three feet tall and will bite your ankles just as soon as they'd give you anything."

Tarja's scratchy cough echoed in my head. Stella stopped laughing and looked at Tarja with wide eyes. I stooped and scooped her into my arms. Tarja didn't like to be held but was allowing me to handle her more and more. I was a cuddler.

"That's Tarja's laughter. I need to know you forgive me for making you a witch. I had no idea what I was doing. The only thought that went through my mind was how the loose magic was going to be handled. I wanted someone as kickass as you to get it. I had no idea the power would have come to me if I hadn't been thinking hard enough to accidentally cast a spell giving them to you. Although, I admit I'm not terribly sorry. The thought of going through this with you is so much better than doing it alone."

Stella sighed and grabbed some grapes from the bowl. "I had no idea you were under so much stress. You should have called me. I know it's been years, but I'm here for you. Becoming a witch is a lot to take in, and I have no idea what I will tell Todd and the kids. They think that concussion damaged my mind."

"It's better that you let them think that. Your daughter will eventually need to know. She will inherit the magic, as well. But your husband needs to focus on keeping our town safe. There are Dark powers at work here. The mundies need him on their side."

Stella had that deer-in-a-headlight look again. "Charley is going to get my magic?"

Nina stepped forward. "I know Charley. Well, I met her at school, but I can tell she'll be able to handle it. Plus, we won't get it right away. Tarja said I won't be able to do much until I mature. I bet Charley will be the same."

"Nina's magic will be stronger, but they will start to show signs of magic in the coming months. We will all help them control their emotions. Keeping emotions from being too explosive is the key to managing magical outbursts. Getting too angry or too excited will make their abilities manifest at the worst possible moments."

Layla rubbed Tarja's head, making my familiar jump from my arms to the island. "That's exactly what we need. Two teenaged witches while we are trying to acclimate their menopausal mothers."

I smacked Layla on the shoulder. "Shut your mouth. Peri-menopause is not the same thing. The hot flashes aren't as intense or frequent."

Stella laughed. "And the random chin hairs haven't

sprouted yet. Laugh lines are another story altogether. Unless there's a way to magic them away?!"

Tarja shook her furry head. *"That is not how your powers work."*

Layla popped the tab on her drink. "There's nothing for the two of you to worry about. You both look great. All you need to focus on is controlling your magic. If you don't, we will be trying to contain your daughters and you guys at the same time. I might be able to go on little sleep, but I can't be in two places at once, and Tsekani is shit at interacting with the human world."

"You said Tarja is your familiar and helps you. Do I get one of my own?"

That was a good question. I glanced at Tarja, who was sitting close to the window at the end of the island, grooming herself. She paused and lifted her head. She was an animal, but there was no doubting the power she exuded or her intelligence. It was those attributes I reacted to before inheriting Hattie's power.

"Only Pleiades receive a familiar. At one point, all witches had one, but that bond was warped when the Tainted Turned, and that affected all familiar bonds. My kind died off in record numbers. Now there are too few of us to go around. We can't leave our witch long enough to procreate. Without new familiars, we cannot bestow them on good witches."

Mythia put the mixer she had retrieved next to the flour and yeast. "I say it's time to try again. With Phoebe under the protection of a UIS agent, we should arrange a visitation with Zeph."

Layla waggled her eyebrows. "What do you say, Tarja? You've always had the hots for Zeph."

A hiss echoed through my head, making the hair on my arms stand on end. Tarja didn't like the reference to Zeph. *"There will be no visit with Luci and Zeph. I am not leaving*

Phoebe, and we are not leaving Camden right now. You of all people know why we cannot risk it."

Stella glanced between Tarja and Layla. "What does she mean about that? Why should you know better? Are you a witch, too?"

Layla shook her head from side to side. "I'm not a witch. I was Made by a Tainted one. I'm a werewolf but not a Born one."

Mythia threw ingredients in the mixer and started the thing. The motor hummed low as it stirred the flour, oil, egg, and water together. "Before you misinform Stella. You're not an abomination. Being Made doesn't make you lower than the Born. You're just as powerful, loyal, and talented."

I paused as I went to grab the grated cheese and toppings from the fridge. Pizza Fridays were becoming my favorite. Mythia loved coming up with themes for meals each day. Nina begged her for pizza day once a week, and we all asked her to keep it going. Her 'za was better than any I'd ever eaten.

"Mythia is right. I wouldn't be alive without you. Your quick actions saved my life. I owe you everything. I haven't talked to the Born that roam around the property, but I can tell you none of them hold a candle to you. You are the only one that came to my aid. And you had to face the bitch that Made you when you helped me. What excuse do the others have for hanging back until you'd done most of the work?"

Layla's cheeks turned pink as she shook her head from side to side. "Hattie saved you. All I did was carry you inside."

"What exactly happened? How did you become a witch, Phoebe? I was so side-tracked by my own transformation that I hadn't stopped to ask about yours. You weren't magical when we had lunch."

My chest twisted with her question. Remembering the events still hurt. Thinking about what Hattie sacrificed for me would always cause a piercing ache. I loaded my arms with everything we'd need and carried it to the island.

"I stopped a Tainted witch named Myrna from attacking Hattie and stealing her power. I was injured in the process." I reached up and rubbed the dragonfly necklace that had saved me from being killed instantly. "Hattie gave me her magic to save my life. It killed her in the process."

Stella gaped at me. "You threw yourself in the middle of a magical fight when you had no power? Why would you do something so stupid? And, before I forget. What's a Tainted?"

I growled and balanced my hands on the marble countertop. "First of all, I had no idea she was a witch. And second. There was no way I was going to walk away and leave Hattie vulnerable. When I approached her, there was nothing to tell me she was a witch. It wasn't until she had attacked that I discovered that little tidbit of information. Myrna is the worst of the worst. She's Tainted."

"Tainted witches are greedy witches that played with Dark powers. They discovered that stealing power from others gave them more magic and prolonged their life. There is no surviving the process. And, the first time a witch takes a life like that, it corrupts her forever."

Stella whistled low in her throat. "Did you mention Irish coffee, Mollie? That sounds good right about now." My mom chuckled and went to the Keurig to brew a cup for Stella.

Stella accepted the mug from my mom and took a sip. That was a lot to unpack, and I knew she'd have questions. "Alright. I can't let the power corrupt me. I think we might want to rethink the familiar thing. Absolute power corrupts absolutely. I have to admit that when I felt the thrill of creating something delicious from a bowl of nasty goop, I kept trying to do it again. I wanted to feel that again. If I'd had a magical cat to warn me, I wouldn't have gone so far. That could have been avoided if I had a guide."

Stella had a point. I never considered it from that point of view because my powers came with Tarja. "How likely is it that we can keep good witches from Turning? If we stop, even one taking the risk now would be worth it. I think we should consider the proposal. Or at least reach out to this Zephyrus."

Layla popped a piece of pepperoni into her mouth. "It's something to think about, Tarja. I've told you for years that familiars would lessen the number of witches Turned each year."

Tarja sighed and laid down on the counter in a patch of sunshine. *"I will think about it. First, we need to find Myrna and ensure she cannot steal any more power. Something major is brewing. I just don't know what it is yet."*

Tarja was right. Myrna was an imminent threat. I didn't know much, but one thing I did know was Pleiades couldn't leave their area for long. The distribution of power needed to be maintained. The idea of being without Tarja made my stomach flip over and turn inside out.

Something told me Stella was onto something with the idea of giving familiars to every witch. I made a vow to ensure it happened as soon as Myrna was no longer a threat.

DOWNLOAD the next book in the Mystical Midlife in Maine series, Laugh Lines & Lost Things HERE!

EXCERPT FROM MAGICAL NEW BEGINNIGS BOOK #1 MIDLIFE WITCHERY

*E*mmie released me and wiped a tear from her eye as she looked around the grounds. "I can see why you don't want to leave here. This place is amazing, mom. Well, aside from the eerie cemetery and mausoleum. I always hated that when we came here as kids, and it isn't any better. Anyway, knowing how much you love it will make being so far from you completely worth it."

I squeezed my oldest daughter's hand and nodded my head in agreement. I never imagined I would feel this way when I came to England to say goodbye to my grandmother. "For the first time since your father died, I feel like I'm home here at Pymm's Pondside. The only downside is not being able to hop in a car and visit you and your brother and sister."

"We don't mind coming to you, mom. You've done more than enough for us. It's about time you have something just for you," Skylar, my youngest daughter told me as she jumped into the conversation. She was leaning against the white picket fence that surrounded the massive garden my grandmother kept in pristine condition. That was one thing I wasn't looking forward to maintaining. The knee that gave me more problems than my son ached at the mere idea of so much bending.

Greyson turned from the pond at the front of the property I'd just inherited and rolled his eyes at his twin. Skylar was my sensitive one, where Emmie was the responsible one of my three kids, and Greyson was hotheaded. "Stop sucking up. Mom isn't going to fly you out to England every time you're homesick."

My head started throbbing with the familiar argument. Emmie had been away at college for two years, but the twins just started. And being my sensitive one, Skylar came home nearly every weekend. The three-hour drive didn't faze her at all, where Greyson almost always remained on campus. By staying in England, I will be making it impossible for them to come home for a weekend visit.

I am a horrible mother because leaving my kids without their home base close by didn't make me change my mind. Every cell in my body screamed that I was supposed to be at Pymm's Pondside. No. It was where I *needed* to be. I've lived the past twenty-two years for someone else. Now was my time.

I wrapped one arm around Greyson and the other around Skylar. "What have I always told you, Grey? It's your job to take care of your sisters. They do enough for you. I expect you to make time for her as we all adjust to this new setup."

Greyson's head dipped, and he took a deep breath. "Sorry, mom. You're right. I won't get lost in myself."

"I won't let you," Emmie added. "I never thought I'd be happy to move back in with you nutjobs, but I'm excited."

Dust billowed into the air as the car I arranged to take them to the airport turned down my dirt drive. Emotion clogged my throat, and my eyes burned with tears. I'd lost so much in my life, and it felt like I was losing them now, too. "I'm going to miss you guys."

Skylar squeezed me tighter. "We will miss you, too, but this isn't forever. You never know. We might decide to move here after college."

I released the twins and embraced Emmie next. "Now, remember you guys are closing on your house before the term begins. The agent will be contacting you, Emmie, to set up the date and time, but all three of you need to be there."

The second I stepped foot onto the property, I called a real estate agent in Salisbury and arranged to sell my house. I swear the gods are on my side because it sold before the week was out. Emmie was all too happy to find a place for her to move into with the twins. In no time, the three found the home they wanted. Thanks to the money from my house's sale, I put in an offer for the kids on the two-story they selected.

"I've got it handled, mom. Don't worry about us. We will be back next summer."

"If you need anything, call me." I hugged them each once more then sent them on their way.

Turning around, I took in my new home. Pymm's Pondside was the name for the white cottage. When I visited as a kid, I thought it was neat that they named their houses here. But to call it a 'cottage' was misleading. The thing was nearly as big as my house in Salisbury, but it had charm coming out of the eaves.

The brown roof reminded me of a thatch design. Every angle was rounded, creating a soft, inviting look to the five-bedroom home. The brown shutters on the windows matched the roof, and the ivy growing up one side was straight out of a fairytale. I'd always thought that, and now it was mine.

I even owned a cemetery. I never thought I'd say that in

MAGICAL MAKEOVER

my life. And the craziest part was that it made me feel closer to the family I'd never known. I turned my head to the left and glanced at the headstones. Towards the back of the place were a couple of mausoleums. Yeah, it's super creepy but also pretty neat. I mean, there was a graveyard a hundred feet from where I slept. Good thing I have always loved them, or I wouldn't have been able to stay in the house.

Turning away from the cemetery, I glanced at the garden I had spent days wondering if I should remove. Not only did I cringe at the thought of so much bending, but I didn't have a green thumb. I wasn't as bad as Violet, my best friend, but plants didn't flourish under my care. And I'm starting a new life now. I admit that I have no desire to weed the damn thing. I was reluctant to pull the plants up. They're a part of the place's charm.

I headed to the pond and smiled as I looked at the large watering hole. I've seen deer, rabbits, and miniature bears drinking late at night or in the early morning. At least I thought they were tiny bears. They looked odd and had large floppy ears, and I swear they understood when I cooed at them. I was excited to have animals so close. And with woods surrounding the entire property, I hoped to see more. The area was lush, thanks to the rainy weather in Northern England.

Opening the small gate in the fence around the garden, I searched for some basil to add to my tomato sandwich for lunch. There were so many herbs and plants, and I knew what maybe a third of them were. Rosemary and mint were the most obvious. The rest I would learn in time if I don't lose it all to weeds.

I found what I was looking for in the far corner closest to the cemetery. My gaze shifted to the fresh grave. My vision blurred when I read my grandmother's name. A pinging started up in my head. That was the only way I could describe it.

Something was hitting the walls of my skull, almost like a bee trapped under a cloche. I've never experienced it before in my life. The stress of the past month must be getting to me.

I took a deep breath and thought about my grandma. Isidora Shakleton was unforgettable and an integral part of the town. Most of the residents of Cottlehill Wilds showed up for her service.

The pinging was gone by the time I turned away and walked back to the house. The inside was just as cozy as it appeared on the outside. The back door went right into the kitchen, where I dumped the basil before heading through the small living room and up the stairs to my bedroom.

The patchwork quilt my grandmother made was still on her bed. I had my clothes and a few of my favorite keepsakes shipped to me. The rest was going to the kids.

I need a new comforter. And sheets. Badly. I made plans to head into the city to pick up a cozy Down quilt and maybe a new mattress. I swear there were more lumps in the thing than there were on my butt and thighs. And that was saying something.

Being my age, it was shocking if you didn't carry an extra fifteen or twenty pounds. I know I certainly had the extra cushion. Along with aches and pains, I thought as I bent to pick up the towels Skylar left on the wood floor.

That was one thing I will not miss. The kids, much like my late husband, never picked up after themselves. And boy, did that get on my last damn nerve. I spent my entire life caring for others—both at work and at home. I swear being a caretaker was woven into my DNA.

After graduating with my bachelor's degree in nursing, I worked full-time in the ICU at a local hospital for twenty years then took care of Tim at the end. Perhaps that was what was so inviting about my grandmother's house. I didn't need to take care of anyone here.

After washing the toothpaste from the sink, I turned and yelped. "What the fuck?" My mouth got away from me when I noticed the towels back on the ground. What the hell was going on? I just picked them up and put them in the laundry basket.

I headed into the other bedrooms and stripped the beds before straightening the covers over the mattresses. By the time I returned to the room where Greyson had slept, the sheets were no longer neatly folded. Instead, I tripped over the tangled mess.

Pausing, I thrust my hands on my hips and glanced around. Was someone there messing with me? I didn't find anything else out of the ordinary, so I picked up the pile, added it to the basket, and then carried my load downstairs.

When I entered the tiny room at the back of the kitchen where the washer and dryer were, I stopped short when I noticed the soap tipped over on its side. "Alright, grandma, if you're haunting the place to scare me, there's no need. I'm not going to make too many changes."

It felt almost as if the house sighed around me. Shaking my head at my idiocy, I put a load on then entered the kitchen. The sight of the scuffed wooden stool sitting at the butcherblock island reminded me of all the days I used to sit there as a kid and listen to my grandmother tell me stories about Fae and witches.

I envied her creativity. I could never come up with the elaborate ones she did. She wove tales about portals, fairies, dragons, and gnomes. When I became a mom and my kids started asking for stories, I used my favorites from the ones she told me.

Skylar's favorite was one about a pixie that sought asylum

with a witch. A vicious beast had been hunting her. She was on the edge of her seat when it came to the part about the pixie barely evading the creature when she came up against a barrier. She pounded her tiny hands on the barrier, begging for help. The witch helped and provided the pixie with some woods to live in, and the fairy gave the witch fresh flowers in return.

Emmie's favorite was about a gnome family escaping from some barghests. While Greyson preferred stories about dragon shifters that needed to get away from the vile king that created them to ravage and kill.

I was making a sandwich while my mind traveled down memory lane when movement outside the window caught my eye. I sucked in a breath and immediately started choking on my food. Smashing the food in my hand, I raced for the back door and burst through.

I was still coughing when I dashed down the steps. After a couple more hacks, I managed to clear my throat. "Can I help you?" It still felt like food was stuck down the wrong pipe.

The woman paused with her hand on an herb in the garden and looked up at me. She looked like she was in her late twenties, maybe early thirties, and had stunning red hair. My hands smoothed down my pink t-shirt when I took in her crop top and flat stomach.

She lifted one hand and smiled. "Oh, hi. You must be Fiona, Isidora's granddaughter. I'm Aislinn. I thought you'd be on a plane home by now. I saw the car leave hours ago."

I crossed my arms over my chest, smearing mayonnaise over my left boob. I was a hot freakin' mess, but I didn't care at the moment. I have no idea how my grandmother did things, but I didn't want people wandering on my property whenever they wanted.

"This is my property, and I have decided to stay. Listen, I'm not sure what arrangement you had with my grandmother, but I would like a heads up before you go prowling around stealing my stuff."

Aislinn's eye bugged out of her head, and her hand dropped to her side. "I apologize. Like I said, I figured you'd be gone. I just needed some thistle for a potion, and Isidora has always allowed me to grab the few ingredients I need in exchange for helping with upkeep in here."

That brought a smile to my lips. My hands dropped, and pieces of tomato fell from between the bread. "In that case, you are more than welcome. Honestly, I was thinking about getting rid of the garden. I swear I have a black thumb. Besides, I have no idea what all this is or what it is for."

Aislinn chuckled and cut a couple of sprigs of the plant she'd been holding. "If you're Isidora's kin, you'll be able to keep things alive, but I am happy to help. Gardening has become my therapy since my husband left me a year ago. Is your husband not staying with you?"

I shook my head from side to side as a lump formed in my throat. Anytime I talked about Tim, I was close to losing my shit. Enough time had passed that I should be beyond this by now. But I knew better than anyone that there was no such thing as closure. Grief was a roller coaster that would catch you off guard when you least expected it. The loss of someone you love never stopped hurting, no matter how much time passed.

"My husband passed away a few years ago. Cancer." I preempted the inevitable questions about what killed him. "My kids went back home to college. They will visit, but they won't be living with me."

"I'm so sorry about your husband. You're starting over. That's good. It'll help to create a life that is separate from him. That way, the grief won't suck you under every time you turn around."

My jaw dropped open at the young woman's insight. I

would never have expected her to be so wise. "Honestly, I never thought about that. I had the hardest time letting him go. Despite how much it hurt to eat at our favorite restaurant and go to our park, I ignored it because it felt like a betrayal to do anything else. It wasn't until I got here and felt this sense of belonging that I started giving more thought to my desire to create a new life for myself."

Aislinn exited through the gate and stopped by my side. She was at least three inches shorter than my five-foot-five frame and skinny as a rail, but she exuded this green aura. I must be thinking that because she enjoys gardening.

"As a Shakleton, you belong here. I need to get home to make this potion, but if you ever need anything, I work at Phoenix Feathers. You should come in some time for a drink. On me."

I extended my clean hand and shook hers. "Thank you. I will be in touch, I'm sure."

I watched her walk away. I missed where she turned off my driveway because standing on the other side of the path was a man. He was muscular and intimidating. I wouldn't say he was gorgeous. He was too scary for that, although his beauty was undeniable.

I lifted my hand and waved at him. "Hi. I'm Fiona. I just moved into my grandmother's house." The guy didn't say a word as he stood with his feet braced apart and his arms crossed over his chest while he narrowed his brown eyes at me.

I waited a few minutes before realizing he was not going to introduce himself. Swallowing hard, I turned back to my house. By the time I got inside the kitchen, he was gone. Maybe I would ask Aislinn who the attractive yet angry man was.

Pymm's Pondside was turning out to be a pain in the butt in so many ways. I wanted to scream when I turned back to the kitchen to see silverware strewn over the island. It felt like the place was haunted. Well, too bad. This was my house, and I wasn't leaving.

I lost my Grams, quit my job, sold my house, and moved to another country. I couldn't exactly pick up where I left off. That life was in the wind now.

Download the first book in the Midlife Magic series, Magical New Beginnings HERE!

EXCERPT FROM PACKING SERIOUS MAGICAL MOJO, BOOK #1 IN THE TWISTED SISTERS' MIDLIFE MAELSTROM SERIES

DANIELLE

I was standing on the lawn of Willowberry Plantation House. The sprawling property was located just outside of New Orleans - one that my five sisters and I just purchased. A silhouette caught my eye close to what used to be the slave quarters. I took a step closer and noticed the stacks of beehives. They were my favorite part of the plantation and one of the reasons I wanted to buy the place. I loved honey bees.

Shaking my head at my superstition, I told myself I knew better. I was born and raised in New Orleans. My family were no strangers to the supernatural. I believed in ghosts, vampires, witches, and voodoo queens. It didn't matter that I had no personal experience. My mom saw the ghost of her grandfather when she was a kid. When she was little, Deandra saw the specter of a woman wearing a floppy pink hat. That was enough for me.

I focused on the next step in the dream I shared with my

sisters. I never thought this day would happen. We started our party planning business after losing our mother to cancer. It was a way to ensure life didn't get in the way and force us to drift apart. I couldn't imagine losing touch with the five women I loved most in life.

Our four brothers were business-minded but didn't have an ounce of creativity and had no desire to be part of our venture, which is how we became the Six Twisted Sisters rather than Kay's Talented Ten.

STS started small with a party for one of our brother's grandchildren and grew to the point where we now needed a venue of our own. I had dreamed of owning one of the beautiful old plantation homes in the area, but never thought my sisters would go for it, let alone put in money of their own.

"I can't believe this is finally ours." I smiled and held my hands out as I twirled in a circle. "We are living the dream, Lia."

Perhaps that silhouette by the beehives had been a ghost. It would be just like our mom to come back and share this day with us. I went on tiptoes, searching the spot I thought I'd seen the shadow.

My older sister, Dahlia, snorted, making me look her way. She was a few years older than me. We'd reached the middle of our lives, but she didn't look forty-five. I hoped that meant I didn't look forty-two. "The only thing missing is the pool and the hot cabana boy."

I chuckled. "We brought Fred, the gardener instead. And look, he's even sweaty."

Lia lifted one brow and thrust her hands on her hips. "And happily married. That does not count. At least we don't have to live here with the others. No way would we hear the end of the amount of work from Kota and Dre." Dahlia was absolutely right about that. Our two oldest sisters hadn't read the inspection report.

I winced. Dreya was the oldest of us six and Dakota was just under her. They put in their share of money and trusted Lia and me when we assured them that we could handle fixing the house and getting it ready to host events. When they find out how bad the house really was, they'd want to kill us for buying this place.

I wasn't sure what they expected, but you couldn't get a plantation this big for under a million-five in this area. We got it for half that *because* of the problems. "Thank God for Phi, she's already making a list of the first issues we need to tackle. We've got this, sis."

Lia nodded and headed toward the car that was packed so full you couldn't see the interior color. "Let's go play reverse Jenga and get all this stuff out before the tires pop under the pressure."

Standing on tiptoe, Lia stood around five feet, six inches and was able to grab the zipper for the bag strapped to the top of her SUV. With a yank and a pull, black vinyl parted and spilled pillows, towels, and blankets on top of her.

A laugh escaped me before I could stop it. Before I knew it we were both laughing as the cargo bag continued to spew its guts at us. I had to cross my legs as I bent over at the waist. No one could make me laugh like my sisters, and I loved it despite the consequences. When we were together, we devolved into laughter that ended with one or more of us dashing to the bathroom. None of us had great bladder control after having our kids. Mine went to shit after I had twins.

We could hear Dea chuckling as she got out of the car. Her laugh was the loudest and most infectious of us all. It warmed my heart when I heard it. "What are y'all laughing about?"

"Lia played Jenga a little too well. Now we'll have to wash

everything before we can sleep tonight." I hugged Phi as she got out of the car next.

Kota slammed Dre's car door and hurried toward the house. "Do not make me laugh."

That, of course, made us all devolve into another fit of giggles as we each grabbed up towels and pillows and headed to the house. Kota was shifting from one flip flop to another with sweat running down her perfect makeup by the time we reached her. "Hurry the eff up. I gotta go."

I chuckled and set my burden on the porch, praying the wood held all of us at once. I already had the key in one hand and inserted it in the lock, and twisted. Dakota was through the door like a shot. "We don't have any TP!"

"Or water," Lia yelled over my shoulder. "We forgot to have it put into our name. She's gonna kill us."

Dreya rolled her eyes. "Do not take a dump in the bathroom, Kota! Or you will be fishing it out."

Phi set her pile in the parlor, to the right of the entrance, and had her phone in her hand. "I'll get the water, electricity, and internet turned on. Tucker is on his way with the first load." Once again, Delphine saved the day.

She was super organized and one of the reasons we were so successful. Each of us had a different talent and helped the business run smoothly. I liked to call myself the queen bee, but not because I was more valuable than the others. It was to get under Dakota and Dreya's skin. They were the two oldest and most outspoken of the six of us. I'm sure it bugged the others, but they kept it to themselves. For me, I wanted to feel needed. The truth was, since my divorce from Hugo, I had been floundering and worried I would end up alone.

Dahlia was moving into the plantation with me was that her husband Leo died a few years back. He was killed at work by some angry kids in the foster system. Maybe she needed me as much as I needed her. I couldn't imagine what

I would do in her shoes. Losing Leo, then mom, had to be very difficult.

I stopped that runaway train before it led me to thoughts that would make me cry, like the fact that our mom wasn't here to see us celebrate this achievement. "Steve is on his way to your place Lia, to pick up the laser engraver and supplies. He has the boys with him, so between the five cars, they should be able to get all of our products along with the machine over here and into the barn," Dreya called out as she returned with another load.

Dreya and Dahlia are the workhorses of the bunch. They dove right in and got to work no matter what we were doing. I jumped and dumped the stuff. I looked around at the faded and peeling wallpaper. The musty smell was likely from the mold they found in the attic. Or perhaps it was the broken sump pump in the basement.

My heart squeezed as I walked out of the house to go back to the car. I paused and looked at the wrap-around porch and our investment. The front deck was one of Lia's favorite things about the place. That and what she called the perfect spot to put a gazebo under some willow trees in our yard.

The holes in the flooring were laughing at me. They seemed much bigger now that we owned the place. Rotten wood, check. Mold, check. Broken window, check. I had poured every penny I'd squeezed from my crappy ex-husband into this house. My sisters had each put everything they had into the place as well. Laughter rang out through the massive house, making me smile despite the crushing weight of the project we had just taken on. That right there was the reason this was going to work. Moments like this were priceless and part of the lesson our mom had tried to teach us for years. It wasn't until she was gone that I understood why she wanted the ten of us to be close. You could always count on your family to have your back. At least I could. That was the legacy I inherited from my mom. She didn't leave behind a house for us to fight over or jewelry. She left us love and laughter.

With a smile on my face, I continued to the car while listening to my sisters through the open door. I stopped short when something blue darted out of the corner of my eye. My heart started racing, and my breath caught in my throat. My heart plummeted when I turned, and all I saw were the beehives.

Deandra's arm wrapped around my shoulders as her infectious laughter died down. "Whatcha looking at, sis? Your bees?"

"Our bees." I considered telling Dea about the ghost I swore I kept seeing, then decided against it. There was no doubt she would believe me. She had personal experience.

Hell, all of my sisters believed in them. We'd grown up with stories, but that didn't mean they wouldn't be freaked the hell out. The only one I was certain wouldn't run away screaming was Lia. She loved the paranormal, particularly witches, as much as our mom had.

Dea wrinkled her nose. "You're the bee whisperer. I'll eat the honey, but that's about it."

I laughed as we paused by the trunk of Lia's overflowing car. "I'm afraid to touch anything. Lia had to contort her body to get this stuff in here."

"Don't be such a baby. I'll hand boxes to you," Dea said with a sigh.

I smiled at her even though she couldn't see me. She knew me so well. I was a hard worker like all of my sisters. I'd be right there with Lia repairing walls and striping the wallpaper and painting. However, tweaking my back while unloading the car wasn't my idea of fun.

"Thanks, Dea. Or not." I grunted as she added a third box. I took off before she could add another.

I was perfectly balanced with the packages, so when a box disappeared, I practically fell into Dahlia. "You looked like you could use help."

I lifted one eyebrow. "Is that the box with your BOB?'

Dahlia made a pfft noise. "I had to sell my vibrators plus my house. How else do you think we got such a reasonable monthly payment on a house with fifteen bathrooms and almost double that number of bedrooms?"

I chuckled as I followed Lia up the stairs to the side of the porch. Not many appreciated Lia's sense of humor like us. We passed the detached kitchen and headed up the side of the house. It was amazing how having my sister with me made me see the holes in the porch differently. Instead of lamenting my decision to pressure my sisters, I was busy creating stories about those who had lounged there on hot summer days two hundred years ago.

"We made the right choice, didn't we?" I hadn't meant to blurt that out. My mouth had a tendency to get away from me.

Dahlia stopped, set her box down, and gave me a side hug. "I don't know how to explain it, but this is where we are supposed to be. Everything in our life has led us here. Me losing Leo, you divorcing his royal highness, even losing mom. None of us would have taken the risk without the loss. We know better than most know how imperative it is to live life to the fullest and enjoy the little moments."

I nodded in agreement. "Keep that in mind when we are in the hot attic cleaning out the mold and sealing the wood."

Lia chuckled and picked up her box. "Can we sleep in the ladies' parlor tonight? I'm not ready to be in a room alone yet. I swear there's something here."

I glanced over my shoulder, wondering if she'd seen the ghost. "Did you see something, too?"

"What do you mean, too? I haven't seen anything. It's more a feeling that I can't explain."

"Don't tell me you guys bought us a haunted house," Dakota said as we entered the house. "We can't afford for this to fail. We're extended as far as possible."

"Lia and I gave up our homes to make this work. Our kids don't have a home to return to during spring break next month," I replied.

Dakota meant well, but I was irritated. Mostly because I worried this would ruin us. I'd quit my nursing job, and Dahlia gave notice at social services. Between the parties, tours, and personalized gifts we planned to offer online, there was no choice. And that was the biggest risk for us. If this failed, Dahlia and I were out of a job while the rest still had theirs.

Dahlia set her box down and took mine from me. "They're coming here and going to work their tails off. I've already warned mine."

I took the olive branch and kept myself out of the muck. The six of us got on each other's nerves at times at time, but because we had each other to vent to, we didn't fully blow up with one another. That was what would make it work.

"I know I haven't thanked you guys yet, but it means a lot to me that you have sacrificed so much for us to achieve this dream." It helped keep things calm when Dakota showed insight like this.

She was the most outspoken of all of us and never hesitated to say what she thought. I both loved and hated that about her. I kept my mouth shut about far too much in life, which is probably why I just went through my second divorce. It hit me that I envied Dakota's ability to avoid the hardest of the work and say what she thought, as well.

I hugged her and then went back out for more. Another two loads and the cars were all empty. Dahlia's clothing and mine were all in the ladies' parlor along with the air mattresses we'd be sleeping on tonight.

My back started bitching at me the moment I laid my eyes on the plastic monstrosity that refused to be contained. "Let's take a look around. It doesn't look like the previous owner moved anything out since our last walk-through. I want to take an inventory to see if we will need trash removal."

Phi held up her iPad. "I'll take notes as we go through. I bet there is stuff we can refurbish and sell. Who knows, in an old place like this, we might find some real treasures." Delphine was the most organized of the six of us.

She was smart enough to be a surgeon. Could have been if she'd wanted. Instead, she decided to become a professor in biological sciences. She and her husband, Tucker, bought a hundred-year-old house and refinished the entire thing from top to bottom, so she would know better than me.

The layout was nothing like I was used to in my old house. The entrance was massive with a beautiful crystal chandelier and twin staircases that bent toward the two wings of the house. Beneath the section where the two met and became one wide staircase was a wide hall.

The aisle leading from the front door was long, and there were a few doors on each side as you proceeded into the house. The first rooms on each side were the parlors. One side was for women and the other for men. They would serve as dressing rooms for weddings.

The dining room and a butler's pantry which was a fancy name for an area that was used as staging for the servants to place food before serving. The library was across from that, along with an office. We would keep the library and restore it.

We didn't have plans for the office or servants' prep area. That is what excited me. I loved planning themed parties down to the last little detail and I would enjoy doing the same with this house.

It was hard to be patient when I wanted it done now so we could start making money. "They could have cleaned the chandelier for us," I grumbled as we reached an area that had been renovated and turned into a kitchen. When this plantation was built, the kitchen was in a separate building to avoid a fire burning down the entire house if one started and also keep the house cooler in the summer.

Lucky for us the outdoor kitchen had been updated with modern appliances and would be the perfect location for caterers to prepare. The iron stairs were solid and clean as we climbed.

"These stairs weren't made for people as big as me," Dakota complained.

Deandra started laughing. "This house will never survive us."

By the time we got to the second floor, we were all laughing so hard that I had to go low with my legs crossed. As I balanced on my hands and tried to stop, I swear a ghost appeared at the end of the hallway. It was a blue-colored woman clad in a dress with a wide skirt, high neckline, and fitted top with poofy sleeves. The woman's hair was twisted on top of her head, and her face was pinched.

Dahlia turned wide, frightened eyes my way. Deandra wiped her eyes and opened the first door. "Where's the bathroom?"

Lia pointed further down the hall. "Third door on the left." Dea ran past everyone and into the bathroom.

Delphine shook her head with a smile. "Are we leaving this floor open for wedding parties?"

"Yeah. That's the plan. The place is big enough, we could

live in the other wing, but we're good with the third floor." It was likely an attic at one point, but whoever updated the house with electricity and air conditioning had converted it into a space with three rooms and a bathroom.

"I love this old brass bed," Dakota said. I went on my tiptoes and looked into the room Dakota was standing outside.

"It's gorgeous. Looks like we will have a few things to work with. That'll save some money." Dreya was the oldest and like a mother figure to us. She was the first to find a solution to saving money. She was also the only one that had stories about the rest of us when we were kids.

"Wow, I didn't realize how many beehives were out there," Delphine remarked from the end of the hall.

Dakota scowled. "What are we going to do with so many beehives? How do we even take care of them?"

Deandra joined us holding a roll of toilet paper. "Maleko and I looked into that, actually. We will need to make sure the structures remain in good condition and have proper ventilation. Bees also need a way in and out that we can block when needed. It also said something about woodlice and termites."

I shivered as I listened. There was a cold spot where we were standing, yet there was no vent spewing cold air down on us. This was where the ghost had been standing. Was she still there?

Delphine shrugged her shoulders. "We can sell the honey if we open a gift shop in the old carriage house."

I was overcome with excitement. "We have to have a gift shop. Tourists love their souvenirs. And homegrown honey will be a literal gold mine."

Dreya nodded in agreement. "You're right about that. We can sell personalized jars as party favors"

I saw a person round the corner from the slave's quarters,

MAGICAL MAKEOVER

and I turned and ran for the stairs. My five sisters were running after me and calling my name. I couldn't tell from the window if it was a ghost, but I wanted to make sure it wasn't anyone messing with our property.

I was across the lawn before I was winded. I paused in the middle of the beehives and looked around. The air was sweet from the honey in the nearby drawers. "I thought I saw someone out here," I told them when they all caught up with me.

The six of us were standing in a circle, searching our property for anyone that shouldn't be there. The only people on the property were us. Fred, the gardener, had already left. All of a sudden, the bees went into a flurry as if someone had agitated their hives. I dropped to my knees, and so did my sisters. Keeping my hands over my head, I watched as they buzzed above our heads.

Kota grunted. "I'm not made to do squats."

"I'm more worried about us being stung. What are they doing? It smells like lavender now," Dreya said. I wished I had an answer for her.

Sniffing the air, I smelled the same thing she did. "I don't recall there being any lavender bushes on the plantation." My skin tingled from the energy produced by the bees. It almost felt like it was vibrating through my blood. Looking at my sisters, I was sure that they felt the same thing. I pointed to the left and commando crawled that way, staying low to the ground.

"I'm not sure what that was," Lia said and rubbed her arms as the bees settled and returned to their hives. "But at least we know the bees are healthy and active. Now, let's talk names. Are we keeping Willowberry Plantation? Or changing it?"

Laughter bubbled up as we helped each other stand up and discuss name ideas for our venue. It would take time and some loud discussions for the six of us to come to an agreement on the name, so I steered us to important tasks while we processed.

We had some shelves to put together in the converted barn, where we planned to have our workshop. It had been a major selling point for us. We just needed the electrical and interior updated to accommodate our laser and other supplies.

My heart lightened, and a smile broke across my face. This was going to work. We finally had our own venue for weddings and other parties.

Download the first book in the Twisted Sisters' Midlife Maelstrom series, Packing Serious Magical Mojo HERE!

EXCERPT FROM THE PRIME OF MY MAGICAL LIFE, SHROUDED NATION BOOK #1

My head snapped up, hitting the shelf as I straightened to see who was entering my store. Placing a bell above the door might have been a mistake. *No, leaving the door unlocked was.* Rubbing the back of my skull where a lump was forming, I walked into the aisle and froze.

This was supposed to be my start on a fresh path in my life. Instead, my ex-husband stood there with a sneer on his face. The disgust rolling off of him was unmistakable. I wasn't ready to face him. Honestly, I hoped I would never see him again.

Crossing my arms over my chest, I forced my facial expression to remain neutral and refused to check my long, brown hair. He could suck it if he didn't approve of the Ponytail. "Why are you here, Caton? I'm not open yet, or can't you read the sign in the window?"

One corner of my ex-husband's mouth lifted and his brown eyes narrowed. "Don't take that tone of voice with me, Eve. You should remember your place. I had to see if the rumors were true. I can't believe you used your settlement for this place. It's an embarrassment."

His words hurt more than I wanted them to. This man had cheated on me and left me for a younger woman. She represented the witches on the Shadow Council. Lucinda was closer to our daughter, Mina's age than ours. *That* was the embarrassment, not my store.

He never believed running a magic shop was worthwhile. I had always dreamed of opening a place where beings of all kinds could purchase potions and remedies, and magical creatures could buy their supplies.

There was a need for my place in Ravenholde. As it was, witches and warlocks were forced to search high and wide for whatever they needed. The Blue Moon would change that.

And I'd worked hard over the past few months to locate suppliers and develop the necessary relationships to procure items. Not to mention the fact that I had to find someone willing to help me buy the place. Caton had managed to come out of the divorce with the lion's share while I was struggling to survive.

And here he was pissing on my dream, making me feel like a failure before it even began. The days of him ruining my life were over. "Get out of my store. I don't answer to you anymore. Nor do I listen to what you have to say. I'm not open for business. You can come back when I am."

Caton took several steps toward me, making me shrink into myself while backing up. "How dare you talk back to me? You would still be living in that hovel if not for me. I made you who you are today. You owe me everything. Something you'd do well to remember."

That did it. I was done letting him keep me under his thumb. When I did something that he didn't approve of, especially if he thought it made him look bad, he berated me.

He tried to make me feel like I was nothing. He preferred it when I depended on him.

I was worth more than he could ever imagine and I was done allowing him to chip away at my self-esteem. Straightening my shoulders, I rolled my eyes. "You must really enjoy your imaginary world. I thought for sure you'd grow up one day. Let me be clear, I owe you nothing. Nor do I think about you when making any decision in my life."

With that, I turned my back to him and moved behind the glass counter I'd found at a mundane owned antique store a few towns over. I'd been looking for something to display tarot cards and my more expensive crystals.

I was acutely aware of Caton stalking toward me as I lifted a box from the floor. Through the glass front, I saw the black slacks and dress shoes as he moved. "You are nothing without me, Eve. You can stop this charade and give up this endeavor before you fail."

Standing up, I dropped the box on the glass top with too much force. "Did you stop taking your medication when you threw everything away? You might want to reconsider. I hear the Shadow Council can't get a handle on the increase in suspicious deaths, and they are now moving to mundane cities and victims. I'll have some items for sale. If you need scrying water or any potions to help reveal the culprit, come see me." I was opening the next day and didn't have time for this bullshit. I needed to finish setting up my store.

Caton leaned forward, his face turning red with his anger. One lock of his dark blonde hair fell over his forehead. "Watch your mouth. You've got little power and no talent. You were lucky I married you. Nobody else would have."

I snapped my fingers, making the tips ignite with flames. "Someone still prefers living in denial. I can see how you're with Lucinda now. You are the lucky one. I should have seen through your bullshit years ago. Your days of stealing from me are over. Get the hell out of my store. And that invitation for help extends to anyone on the council except you and Lucinda."

I flicked my wrist, activating the wards I'd placed in and around my shop. There was a moment of pure joy when Caton's eyes widened as the spell forced him down the aisle. I barely managed to open the doors with my telekinesis before he crashed into the panel.

I'd have been pissed if his body broke the glass topped panel. Ayesha had helped me finish painting the store name and logo onto the surface the day before. We had the large picture windows to do next.

My heart was in my throat when I followed him down the aisle and slammed the door as he was dumped on his ass. Control of my telekinesis was sketchy at best, and I had no desire to flop in front of him.

After locking the deadbolt, I watched as Caton stood up and brushed himself off. I winced when he glared at me and muttered something under his breath. Given the way he concentrated on me and my shop, I knew it wasn't good.

The sparks that flew when his spell hit my wards made me jump back as a scream escaped from my lips. That turned into a laugh when Caton's suit jacket caught on fire. He'd tried to burn my store down.

In my anger, I had the door open, and I was in Caton's face before reason resurfaced. "You never did learn when to quit. Take your stupidity and stay away from me. My store is protected by more than just wards. They're the strongest protections out there. And will be available to purchase in a few weeks."

Caton lifted his chin and opened his mouth to reply when Ayesha arrived. The Fae leader slammed her car door, breaking the moment. "Fancy meeting you here, Caton. Did you come to support the wife you let get away? I still don't understand how you left her for Lucinda. Then again, we can't all have good taste."

Caton shifted his glare from me to Ayesha. "So, you're behind Eve's latest venture. I was just telling her how pathetic this place is. I will relish its failure even more, knowing it will reflect on you both."

Ayesha's face split into a grin as she walked up the steps and looped her arms through mine. "It will be fun to watch Eve soar without you dragging her down. Your humiliation has already started, Caton. Look around. Countless townspeople have already seen your attempt to attack your ex-wife blow up in your face. Quite literally, it seems."

The tight band around my chest loosened when I realized she was right. Several people were focused on the three of us. The charred holes in Caton's jacket were lingering proof of what he had tried to do.

"You failed to sabotage my new venture, and managed to show the community how much talent I have. I couldn't have asked for better marketing. It's the least you could do after all you put me through." I still hated that I'd given this man the best twenty years of my life.

You're only forty-two years old, not one hundred. The best is yet to come. My life was far from over and I needed to keep reminding myself of that. Ayesha turned, pulling me with her, and walked me back inside my store.

After shutting the door, I locked it and extricated myself from my mentor. Ayesha had been there for me when Caton left me. I was devastated and humiliated that I hadn't seen him for who he really was sooner.

The signs had been there, but I'd chosen to ignore them in favor of keeping Mina's life stable. The desire to leave him had become the only thought in my head too many times over the years. Regret was a bitter pill to swallow.

"Don't," Ayesha told me. "Do not give his words or his

thoughtless actions space in your mind. You need it for all the skills you've honed over the past few months."

I sighed and walked to the back of the store, away from the prying eyes on the street. I didn't want anyone to see me break down. "But what if he's right? I'm doing magic that shouldn't exist. No one has ever combined Fae methods with witchcraft."

Ayesha pulled me to the stairs that lead up to my apartment above the shop. The old Victorian was converted into two separate spaces a couple of decades ago by a fame demon when she opened Ravenholde's first bakery.

My parents used to take me to Callaleh's place for cupcakes as a kid. She made my birthday cake every year until she closed up shop and moved to Wilmington, North Carolina, taking her store with her.

"Just because something hasn't been done before doesn't mean it shouldn't be. You are allowing Caton to get into your head again. It took us months to undo the damage he'd done. You are far more talented than him or Lucinda. You belong on the council, not her." She flicked her hand. "Regardless, you are where you're meant to be. There are big things in store for you." Ayesha's pep talk soothed the hurt that I was yet to banish, making it easier to reclaim my determination to succeed.

I had no desire to make decisions that affected the entire Shrouded Nation. I was happy in my corner of the world, helping where I could. And her belief in me was the reason I'd come to rely on her friendship and guidance. Crossing to the stove, I put the kettle on to boil and grabbed the canister of assorted tea bags I kept on hand.

Ayesha wasn't a witch with the power of premonition, but her last words struck me as foreboding. "Having anything beyond the Blue Moon in the future sounds ominous. Should I be afraid?"

Ayesha shook her head and blinked her eyes several times. "Honestly, I'm not sure. You know I don't get glimpses of the future. It's more of a feeling than an omen. This store was always meant for you and you know it. You'd have opened it years ago if you hadn't allowed Caton to stop you. Did he ever find out that you made potions and tinctures on the side throughout your marriage?"

I shook my head and placed the tea, sugar, and milk on the table along with the mugs, then turned back to the pantry to grab some cookies. "He was clueless about anything that didn't involve him. He saw me as an accessory to pull out when he needed and stuck me on the shelf when he didn't. I doubt the people that came to me talked much about it. The shifters, especially. They would have been looked down upon for going to a witch for help, you know that."

Ayesha frowned as I retrieved the kettle when it whistled like a train. "I've tried to overcome the prejudices separating the species for years. There will come a day when those in charge will realize we have to band together to survive. I've never understood the animosity between some. Particularly the hatred shifters feel toward witches. I get vampires and shifters hating one another. They're natural enemies in many ways, but we can overcome these differences. You opening the Blue Moon is the first step. No witch has ever catered to all the species like you will."

Pouring the hot water into our mugs, I smiled, thinking about the work I'd accomplished lately. It helped to forget everything I'd lost when Caton left me the second Mina went away to college. In some ways, losing my daughter was worse than the divorce. Neither was the house or the status I once had.

Refusing to go down that road and get lost in grief and concern, I focused on Ayesha. The Fae had long white hair that flowed to her waist. She looked younger than me, despite being over seven hundred years old. Until you looked into her eyes. They were the color of Scotland moss in the springtime and had an ancient quality to them.

"I'm only able to open this place because you helped me purchase the house. Speaking of which. I have another payment for you." I grabbed the envelope from my purse and handed it to her.

She narrowed her eyes. "I told you not to worry about payments until you started making money. The support from Caton is supposed to be used for your food."

I lifted one shoulder. "The sooner I can pay you back, the faster I will truly feel like this is mine. Not that I mind being in business with you. You didn't just save my life, you're my only true friend. I want to stand on my own two feet. I need to prove it to myself more than anyone else. I hope you understand."

Ayesha dunked her tea bag in and out of her cup. "It's your time to shine, Eve. Don't let anyone tell you differently. Especially not those witches that act like they care about you. They'll come around to see what you're doing, but their sentiment will be as fake as they are."

I laughed at that. She wasn't wrong about the people I'd grown up with. They never really liked me in high school and only started coming around after Caton married me. They wanted to be close to the head warlock, not me. Only my best friend, Arabelle, was there for me growing up.

She moved to the west coast right after high school. I was missing her dearly when I went to college and met Caton. Belle and I maintained contact through the phone and later on social media, but without having her here I never confided in her about things in my life. It was easier to maintain the façade that I was happy and everything was great.

"I don't know. I thought I'd go to the dark side and become one of Caton's simpering fools. It seems to be all the

MAGICAL MAKEOVER

rage in the witching and warlock worlds," I joked, though the simpering part was one hundred percent accurate.

Ayesha rolled her eyes while laughing. "Har, har my friend. You're a real comedian. What did Caton want anyway?"

That question killed my laughter instantly. "What do you think? He wanted to tell me to close the store and give up because I would fail and was an embarrassment."

Ayesha scowled as she stirred her tea a little too briskly, making it slosh over the sides. "That's because he's worried that you'll show him and his chippie up. If he'd put that much effort into his role on the council, we might get out of this mess before the mundanes discover us."

The shift in topic to the recent string of murders was sobering. "That's what I told him. I might have also taunted him with an offer of potions to help reveal the vampire behind these deaths."

Ayesha's frown lifted a bit at that. "I bet he didn't like that. Using one of your potions will be the perfect way to stick it to him and prove your worth. Although Darick swears none of his vampires are responsible. I believe him. He has too much to lose if he's lying. And if it's a rogue, seeing his or her face won't be all that helpful."

My gut churned as I considered the ramifications of the vamp being rogue. "Whoever is doing this is escalating their attacks and needs to be stopped before they kill enough mundanes to make their police link their cases to ours."

Ravenholde was populated by supernaturals, but we were located close to mundane cities and towns. Years ago, when a nearby Sherriff realized we had no police force, he incorporated our town into his service area. Patrol officers had discovered two of the victims here before the Shadow Council could cover them up.

Ayesha nodded in agreement. "This situation is close to

exploding all over us. The council has been meeting nightly and we each leave with areas to search for cases. There were victims close to Roanoke last night. Once it reaches the city where they have more resources, it'll only be a matter of time until they call in the FBI and Ravenholde is inundated."

I hated being on the sidelines. I felt like I had a voice when I gave Caton ideas to help solve problems that the council faced. Through Ayesha, I discovered that he suggested my ideas more than once to his peers, although he never admitted as much to me.

Now, I had no way to locate the vampire rampaging my town and the surrounding areas. I lifted my lukewarm tea to my lips. "Unless you can get your hands on something personal for me to scry with, it might help map the victims and determine if there is a pattern to who he's choosing. Maybe you can predict where he will go next."

Ayesha clapped my shoulder. "I like the way you think, Eve. Now let's get your store set up for your grand opening tomorrow."

My nerves jumped for very different reasons as I put our cups in the sink and headed downstairs. My lifelong dream was coming true. In a matter of hours, I would open the Blue Moon and I couldn't wait. No more hiding and making potions for people under Caton's nose. I'd prove to him how valuable the community would find my goods and services. *Let's see what tomorrow brings.*

CLICK HERE to continue reading Prime of my Magical Life, book 1 in the exciting new Supernatural Midlife Series.

AUTHORS' NOTE

Reviews are like hugs. Sometimes awkward. Always welcome! It would mean the world to me if you can take five minutes and let others know how much you enjoyed my work.

Don't forget to visit my website: www.brendatrim.com and sign up for my newsletter, which is jam-packed with exciting news and monthly giveaways. Also, be sure to visit and like my Facebook page https://www.facebook.com/AuthorBrendaTrim to see my daily posts.

Never allow waiting to become a habit. Live your dreams and take risks. Life is happening now.

DREAM BIG!

XOXO,

Brenda

CLICK THE SITE BELOW TO STALK BRENDA:

Amazon

BookBub

Facebook

Brenda's Book Warriors FB Group

AUTHORS' NOTE

Booksprout
Goodreads
Instagram
Twitter
Website

ALSO BY BRENDA TRIM

Midlife Witchery:

Magical New Beginnings Book 1

Mind Over Magical Matters

Magical Twist

My Magical Life to Live

Forged in Magical Fire

Like a Fine Magical Wine

Magical Yule Tidings

Magical Complications

Magical Delivery

Magical Moxie

In the Goddess's Magical Snare

Hunting for Magical Meaning

Meddling in Magical Pursuits

Guardians Of Magical Power

Twisting The Magical Fires

Mystical Midlife in Maine

Magical Makeover

Laugh Lines & Lost Things

Hellmouths & Hot Flashes

Holiday with Hades

Saggy But Witty in Crescent City

Nasty Curses & Big Purses

Fae Forged Axes & Chin Waxes

Demonic Stones & Creaky Bones

Underworld Frights & Sleepless Nights

Pixie Dust & Brain Rust

Magical Hands & Silver Strands

Deadly Quips & Furry Lips

Twisted Sisters' Midlife Maelstrom

Packing Serious Magical Mojo

Cadaver on Canal Street

Seances & Second Line Parades

French Quarter Fae

King's Day Magical Mischief

Etou-Fae the Hard Way

Hurricanes, Heroes, & Hail Marys

Royal Street Romp

Levees, Lost Crowns & Loa

Supernatural Midlife Mystique Series:

The Prime of my Magical Life

All Good Magic Comes to an End

Sweet Magical Destruction

It Takes a Demon to Know One

The Demon is in the Details

Magic is Only Skin Deep

A Demon is as a Demon Does

Fork in the Magical Quest

The Dark Warrior Alliance

Dream Warrior (Dark Warrior Alliance, Book 1)

Mystik Warrior (Dark Warrior Alliance, Book 2)

Pema's Storm (Dark Warrior Alliance, Book 3)

Isis' Betrayal (Dark Warrior Alliance, Book 4)

Deviant Warrior (Dark Warrior Alliance, Book 5)

Suvi's Revenge (Dark Warrior Alliance, Book 6)

Mistletoe & Mayhem (Dark Warrior Alliance, Novella)

Scarred Warrior (Dark Warrior Alliance, Book 7)

Heat in the Bayou (Dark Warrior Alliance, Novella, Book 7.5)

Hellbound Warrior (Dark Warrior Alliance, Book 8)

Isobel (Dark Warrior Alliance, Book 9)

Rogue Warrior (Dark Warrior Alliance, Book 10)

Shattered Warrior (Dark Warrior Alliance, Book 11)

King of Khoth (Dark Warrior Alliance, Book 12)

Ice Warrior (Dark Warrior Alliance, Book 13)

Fire Warrior (Dark Warrior Alliance, Book 14)

Ramiel (Dark Warrior Alliance, Book 15)

Rivaled Warrior (Dark Warrior Alliance, Book 16)

Dragon Knight of Khoth (Dark Warrior Alliance, Book 17)

Ayil (Dark Warrior Alliance, Book 18)

Guild Master (Dark Alliance Book 19)

Maven Warrior (Dark Alliance Book 20)

Sentinel of Khoth (Dark Alliance Book 21)

Araton (Dark Warrior Alliance Book 22)

Cambion Lord (Dark Warrior Alliance Book 23)

Omega (Dark Warrior Alliance Book 24)

Dragon Lothario of Khoth (Dark Warrior Alliance Book 25)

Cunning Warrior (Dark Warrior Alliance Book 26) Coming September 2023

Dark Warrior Alliance Boxsets:
Dark Warrior Alliance Boxset Books 1-4
Dark Warrior Alliance Boxset Books 5-8
Dark Warrior Alliance Boxset Books 9-12
Dark Warrior Alliance Boxset Books 13-16
Dark Warrior Alliance Boxset Books 17-20

Hollow Rock Shifters:
Captivity, Hollow Rock Shifters Book 1
Safe Haven, Hollow Rock Shifters Book 2
Alpha, Hollow Rock Shifters Book 3
Ravin, Hollow Rock Shifters Book 4
Impeached, Hollow Rock Shifters Book 5
Anarchy, Hollow Rock Shifters Book 6
Allies, Hollow Rock Shifters Book 7
Sovereignty, Hollow Rock Shifters Book 8

Bramble's Edge Academy:
Unearthing the Fae King
Masking the Fae King
Revealing the Fae King

Midnight Doms:
Her Vampire Bad Boy
Her Vampire Suspect
All Souls Night

BRENDA TRIM
AND
TAMI JULKA
Want a FREE Book?
Click HERE and join
my mailing list to
get an ecopy of
Heat in The Bayou!